Awakened

A House of Night Novel

Awakened

P.C. and KRISTIN CAST

Book Eight of the
HOUSE OF NIGHT
Series

www.atombooks.net

ATOM

First published in the United States in 2011 by St Martin's Press
First published in Great Britain in 2011 by Atom
This paperback edition published in 2011 by Atom

A CIP catalogue record for this book
is available from the British Library.

ISBN 978-1-905654-85-7

Typeset in Minion Pro
Printed and bound by CPI Group (UK) Ltd, Croydon, CR0 4YY

Papers used by Atom are from well-managed forests
and other responsible sources.

MIX
Paper from
responsible sources
FSC® C104740

Atom
An imprint of
Little, Brown Book Group
100 Victoria Embankment
London EC4Y 0DY

An Hachette UK Company
www.hachette.co.uk

www.atombooks.net

Kristin and I would like to dedicate this book to LGBT teens.

Gender preference does not define you.

Your spirit defines you.

It gets better.

We heart you.

No matter what "they" say, life is really about love, always love.

ACKNOWLEDGMENTS

As always, we would like to thank our agent, Meredith Bernstein, without whom the House of Night would not exist.

THANK YOU to our Little, Brown UK family—and especially to our editor Samantha Smith.

And a special WE HEART YOU to our Scottish fans. Y'all make us smile . . .

CHAPTER ONE

Neferet

A disquieting sense of irritation awakened Neferet. Before she had truly departed that amorphous place between dreams and reality, she reached out with her long, elegant fingers and felt for Kalona. The arm she touched was muscular. His skin was smooth and strong and pleasing beneath her fingertips. All it took was that small, feather-like caress. He stirred and turned eagerly to her.

"My Goddess?" His voice was husky with sleep and the beginnings of renewed desire.

He annoyed her.

They all annoyed her because they were not *him*.

"Leave me . . . Kronos." She had to pause, and search her memory to remember his ridiculous, overly ambitious name.

"Goddess, have I done something to displease you?"

Neferet glanced up at him. The young Son of Erebus Warrior was reclining on the bed beside her, his handsome face open, his expression willing, his aquamarine eyes just as striking in the dimness of her candlelit bedroom as they had been earlier that day when she'd watched him training in the castle courtyard. He'd stirred her desires then, and with one inviting look from her, he'd willingly come to her and futilely, though enthusiastically, attempted to prove that he was god in more than namesake alone.

The problem was that Neferet had been bedded by an immortal, thus she knew all too intimately just how much of an imposter this Kronos truly was.

"Breathe," Neferet said, meeting his blue eyes with a bored glance.

"Breathe, Goddess?" His brow, decorated by a tattoo pattern that was supposed to represent ball and mace weaponry, but to Neferet appeared more like frilly Fourth of July fireworks, furrowed in confusion.

"You asked what you'd done to displease me and I told you: you're breathing. And in much too close a proximity to me. *That* displeases me. It's time you depart my bed." Neferet sighed and flicked her fingers at him in dismissal. "Go. Now."

She almost laughed aloud at his undisguised look of hurt and shock.

Had the youth really believed he could replace her divine Consort? The impertinence of the thought fueled her anger.

In the corners of Neferet's bedchamber, shadows within shadows quivered in anticipation. Though she didn't acknowledge them, she felt their stirrings. It pleased her.

"Kronos, you were distracting, and for a brief time you gave me a measure of pleasure." Neferet touched him again, this time not so gently, and her fingernails left twin raised welts down his thick forearm. The young warrior didn't flinch or pull away. Instead he trembled beneath her touch and his breathing deepened. Neferet smiled. She'd known this one needed pain to feel desire the instant his eyes had met hers.

"I would give you more pleasure, if you allowed it," he said.

Neferet smiled. Her tongue flicked out slowly, licking her lips as she watched him watch her. "Perhaps in the future. Perhaps. For now what I require of you is to leave me and, of course, to continue to worship me."

"Would that I could show you how much I long to worship you *again*." The last word was spoken as a verbal caress, and—mistakenly—Kronos reached for her.

As if it was his right to touch her.

As if her wishes were subservient to his needs and desires.

One small echo from Neferet's distant past—a time she thought she'd buried with her humanity—seeped from the entombed memories. She felt her father's touch and even smelled the reek of his rancid, alcohol-soaked breath as her childhood invaded the present.

Neferet's response was instantaneous. As easily as breathing, she lifted her hand from the warrior's arm and held it, palm outward, at the closest of the shadows lurking at the edges of her chamber.

Darkness responded to her touch even more quickly than had Kronos. She felt its deadly chill and reveled in the sensation, especially as it banished the rising memories. With a nonchalant motion, she scattered the Darkness at Kronos, saying, "If it is pain you so desire, then taste my cold fire."

The Darkness Neferet hurled at Kronos penetrated his young, smooth skin eagerly, slicing ribbons of scarlet through the forearm she had so recently caressed.

He moaned, though this time more in fear than passion.

"Now do as I command. Leave me. And remember, young warrior, a goddess chooses when and where and how she is touched. Do not overstep yourself again."

Gripping his bleeding arm, Kronos bowed low to Neferet. "Yes, my Goddess."

"Which goddess? Be specific, Warrior! I have no desire to be called by ambiguous titles."

His response was instantaneous. "Nyx Incarnate. That is your title, my Goddess."

Her narrowed look softened. Neferet's face relaxed into its mask of beauty and warmth. "Very good, Kronos. Very good. See how easy it is to please me?"

Caught in her emerald gaze, Kronos nodded once, then fisting his right hand over his heart he said, "Yes, my Goddess, my Nyx," and backed reverently from her chamber.

Neferet smiled again. It was unimportant that she was not actually Nyx Incarnate. The truth was Neferet wasn't interested in being cast in the role of an incarnate goddess. "That implies I am lesser than a goddess," she spoke to the shadows gathered around her. What was important was power—and if the title Nyx Incarnate aided her in the acquisition of power, especially with the Sons of Erebus Warriors, then that was the title by which she would be called. "But I aspire to more—much more than standing in the shadow of a goddess."

Soon she would be ready to take her next step, and Neferet knew some of the Sons of Erebus would be manipulated into standing beside her. Oh, not enough of them to actually sway a battle with their physical force, but enough of them to fragment the Warriors' morale by setting brother against brother. *Men,* she thought disdainfully, *so easily fooled by the masks of beauty and title, and so easily used to my advantage.*

The thought pleased her but wasn't distracting enough to keep Neferet from restlessly leaving her bed. She wrapped a sheer silk robe around herself and moved from her chamber out into the hallway. Before she'd given conscious thought to her actions she was heading to the stairwell that would take her to the bowels of the castle.

Shadows within shadows drifted after Neferet, dark magnets drawn by her increasing agitation. She knew they moved with her. She knew they were dangerous and that they fed on her unease, her anger, her restless mind. But, oddly, she found a measure of comfort in their presence.

She paused only once in her downward descent. *Why am I going to him again? Why am I allowing him to invade my thoughts tonight?* Neferet shook her head as if to dislodge the silent words and spoke into the narrow, empty stairwell, addressing the Darkness that hovered attentively around her. "I go because it is what I wish to do. Kalona is my Consort. He was wounded serving me. It is only natural that I think of him."

With a self-satisfied smile Neferet continued down the winding stairwell, easily repressing the truth: that Kalona had been wounded because she had entrapped him, and the service he performed for her was a forced one.

She reached the dungeon, carved centuries ago from the rocky earth that made up the Isle of Capri at the bottommost level of the castle, and moved silently down the torch-lit hallway. The Son of Erebus Warrior standing watch outside the barred room couldn't hide his jolt of surprise. Neferet's smile widened. His shocked look, tinged with fear, told her that she was getting better and better at appearing to materialize from nothing but shadows and night. That lightened her mood, but not enough to add the softness of a smile to temper the cruel edge of command in her voice.

"Leave. I wish to be alone with my Consort."

The Son of Erebus hesitated only a moment, but that slight pause was enough for Neferet to make a mental note about being sure in the next few days that this particular Warrior would be called back to Venice. Perhaps because of an emergency regarding someone close to him . . .

"Priestess, I leave you to your privacy. But know that I am within the sound of your voice and will respond to your call should you need me." Without meeting her eyes, the Warrior fisted his hand over his heart and bowed—though too slightly to suit her.

Neferet watched him retreat down the narrow hallway.

"Yes," she whispered to the shadows. "I can feel that something quite unfortunate is going to happen to his mate."

Smoothing the sheer silk of her wrap, she turned to the closed wooden door. Neferet drew a deep breath of the damp dungeon air. She swept the thick fall of her auburn hair back from her face, baring her beauty as if girding herself for battle.

Neferet waved her hand at the door and it opened for her. She stepped into the room.

Kalona lay directly on the earthen floor. She'd wanted to make a bed for him, but discretion had dictated her actions. It really wasn't that she was keeping him imprisoned. She was simply being wise. He had to complete his mission for her—that was what was best for him. If his body regained too much of its immortal strength, it would be a distraction for Kalona, an unfortunate distraction. Especially as he'd sworn to act as her sword in the Otherworld and to rid them of the inconvenience Zoey Redbird had created for them in this time, this reality.

Neferet approached his body. Her Consort lay flat on his back, naked, with only his onyx wings as a veil-like covering. She sank gracefully to her knees and then reclined, facing him, on the thick fur pelt she'd ordered placed beside him for her convenience.

Neferet sighed. She touched the side of Kalona's face.

His flesh was cool, as it always was, but lifeless. He showed no reaction whatsoever to her presence.

"What is taking so long, my love? Could you not have disposed of one annoying child more quickly?"

Neferet caressed him again; this time her hand slid from his face down the curve of his neck, over his chest, to rest on the indentations that defined the corded muscles of his abdomen and waist.

"Remember your oath and fulfill it so that I might open my arms and my bed to you again. By blood and Darkness you have sworn to prevent Zoey Redbird from returning to her body, thus destroying her so that I might rule this magickal modern world." Neferet caressed the fallen immortal's slim waist again, smiling secretly to herself. "Oh, and of course you shall be by my side while I rule."

Invisible to the Sons of Erebus fools who were supposed to be the High Council's spies, the black, spider-like threads that held Kalona trapped against the earth shivered and shifted, brushing their frigid tentacles against Neferet's hand. Distracted momentarily by their alluring chill, Neferet opened her palm to Darkness and allowed it to twine around her wrist, cutting ever so slightly into her flesh—not enough to cause her pain that was unbearable—only enough to temporarily sate its unending lust for blood.

Remember your sworn oath . . .

The words sloughed around her like the winter wind through denuded branches.

Neferet frowned. She need not be reminded. Of course she was aware of her oath. In exchange for Darkness doing her bidding— entrapping Kalona's body and forcing his soul to the Otherworld— she had agreed to sacrifice the life of an innocent Darkness had been unable to taint.

The oath remains. The bargain holds, even should Kalona fail, Tsi Sgili . . .

Again the words whispered around her.

"Kalona will not fail!" Neferet shouted, utterly incensed that even Darkness would dare chastise her. "And should he, I have bound his spirit as mine to command as long as he is immortal, so even in failure there is victory for me. But he will not fail." She repeated the words, slowly and distinctly, regaining control over her increasingly volatile temper.

Darkness licked her palm. The pain, slight though it was, pleased her, and she gazed at the tendrils affectionately, as if they were simply overeager kittens vying for her attention.

"Darlings, be patient. His quest is not complete. My Kalona is still but a shell. I can only assume Zoey languishes in the Otherworld—not fully living and, unfortunately, not yet dead."

The threads that held her wrist quivered, and for an instant Neferet thought she heard the mocking ring of laughter rumbling in the distance.

But she had no time to consider the implications of such a sound—whether it was real or just an element of the expanding world of Darkness and power that consumed more and more of what she once knew as reality—because at that instant Kalona's entrapped body jerked spasmodically and he drew a deep, gasping breath.

Her gaze went instantly to his face, so she witnessed the horror of his eyes opening, even though they were nothing but empty, bloody sockets.

"Kalona! My love!" Neferet was on her knees, bending over him, her hands fluttering around his face.

The Darkness that had been caressing her wrists throbbed with a sudden jolt of power, causing her to flinch before they shot from her body and joined a myriad of sticky tendrils that, web-like, hovered and pulsed against the stone ceiling of the dungeon.

Before Neferet could form a command to call a tendril to her—to order an explanation for such bizarre behavior—a blinding flash of light, so bright and shining that she had to shield her eyes from it, exploded from the ceiling.

The web of Darkness caught it, slicing through the light with inhumane sharpness and entrapping it.

Kalona opened his mouth with a soundless scream.

"What is it? I demand to know what is happening!" Neferet cried.

Your Consort has returned, Tsi Sgili.

Neferet stared as the globe of imprisoned light was wrenched from the air and, with a terrible hissing, Darkness plunged Kalona's soul through the sockets of his eyes and back into his body.

The winged immortal writhed in pain. His hands lifted to cover his face, and he drew panting, ragged breaths.

"Kalona! My Consort!" As she would have done when she was a young healer, Neferet moved automatically. She pressed her palms over Kalona's hands, quickly and efficiently centered herself, and said, "Soothe him . . . remove his pain . . . make his agony like the red sun setting into the horizon—gone after a momentary slash through the waiting night sky."

The shudders that wracked Kalona's body began to lessen almost instantly. The winged immortal drew a deep breath. Though his hands trembled, he clasped Neferet's tightly, removing them from his face. Then, opened his eyes. They were the deep amber color of whisky, clear and coherent. He was completely himself again.

"You've returned to me!" For a moment Neferet was so filled with relief that he was awake and aware that she almost wept. "Your mission is complete." Neferet brushed away the tentacles that clung stubbornly to Kalona's body, frowning at them because they seemed so reluctant to withdraw their hold on her lover.

"Take me from the earth." His voice was gravelly with disuse, but his words were lucid. "To the sky. I need to see the sky."

"Yes, of course, my love." Neferet waved at the door and it re-opened. "Warrior! My Consort awakens. Help him to the castle rooftop!"

The Son of Erebus who had annoyed her so recently obeyed her command without question, though Neferet noted he looked shocked at Kalona's sudden reanimation.

Wait until you know the whole of it. Neferet speared him a superior smirk. *Very soon you and the other Warriors will take orders only from me—or you will perish.* The thought pleased her as she followed the two men out of the bowels of the ancient fortress of Capri, up and up until finally they emerged from the long length of stone steps onto the rooftop.

It was past midnight. The moon hung toward the horizon, yellow and heavy though not yet full.

"Help him to the bench and then leave us," Neferet ordered, gesturing to the ornately carved marble bench that rested near the edge of the castle's rooftop, affording a truly magnificent view of the glistening Mediterranean. But Neferet had no interest in the beauty that surrounded her. She waved away the Warrior, dismissing him from her mind even though she knew he would be notifying the High Council that her Consort's soul had returned to his body.

That didn't matter now. That could be dealt with later.

Only two things mattered now: Kalona had returned to her, and Zoey Redbird was dead.

CHAPTER TWO

Neferet

"Speak to me. Tell me everything slowly and clearly. I want to savor each word." Neferet went to Kalona, kneeling before him, stroking the soft, dark wings that unfurled loosely around the immortal as he sat on the bench, face raised to the night sky, bronzed body bathed in the golden glow of the moon. She tried to keep herself from trembling in anticipation of his touch—of the return of his cold passion, his frozen heat.

"What would you have me say?" He didn't meet her eyes. Instead he opened his face to the sky, as if he could drink in the heavens above them.

His question took her aback. Her lust abated and her hand ceased stroking his wing.

"I would have you give me the details of our victory so that I might savor the retelling of it with you." She spoke slowly, thinking that perhaps his brain might still be slightly addled from the recent displacement of his soul.

"*Our* victory?" he said.

Neferet's green eyes narrowed. "Indeed. You are my Consort. Your victory is mine, as mine is yours."

"Your kindness is almost divine. Have you become a goddess during my absence?"

Neferet studied him closely. He still wasn't looking at her; his voice was almost expressionless. Was he being impudent? She shrugged off his question, though she continued to watch him closely. "What happened in the Otherworld? How did Zoey die?"

She knew what he would say the instant his amber eyes finally found hers, though childishly she covered her ears and began to shake her head back and forth, back and forth as he spoke the words that were like a sword stroke to her soul.

"Zoey Redbird is not dead."

Neferet stood and forced her hands from her ears. She stalked several paces from Kalona, staring unseeingly out at the liquid sapphire of the night sea. She breathed slowly, carefully, attempting to control her seething emotions. When finally she knew she could do so without shrieking in anger to the sky, she spoke.

"Why? Why did you not complete your quest?"

"It was your quest, Neferet. Never mine. You forced me to return to a realm from which I'd been banished. What happened was predictable: Zoey's friends rallied about her. With their aid she healed her shattered soul and found herself again."

"Why did you not stop it from happening?" Her voice was frigid. She didn't so much as glance at him.

"Nyx."

Neferet heard the name leave his lips as if he'd spoken a prayer—soft, low, reverent. Jealousy speared her.

"What of the goddess?" She almost spat the question.

"She intervened."

"She did what?" Neferet whirled around. Disbelief tinged with fear made her words breathless, incredulous. "Do you expect me to believe that Nyx actually interfered with mortal choice?"

"No," Kalona said, sounding weary again. "She didn't interfere; she intervened, and only after Zoey had already healed herself. Nyx blessed her for it. That blessing was part of her and her Warrior's salvation."

"Zoey lives." Neferet's voice was flat, cold, lifeless.

"She does."

"Then you owe me the subservience of your immortal soul." She started to walk away from him, toward the rooftop exit.

"Where are you going? What will happen next?"

Disgusted by what she perceived as weakness in his voice, Neferet turned to him. She drew herself up tall and proud, and held out her arms so that the sticky threads that pulsed around her could brush her skin freely, caressingly.

"What will happen next? It is quite simple. I will ensure Zoey is drawn back to Oklahoma. There, on my own terms, I will complete the task you failed."

To her retreating back the immortal asked, "And what of me?"

Neferet paused and glanced over her shoulder. "You will return to Tulsa, too, only separately. I have need of you, but you cannot be with me publically. Do you not remember, my love, that you are a killer now? Heath Luck's death was your doing."

"*Our* doing," he said.

She smiled silkily. "Not according to the High Council." She met his eyes. "This is what is going to happen. I need you to regain your strength quickly. By dusk tomorrow I will have to report to the High Council that your soul has returned to your body, and that you confessed to me you killed the human boy because you thought his hatred for me a threat. I will tell them because you believed you were protecting me, I was merciful in your punishment. I only had you flogged one hundred strokes and then banished you from my side for one century."

Kalona struggled to sit. Neferet was pleased to see anger flash in his amber eyes.

"You expect to be bereft of my touch for a century?"

"Of course not. I will graciously allow you to return to my side after your wounds have healed. Until then I will still have your touch; it will simply be away from the prying eyes of the public."

His brow lifted. She thought how arrogant he looked, even weakened and defeated.

"How long do you expect me to skulk in the shadows, pretending to heal from nonexistent wounds?"

"I expect you to be absent from my side until your wounds *do* heal." With a quick, precise movement, Neferet brought her wrist to her lips and bit deeply, instantly drawing a circle of blood. Then she began to make a swirling motion with her uplifted arm, sifting through the air while sticky threads of Darkness slithered greedily around her wrist, attaching to the blood like leeches. She ground her teeth together, forcing herself to remain unflinching, even when the sharpness of the tentacles stabbed her over and over. When they seemed bloated enough, Neferet spoke softly, lovingly to them. "You've taken your payment. Now you must do my bidding." She looked from the throbbing strands of Darkness to her immortal lover. "Lash him deeply. One hundred times." Neferet hurled Darkness at Kalona.

The weakened immortal only had time to unfurl his wings and begin to vault for the edge of the castle's roof. The razor threads caught him midstride. They wrapped around his wings at the sensitive base where they met his spine. Instead of leaping from the rooftop he was trapped, pinned against the ancient stone of the balustrade while Darkness began to slowly, methodically, slice furrows into his naked back.

Neferet watched only until his proud, handsome head sagged in defeat and his body jerked convulsively with every cutting stroke.

"Do not mar him permanently. I plan to enjoy the beauty of his skin again," she said before turning her back on Kalona and walking purposefully from the blood-soaked rooftop.

"It seems I must do everything myself, and there is so much to do . . . so much to do . . . ," she whispered to the Darkness that flitted about her ankles.

From the shadows within shadows Neferet thought she caught the outline of a massive bull watching her with approval and pleasure.

Neferet smiled.

CHAPTER THREE

Zoey

For the zillionth time I thought about what an amazing place Sgiach's throne room was. She was an ancient vampyre queen, the Great Taker of Heads, uber-powerful and surrounded by her own personal Warriors known as Guardians. Hell, way back in the day she'd even taken on the Vampyre High Council and won, but her castle wasn't a nasty-outdoor-plumbing-medieval-version-of-camping (gross). Sgiach's castle was a fortress, but it was—as they say over here in Scotland—a posh castle. I swear the view from any of the sea-facing windows, but especially her throne room, is so incredible that it looks like it should be on HD TV and not in front of me, in real life.

"It's beautiful here." Okay, talking to myself—especially so soon after being, well, kinda sorta *crazy* in the Otherworld—might possibly be a not-so-good idea. I sighed and shrugged. "Whatever. With Nala not here, Stark mostly out of it, Aphrodite doing stuff I'd rather not imagine with Darius, and Sgiach off doing something magickal or kicking ass in superhero-like training with Seoras, talking to myself seems like the only option."

"I was simply checking my email—nothing magickal or ass-kicking about that."

I suppose she should have made me jump. I mean, the queen seemed to materialize from the air beside me, but I guess being all shattered and crazy in the Otherworld had given me a pretty high spookiness tolerance. Plus, I felt a weird bond with this vampyre queen. Yeah, she was awe-inspiring and had mad powers and all, but in the weeks since Stark and I had come back, she had been a fixture by my side. While Aphrodite and Darius played gross kissy-face and walked hand in hand on the beach, and while Stark slept and slept and slept, Sgiach and I had spent time together. Sometimes talking—sometimes not. She was, I'd decided days ago, the coolest woman, vamp or not, I'd ever met.

"You're kidding, right? You're an ancient warrior queen who lives in a castle on an island no one can get to without you letting them, *and you're checking your email*? Sounds like magick to me."

Sgiach laughed. "Science often feels more mysterious than magick, or at least I have always thought so. Which reminds me—I have been considering how odd it is that daylight affects your Guardian with such debilitating severity."

"It's not just Stark. I mean, it's been worse with him recently 'cause, well, 'cause he's hurt." I paused, tripping over the words and not wanting to admit how hard it was to see my Warrior and Guardian so obviously messed up. "This really isn't normal for him. He can usually stay conscious during the day, even if he can't stand direct sunlight. All the red vampyres and fledglings are the same about it. Sun does them in."

"Well, young queen, it could be a distinct disadvantage that your Guardian is unable to protect you during the daylight hours."

I gave a shoulder shrug, even though her words sent a shiver of what might be premonition down my spine. "Yeah, well, recently I've learned to take care of myself. I think I can handle a few hours a day on my own," I said with a sharpness that surprised even me.

Sgiach's green-amber gaze caught me. "Do not allow it to make you hard."

"It?"

"Darkness and the struggle against it."

"Don't I have to be hard to fight?" I remembered skewering Kalona to the wall of an Otherworld arena with his own spear, and my stomach clenched.

She shook her head and the fading daylight caught the streak in her silver hair, making it glisten like cinnamon and gold mixed together. "No, you must be strong. You must be wise. You must know yourself and trust only those who are worthy. If you allow the battle against Darkness to harden you, you will lose perspective."

I looked away, staring out at the gray-blue waters that surrounded the Isle of Skye. The sun was setting into the ocean, reflecting delicate pink and coral colors across the darkening sky. It was beautiful and peaceful and looked utterly normal. Standing here it was hard to imagine that hanging around in the world out there was evil and Darkness and death.

But Darkness was out there, probably multiplied times a gazillion. Kalona hadn't killed me, and that was really, really gonna piss off Neferet.

Just the thought of what that meant, that I was going to have to deal with her and Kalona and all the horrible bullpoopie that went along with them again made me feel incredibly tired.

I turned away from the window, squared my shoulders, and faced Sgiach. "What if I don't want to fight anymore? What if I want to stay here, at least for a while? Stark's not himself. He needs to rest and get better. I've already sent that message to the High Council about Kalona. They know he murdered Heath and then came after me, and that Neferet was all involved in it and has allied herself with Darkness. The High Council can handle Neferet. Hell, *adults* need to handle her and the nasty evil mess she keeps trying to make out of life."

Sgiach didn't say anything, so I took a breath and kept on babbling. "I'm a kid. Seventeen. Barely. I'm crappy at geometry. My Spanish sucks. I can't even vote yet. Fighting evil isn't my responsibility—graduating from high school and, hopefully, making the Change is. My soul's been shattered and my boyfriend's been killed. Don't I deserve a break? Just a little one?"

Utterly surprising me, Sgiach smiled and said, "Yes, Zoey, I believe you do."

"You mean I can stay here?"

"For as long as you wish. I know what it is to feel the world press too tightly around. Here, as you said, the world is only allowed to enter at my command—and mostly I command it to stay away."

"What about the fight against Darkness and evil and whatnot?"

"It will be there when you return."

"Wow. Seriously?"

"Seriously. Stay here on my isle until your soul is truly rested and restored, and your conscience tells you to return to your world and your life there."

I ignored the little pang I felt at the word *conscience*. "Stark can stay, too, right?"

"Of course. A queen must always have her Guardian by her side."

"Speaking of," I said quickly, glad to steer the subject away from questions of conscience and battling evil, "how long has Seoras been your Guardian?"

The queen's eyes softened and her smile became sweeter, warmer, and even more beautiful. "Seoras became my Oath Bond Guardian more than five hundred years ago."

"Holy crap! Five hundred years? How old are you?"

Sgiach laughed. "After a certain point, don't you think age is irrelevant?"

"And it isna polite to ask a lassie's age."

Even if he hadn't said anything, I would have known Seoras had come in the room. Sgiach's face changed when he was around. It was like he turned on a switch and made something soft and warm glow inside her. And when he gazed back at her, just for a moment, he didn't look so gruff and battle-scarred and I'd-rather-kick-your-butt-than-talk-to-you.

The queen laughed and touched her Guardian's arm with an intimacy that made me hope Stark and I could find even a little piece of what the two of them had. And if he called me lassie after five hundred years, that would be pretty cool, too.

Heath would have called me lassie. Well, more like girl. Or maybe just Zo—forever just his Zo.

But Heath was dead and gone and he'd never call me anything again.

"He's waiting for yu, young queen."

Shocked, I stared at Seoras. "Heath?"

The Warrior's look was wise and understanding—his voice gentle. "Aye, yur Heath probably does await yu somewhere in the future, but it is of yur Guardian I speak."

"Stark! Oh, good, he's awake." I know I sounded guilty. I didn't mean to keep thinking about Heath, but it was hard not to. He'd been part of my life since I was nine—and dead only for a few weeks. I mentally shook myself, bowed quickly to Sgiach, and started for the door.

"He isna in your chamber," Seoras said. "The boy is near the grove. He asked that you meet him there."

"He's outside?" I paused, surprised. Since Stark had come back from the Otherworld, he'd been too weak and out of it to do much more than eat, sleep, and play computer games with Seoras, which was actually a super weird sight—it was like high school meets *Braveheart* meets *Call of Duty*.

"Aye, the lassie's done fussin' about with his makeup the now and is actin' like a proper Guardian again."

I put my fist on my hip and narrowed my eyes at the old Warrior. "He almost died. You cut him to pieces. He was in the Otherworld. Give him a little break. Jeesh."

"Aye, well, he dinna *actually* die, did he?"

I rolled my eyes. "You said he's at the grove?"

"Aye."

"Okie dokie."

As I hurried through the doorway, Sgiach's voice followed me. "Take that lovely scarf you bought in the village. It is a cold evening."

I thought it was a kinda strange thing for Sgiach to say. I mean, yeah, it was cold (and usually wet) on Skye, but fledglings and vamps don't feel changes in weather like humans do. But whatever. When a warrior queen tells you to do something, it's usually best to do it. So I detoured to the huge room I shared with Stark and grabbed the scarf I'd draped over the end of the canopied bed. It was cream-colored cashmere, with threads of gold woven through it, and I thought it probably looked prettier hanging against the crimson bed curtains than it did around my neck.

I paused for a second, looking at the bed I'd been sharing with Stark for the past weeks. I'd curled up with him, held his hand, and rested my head on his shoulder while I watched him sleep. But that was it. He hadn't even tried to tease me about making out with him.

Crap! He's hurt bad!

I mentally cringed as I recounted how many times Stark had suffered because of me: an arrow had almost killed him because he'd taken the shot that had been meant for me; he'd had to be sliced up and then destroyed a part of himself to pass into the Otherworld to join me; he'd been mortally wounded by Kalona because he'd believed it was the only way to reach what was shattered inside me.

But I'd saved him, too, I reminded myself. Stark had been right—watching Kalona brutalize him had made me pull myself together, and because of that Nyx had forced Kalona to breathe a sliver of immortality into Stark's body, returning his life and paying the debt he owed for killing Heath.

I walked through the beautifully decorated castle, nodding to the Warriors who bowed respectfully to me, and thought about Stark, automatically picking up my pace. What was he thinking, dragging himself outside after what he'd been through?

Hell, I didn't know what he was thinking. He'd been different since we'd been back.

Well, of course he's been different, I told myself sternly, feeling crappy and disloyal. My Warrior had made an Otherworld journey, died, been resurrected by an immortal, and then yanked back into a body that was weak and wounded.

But before then. Before we'd returned to the real world, something had happened between us. Something had changed for us. Or at least I'd thought it had. We'd been super intimate in the Otherworld. His drinking from me had been an incredible experience. It'd been *more* than sex. Yeah, it'd felt good. Really, *really* good. It had healed him, strengthened him, and—somehow—it had fixed whatever had still been broken inside me, allowing my tattoos to return.

And this new closeness with Stark had made losing Heath bearable.

So why was I feeling so depressed? What was wrong with me? Crap. I didn't know.

A mom would know. I thought about my mom and felt an unexpected and terrible loneliness. Yeah, she'd messed up and basically chosen a new husband over me, but she was still my mom. *I miss her,* the little voice inside my head admitted. Then I shook my head. No. I still had a "mom." My grandma was that and more to me.

"It's Grandma I miss." And then, of course, I felt guilty because since I'd been back I hadn't even called her. Okay, sure, I knew that Grandma would feel that my soul had returned—that I was safe. She'd always been super intuitive, especially about me. But I should have called her.

Feeling really disappointed in myself and sad, I chewed my lip and wrapped the cashmere scarf around my neck, holding the ends close while I made my way across the moat-like bridge and the cold wind whipped around me. Warriors were lighting the torches and I greeted the guys who bowed to me. I tried not to look at the creepy impaled skulls that framed the torches. Seriously. Skulls. Like of real dead people. Well, they were all old and shriveled and pretty much meatless, but still, *disgusting.*

Keeping my eyes carefully averted, I followed the raised pathway over the boggy area that surrounded the land side of the castle. When I got to the narrow road I turned left. The Sacred Grove began just a little way from the castle, seeming to stretch endlessly into the distance on the other side of the street. I knew where it was not because I remembered being carried, corpselike, past it on my way to Sgiach. I knew where it was because during the past weeks, while Stark had been recovering, I'd felt myself drawn to the grove. When I hadn't been with the queen, or Aphrodite, or checking on Stark, I'd been taking long walks inside it.

It reminded me of the Otherworld, and the fact that this memory comforted and creeped me out at the same time scared me.

Still, I'd visited the Sacred Grove, or as Seoras called it, the

Croabh, but I'd always come to it during daylight hours. Never after sunset. Never at night.

I walked along the road. Torches lined the street. They cast flickering shadows against the edge of the grove, lending enough light so that I could make out a hint of the mossy, magickal world within the boundary of ageless trees. It looked different without the sun making a living canopy of branches. It wasn't familiar anymore, and I felt a prickly sensation across my skin, like my senses were on super alert.

My eyes kept being pulled to the shadows within the grove. Were they blacker than they should be? Was there something *not quite right* lurking inside there? I shivered, and that's when a movement farther down the street caught at the edge of my vision. My heart skittered around in my chest while I peered ahead of me, half expecting wings and coldness, evil and madness . . .

Instead what I saw had my heart skittering for other reasons.

Stark was there, standing in front of two trees that were twisted together to form one. The trees' interwoven branches were decorated with strips of cloth knotted together—some were brightly colored, some were worn and faded and tattered. It was the mortal version of the hanging tree that had stood before Nyx's Grove in the Otherworld, but just because this one was in the "real" world didn't mean it was any less spectacular. Especially when the guy standing in front of it, staring up at its branches, was wearing the earth-colored MacUallis plaid, in the traditional Warrior way, complete with dirk and sporran and all sorts of sexy metal-studded leather accoutrements (as Damien would say).

I stared at him as if I hadn't seen him for years. Stark looked strong and healthy and totally gorgeous. I was distracting myself by wondering what exactly Scottish guys did, *or didn't,* wear under those kilts when he turned to face me.

His smile lit up his eyes. "I can practically hear you thinking."

My cheeks got instantly warm, especially since Stark did have the ability to sense my emotions. "You're not supposed to be listening in unless I'm in danger."

His grin turned cocky and his eyes sparkled mischievously. "Then don't think so loud. But you're right. I shouldn't have been listening in 'cause what I was getting from you was the opposite of what I'd call danger."

"Smart-ass," I said, but I couldn't help grinning back.

"Yep, that's me, but I'm your smart-ass."

Stark held out his hand to me as I reached his side, and our fingers twined together. His touch was warm—his hand strong and steady. This close to him I could see that he still had shadows under his eyes, but he wasn't as deadly pale as he had been. "You're yourself again!"

"Yeah, it's taken me a while; my sleep's been weird—not as restful as it should be, but it's like a switch flipped inside me today and I finally recharged."

"I'm glad. I've been so worried about you." As I said it I realized how true that was, and I also blurted, "I've missed you, too."

He squeezed my hand and tugged me closer to him. All of his cocky kidding evaporated. "I know. You've felt distant and scared. What's up with that?"

I started to tell him he was wrong—that I was just giving him some space to get well, but the words that formed and slipped from my lips were more honest. "You've been hurt a lot because of me."

"Not because of *you*, Z. I've been hurt because that's what Darkness does—it tries to destroy those of us who fight for Light."

"Yeah, well, I wish Darkness would pick on someone else for a while and let you rest."

He bumped me with his shoulder. "I knew what I was getting

into when I swore myself to you. I was cool with it then—I'm cool with it now—and I'll still be cool with it fifty years from now. And, Z, it really doesn't make me sound very manly and Guardian-like when you say Darkness is 'picking on' me."

"Look, I'm being serious. You want to know what's up with me, well, I've been worried that you might have been hurt too bad this time." I hesitated, fighting unexpected tears as I finally understood. "So bad that you weren't gonna get well. And then you would leave me, too."

Heath's presence was so tangible there between us that I half expected to see him step from the grove and say *Hey there, Zo. No crying. You snot way too much when you cry.* And of course that thought made it even harder for me *not* to bawl.

"Listen to me, Zoey. I'm your Guardian. You're my queen; that's more than a High Priestess, so our bond is even stronger than a regular Oath Sworn Warrior's."

I blinked hard. "That's good, 'cause it feels like bad stuff keeps trying to tear me away from everyone I love."

"Nothing will ever take me away from you, Z. I've sworn my oath on it." He smiled, and there was such confidence and trust and love in his eyes that he made my breath catch in my throat. "You'll never get rid of me, *mo bann ri*."

"Good," I said softly, leaning my head against his shoulder as he drew me inside the half circle of his arm. "I'm tired of the whole leaving thing."

He kissed my forehead, murmuring against my skin, "Yeah, me, too."

"Actually, I think the truth is that I'm tired. Period. I need to recharge, too." I looked up at him. "Would it be okay with you if we stayed here? I-I just don't want to leave and go back to . . . to . . ." I hesitated, not sure how to put what I was feeling into words.

"To everything—the good and the bad. I know what you mean," said my Guardian. "It's cool with Sgiach?"

"She said we could stay as long as my conscience lets me," I said, smiling a little wryly. "And right now my conscience is definitely letting me."

"Sounds good to me. I'm in no rush to get back to all the Neferet drama that's gotta be waiting for us."

"So we stay for a while?"

Stark hugged me. "We stay until you say to go."

I closed my eyes and rested in Stark's arms, feeling like a huge weight had been taken off me. When he asked, "Hey, would you do something with me?" my response was instant and easy: "Yep, anything."

I could feel him chuckling. "That answer makes me want to change what I was gonna ask you to do."

"Not *that* kind of anything." I gave him a little shove, even though I was feeling waves of relief that Stark was definitely acting like Stark again.

"No?" His gaze went from my eyes to my lips, and he suddenly looked less cocky and more hungry—and that look made my stomach shiver. Then he bent and kissed me, hard and long, and he completely took my breath away. "Are you sure you don't mean *that* kind of anything?" he asked, his voice lower and gruffer than usual.

"No. Yes."

He grinned. "Which is it?"

"I don't know. I can't think when you kiss me like that," I told him honestly.

"Then I'll have to do more of that kind of kissing," he said.

"Okay," I said, feeling light-headed and weirdly weak-kneed.

"Okay," he repeated. "But later. Right now I'm going to show you how strong a Guardian I am and stick to the original question I was gonna ask you." He reached into the leather satchel that was strapped across his body and pulled out a long, narrow strip of the MacUallis plaid, lifting it so that it floated gently on the breeze. "Zoey Redbird, would you tie your wishes and your dreams for the future with me in a knot on the hanging tree?"

I hesitated for only a second—only long enough to feel the sharp pain that was the absence of Heath, the absence of a future thread that could never be—and then I blinked my eyes clear of tears and answered my Guardian Warrior.

"Yes, Stark, I'll tie my wishes and dreams for the future with you."

CHAPTER FOUR

Zoey

"I have to do *what* to my cashmere scarf?"

"Tear a strip from it," Stark said.

"Are you sure?"

"Yeah, I got the instructions straight from Seoras. That and a bunch of smart-ass comments about my education being sadly lacking and something about not knowing my arse from my ear or my elbow, and also something about me being a fanny, and I don't know what the hell that means."

"Fanny? Like a girl's name?"

"I don't think so . . ."

Stark and I shook our heads, in total agreement about Seoras and his weirdness. "Anyway," Stark continued, "he said the pieces of fabric have to be from something that's mine and something that's yours, and it has to be special to each of us." He smiled and tugged at my shimmery, expensive, beautiful new scarf. "You like this thing a lot, don't you?"

"Yeah, enough that I don't want to rip it up."

Stark laughed, pulled his dirk from the sheath at his waist, and handed it to me. "Good, then that tied with my plaid will make a strong knot between us."

"Yeah, that plaid didn't cost you eighty euros, which is more than a hundred dollars. I think," I muttered as I reached for the dirk.

Instead of letting me take the dirk from him, Stark hesitated. His eyes found mine. "You're right. It didn't cost me money. It cost me blood."

My shoulders slumped. "I'm sorry. Listen to me, whining about money and a scarf. Ah, hell! I'm starting to sound like Aphrodite."

Stark flipped the dirk around so that it pressed against his chest over his heart. "If you turn into Aphrodite I'm going to stab myself."

"If I turn into Aphrodite, stab me first." I reached for the dirk, and this time he gave it to me.

"Deal." He grinned.

"Deal," I said, and then I pierced the fringy edge of my new scarf and with one quick yank ripped a long, slender piece from it. "Now what?"

"Pick a branch. Seoras said I'm supposed to hold my piece, and you hold yours. We tie them together, and the wish we make for us will be tied together."

"Really? That's super romantic."

"Yeah, I know." He reached out and traced my cheek with one finger. "It makes me wish I'd made it up, just for you."

I looked into his eyes and said exactly what I was thinking. "You're the best Guardian in the world."

Stark shook his head, his expression tight. "I'm not. Don't say that."

As he had done to me, I traced his cheek with a finger. "For me, Stark. For me you're the best Guardian in the world."

He relaxed a little. "For you, I'll try to be."

I looked from his eyes to the ancient tree. "There." I pointed to a low-hanging branch that forked, creating with leaves and limbs what looked like a perfect heart. "That's our place."

Together we went to the tree. Then, like Sgiach's Guardian had instructed, Stark and I tied the earth-colored MacUallis plaid and my shimmery length of cream together. Our fingers brushed and as we looped the last part of the knot, our eyes met.

"My wish for us is that our future is strong, just like this knot," Stark said.

"My wish is that our future is together, just like this knot," I said.

We sealed our wishes with a kiss that made me breathless. I was leaning into Stark to kiss him again when he took my hand in his and said, "Would you let me show you something?"

"Okay, sure," I said, thinking that just about then I'd let Stark show me anything.

He started leading me into the grove, but he felt my hesitation because he squeezed my hand and smiled down at me. "Hey, there's nothing here that can hurt you, and if there was I'd pro-tect you. I promise."

"I know. Sorry." I swallowed past the weird little knot of fear that had formed in my throat, squeezed his hand back, and we walked into the grove.

"You're back, Z. Really back. And you're safe."

"Doesn't it remind you of the Otherworld, too?" I spoke qui-etly and Stark had to bend to hear me.

"Yeah, but in a good way."

"Me, too, most of the time. I feel stuff here that makes me think of Nyx and her realm."

"I think it has something to do with how old this place is, and how apart from the world it's been. Okay, it's over here," he said. "Seoras was telling me about this, and I thought I saw it just before you came up. This is what I wanted to show you." Stark pointed ahead and to the right of us, and I gasped in pleasure. One of the trees was glowing. From within the craggy lines in its thick bark, a soft blue light glistened, as if the tree had luminous veins.

"It's amazing! What is it?"

"I'm sure there's a scientific explanation—probably something about phosphorous plants and stuff, but I'd rather believe it's magick, Scottish magick," Stark said.

I looked up at him, smiled, and tugged at his plaid. "I like calling it magick, too. And speaking of Scottish stuff, I'm seriously liking you in this outfit."

He glanced down at himself. "Yeah, weird that what's basically a dress made out of wool can look so manly."

I giggled. "I'd like to hear you tell Seoras and the rest of the Warriors that they're wearing woolly dresses."

"Hell, no. I just came from the Otherworld, but that doesn't mean I have a death wish." Then he seemed to reconsider what I'd just said, and added, "You like me in this, huh?"

I crossed my arms and walked a circle around him, giving him a serious once-over while he watched me. The colors of the MacUallis plaid always reminded me of the earth—weirdly enough, Oklahoma red dirt earth to be specific. That distinctive rusty brown was mixed with lighter just-changed-leaves and bark-like gray-black, lighter just-changed-leaves. He wore it the ancient way, like Seoras had taught him, pleating all those yards of material by hand and then wrapping himself into it and securing it with belts and cool old brooches (except I didn't think Warrior guys called them brooches). He had another piece of plaid that he could pull up over his shoulders, which was a good thing because except for the crisscross leather belt things, all he wore over his chest was a sleeveless T-shirt that left lots of his skin bare.

He cleared his throat. His half grin made him look a little boyish and kinda nervous. "So? Do I pass your inspection, my queen?"

"Totally." I grinned. "With a big A-plus."

I liked it that even though he was a big, tough Guardian, he looked relieved. "Glad to hear it. Check out how handy all this wool is." He took my hand and led me closer to the glowing tree, and sat down, spreading part of his plaid out over the moss. "Have a seat, Z."

"Don't mind if I do," I said, curling up beside him. Stark pulled me into his arms and flipped up the edge of the kilt over me so that I was warm, cocooned in what felt like a lovely Warrior-and-plaid sandwich.

We lay there like that for what seemed like a long time. We didn't talk. Instead we sank into a beautiful, comfortable silence. It felt right to be in Stark's arms. Safe. And when his hands started to move, tracing the pattern of my tattoos, first on my face and then down my neck, that felt right, too.

"I'm glad they came back," Stark said softly.

"It was because of you," I whispered back. "Because of what you made me feel in the Otherworld."

He smiled and kissed my forehead. "You mean scared and freaked out?"

"No," I said, touching his face. "You made me feel alive again."

His lips went from my forehead to my mouth. He kissed me deeply and then, against my lips, he said, "That's good to hear, 'cause the whole thing with Heath, and almost losing you, has made me know something for real that I only kinda knew before. I can't live without you, Zoey. Maybe I'll only be your Guardian, and you'll have another consort or even a mate, but whoever else you have in your life won't change who I am to you. I'll never get pissed and selfish again and leave you. No matter

what. I'll deal with other guys, and it won't change us. I swear."
He sighed then and pressed his forehead against mine.

"Thank you," I said. "Even if it does kinda sound like you're giving me away to other guys."

He leaned back, frowned at me, and said, "That's just bullshit, Z."

"Well, you just said that it's cool with you if I'm with—"

"No!" He shook me a little. "I didn't say I was cool with you being with other guys. I said I wouldn't let it break up what we have."

"What do we have?"

"Each other. For always."

"That's enough for me, Stark." I twined my arms around his shoulders. "Would you do something with me?"

"Yep, anything," he echoed my answer, making both of us smile.

"Kiss me like you did before so that I can't think."

"I can handle that," he said.

Stark's kiss started out as slow and sweet, but it didn't stay that way for long. As his kiss deepened, his hands began to explore my body. When he found the bottom edge of my T-shirt he hesitated, and it was during that tiny moment of hesitation that I made my decision. I wanted Stark. I wanted all of him. I pulled away from him so that I could look into his eyes. We were both breathing hard and he automatically leaned toward me, like he couldn't stand not being pressed against my body.

"Wait." I put my hand flat against his chest.

"Sorry." His voice sounded gruff. "I didn't mean to come on too strong."

"No, that's not it. You're not coming on too strong. I just wanted to . . . well . . ." I hesitated, trying to make my mind work through the fog of desire I was feeling for him. "Ah, hell. I'll show you what I want." Before I could get shy or embarrassed, I stood up. Stark was watching me with an expression that was curiosity mixed with heat, but when I pulled off my shirt, undid and stepped out of my jeans, the curiosity went away and his eyes seemed to darken with the heat. I lay back down within the safety of his arms, loving the sensation of the roughness of his plaid against the smoothness of my naked skin.

"You're so beautiful," Stark said, tracing the pattern of my tattoo that wrapped around my waist. His touch made me tremble. "Are you scared?" he asked, pulling me closer.

"I'm not trembling because I'm scared," I whispered against his lips between kisses. "I'm trembling because of how much I want you."

"You're sure?"

"Totally sure. I love you, Stark."

"I love you, too, Zoey."

Stark took me in his arms then, and with his hands and his lips, he blocked out the world, making me think only about him—want only to be with him. His touch banished the ugly memory of Loren, and the mistake I'd made giving myself to him, into the mists of the past. At the same time Stark soothed the hurt inside me left by Heath's loss. I would always miss Heath, but he had been human, and as Stark made love to me I understood that I would have had to say goodbye to Heath eventually.

Stark was my future—my Warrior—my Guardian—my love.

When Stark unwrapped the MacUallis plaid from around his body and lay naked beside me, he bent and I felt his tongue first against the pulse at my neck, and then a brief, questioning touch of his teeth.

"Yes," I said, surprised by the breathless, unfamiliar sound of my voice. I shifted my body so that Stark's lips pressed more firmly against my neck, while I kissed the strong, smooth slope where his shoulder met his biceps. With my own wordless question, I let my teeth graze his skin.

"Oh, goddess, yes! Please, Zoey. Please."

I couldn't wait any longer. I nicked his skin at the same moment he bit gently into my neck, and with the warm, sweet taste of his blood my body was filled with our shared feelings. The bond between us was like fire—it burned and consumed, almost painful in its intensity. Almost unbearable in its pleasure. We clung to each other, mouths pressed against skin, body against body. All I could feel was Stark. All I could hear was the pounding of our hearts beating in time together. I couldn't tell where I ended and he began. I couldn't tell which pleasure was mine, and which was his. Afterward while I lay in his arms, our legs twined together, our bodies still slick with sweat, I sent a silent prayer to my Goddess: *Nyx, thank you for giving Stark to me. Thank you for letting him love me.*

We didn't leave the grove for hours. Later I would remember that night as one of the happiest of my life. In the chaos of the future, the memory of being wrapped in Stark's arms, sharing touches and dreams, and for that moment in time being completely, utterly content, would be something I cherished, like the warm glow of candlelight on the darkest of nights.

Much later we walked slowly back to the castle. Our fingers were threaded together, our sides brushed intimately. We'd just crossed the moat bridge, and I'd been so wrapped up in Stark that I hadn't even noticed the staked heads. Actually, I hadn't noticed much of anything until Aphrodite's voice intruded.

"Oh, for shit's sake. Could you two be more obvious?"

I lifted my head dreamily from Stark's shoulder and saw Aphrodite standing in a pool of torchlight at the entrance to the castle, toe tapping in annoyance.

"My beauty, leave them be. They've earned their piece of happiness." Darius's deep voice came from the shadows beside her.

One fine blond eyebrow lifted mockingly. "I don't think happiness is the piece she just gave Stark."

"Seriously, even your crudeness can't bother me right now," I told her.

"It can bother me, though," Stark said. "Shouldn't you be pulling the wings off seagulls or the claws off crabs?"

Aphrodite acted like Stark hadn't spoken and walked up to me. "Is it true?"

"Is what true? That you're a pain in the butt?" I said.

Stark snorted. "That's definitely true."

"If it's true, then you're gonna have to tell him. I'm not listening to him blubber." Aphrodite waved her iPhone around, using it to punctuate her words.

"Jeesh, you're acting super crazy, even for you," I said. "Do you need shopping therapy intervention? Is. What. True?" I spoke slowly, pretending she was an English-as-a-second-language-learner.

"Is it true what the Queen of Every Damn Thing Skye just told me—that you're not leaving with us tomorrow? That you're staying here?"

"Oh." I shuffled my feet, wondering why I should feel guilty. "Yeah, that's true."

"Great. Just great. Then, like I said before, *you* tell him."

"Who him?"

"Jack. Here. He's gonna burst into snotty tears and ruin his makeup, which will make him boo-hoo even more. And I want nothing to do with gay snot. At all." Aphrodite punched the screen of her phone. It was ringing when she handed it to me.

Jack sounded sweet but defensive when he answered. "Aphrodite, if you're going to say something else mean about the Ritual, then I think you should just say nothing at all. Plus, I'm not going to listen to you because I'm busy defying gravity. So there."

"Uh, hi, Jack," I said.

I could almost see his smile blaze through the phone. "*Zoey!* Hi! Oooh, it's so cool that you're not dead, or even dead-like. Oh, oh, did Aphrodite tell you what we're planning for tomorrow after you get back? Ohmigoddess, it's going to be so totally cool!"

"No, Jack. Aphrodite didn't tell me 'cause—"

"Goodie! I get to tell you. So, we're going to have a special Dark Daughters and Sons Ritual of Celebration, like with proper nouns and such, because you being un-shattered is a big deal."

"Jack, I have to—"

"No, no, no, you don't have to do anything. I have it all handled. I even have the food planned, well, with Damien's help, of course. I mean . . ."

I sighed and waited for him to take a breath.

"See, told ya," Aphrodite said under her breath while Jack gushed. "He's going to bawl when you burst his little pink bubble."

". . . and my favorite part is when you come into the circle I'm going to be singing 'Defying Gravity.' You know, like Kurt did on *Glee,* except I'm going to actually hit that high note. So what do you think?"

I closed my eyes, took a deep breath, and said, "I think you're a really good friend."

"Oooh! Thank you!"

"*But* let's postpone the Ritual."

"Postpone? How come?" His voice already sounded trembly.

"Because . . ." I hesitated. Crap. Aphrodite was right. He probably *was* going to cry.

Stark pried the phone gently from my hand and tapped the speaker button.

"Hey there, Jack," he said.

"Hi, Stark!"

"Could you do me a favor?"

"Ohmigoddess! Of course!"

"Well, I'm still kinda out of it from the Otherworld thing and all. Aphrodite and Darius are coming back tomorrow, but Zoey is going to stay here on Skye with me while I get stronger. So could you let everyone know that we won't be back in Tulsa for a couple more weeks or so? Just pass the word for me and smooth everything over?"

I held my breath, waiting for the tears, but instead Jack sounded totally grown and mature. "Absolutely. Don't worry about anything, Stark. I'll let Lenobia and Damien and everyone know. And Z, no problem. We can definitely postpone. It'll just give me more time to practice my song and figure out how to make origami swords for decorations. I thought I'd hang them with fishing line, that see-through stuff, so it would look like, you know, they're *defying gravity*."

I smiled and mouthed *thank you* to Stark. "Sounds perfect, Jack. I won't worry about a thing if I know you're in charge of the decorations and the music."

Jack's happy laughter bubbled. "It's going to be a great Ritual! You wait and see. Stark, just get well. Oh, and Aphrodite, you shouldn't assume that I'm going to burst into tears at the first hint of a change in party plans."

Aphrodite frowned at the phone. "How the hell did you know that's what I assumed?"

"I'm gay. I know things."

"Whatever. Say goodbye, Jack. My phone's roaming," Aphrodite said.

"Goodbye, Jack!" Jack said, giggling, while Aphrodite snatched the phone from Stark and ended the call.

"That went better than you thought it was going to go," I said to Aphrodite.

"Yeah, 'she' took it well. Wonder how that other one will take it, since she's exponentially worse than Miss Jack."

"Look, Aphrodite, Damien isn't a fluttery gay, not that there's anything wrong with that. But I really wish you'd be nicer about both of them."

"Oh, please. I'm not talking your gays. I'm talking about Neferet."

"Neferet!" My voice was sharp. I hated even saying her name. "What have you heard from her?"

"Nothing, and that's exactly what I'm worried about. But, hey, Z, don't lose any sleep over it. After all, you're going to be here, on Skye, with a gazillion big, strong guys—and Stark—to protect you, while the rest of us mere mortals get on with the whole good versus evil, Darkness v. Light, epic battle, blah, blah, et cetera, ad nauseam." Aphrodite turned and stomped up the front stairs of the castle.

"Aphrodite's a mere mortal? I thought her pain-in-the-ass level was well beyond mere," Stark said.

"I heard that!" Aphrodite called over her shoulder. "Oh, and FYI, Z, I had a luggage emergency, as in I didn't have enough of it, so I'm confiscating that suitcase you bought the other day. I'm off to do some power packing. Later, peasants." She slammed the thick, wooden door to the castle, which really took some doing.

"She's magnificent," Darius said, smiling proudly as he vaulted the steps and followed Aphrodite.

"I can think of a lot of *m* words that she could be. *Magnificent* isn't one of them," Stark grumbled.

"*Mental* and *mean* pop into my head," I said.

"*Manure* pops into mine," Stark said.

"Manure?"

"I think she's full of shit, but it's too many words and doesn't start with an *m,* so that's as close as I could get," he said.

"Heehees," I said. Then I linked my arm with his. "You're just trying to distract me from the Neferet stuff, aren't you?"

"Is it working?"

"Not really."

Stark's arm slid around me. "Then I'll have to work on my distraction skills."

Arm in arm, we walked to the castle entrance. I let Stark amuse me with his list of *m* words that fit Aphrodite better than *magnificent,* and tried to regain the sense of contented happiness I'd felt so recently and so briefly. I kept telling myself that Neferet was a world away—and the adults of that world could handle her. As Stark opened the castle door for me, something pulled my vision upward and my eyes caught on the flag that waved proudly over Sgiach's domain. I paused, appreciating the beauty of the powerful black bull with the shape of the glittering Goddess within his body. Just then, a trail of mist lifted from the waters that flanked the castle, altering my sight of the flag and changing the black bull to ghostly white as it blanked out the Goddess image completely.

Fear skittered through my body.

"What is it?" Instantly alert, Stark moved to my side.

I blinked. The fog dissipated and the flag shifted back into its proper form.

"Nothing," I said quickly. "Just me being paranoid."

"Hey, I'm right here. You don't have to be paranoid; you don't have to worry. I can protect you."

Stark took me into his arms and held me tightly, blocking the outside world and what my gut was trying to tell me.

CHAPTER FIVE

Stevie Rae

"You ain't yourself. You know that?"

Stevie Rae looked up at Kramisha. "All I'm doin' is just sittin' here, minding *my own* business." She paused, letting the *unlike you* implication sink in. "How is that not being myself?"

"You picked the darkest, creepiest corner stuck all over here. You blew them candles out so it'd be even darker. And you sitting here moping so loud I can almost hear your thoughts."

"You can't hear my thoughts."

The hard edge to Stevie Rae's voice had Kramisha's eyes widening. "'Course I can't. They's no need for you to get all huffy. I said *almost*. I ain't Sookie Stackhouse. Plus, even if I was I wouldn't listen in to your thoughts. That'd be rude and my mama raised me better than that." Kramisha sat next to Stevie Rae on the little wooden bench. "Speaking of—am I the only one who thinks that werewolf is hotter than Bill and Eric put together?"

"Kramisha, do not mess up season three of *True Blood* for me. I haven't finished my DVDs of season two."

"Well, I'm just sayin', prepare for some serious four-footed hotness."

"Seriously. Don't you dare tell me anything else."

"Okay—okay, but the whole wolf-monster-hotness-guy thing is somethin' I need to talk to you 'bout."

"This bench is made of wood. Wood equals earth. Which means I can probably figure out a way to make it smack the living crap right outta you if you mess up *True Blood* for me."

"Would you please relax? I'm already offa that. I got somethin' else we gotta discuss before we go into what I know is gonna be one majorly boring Council Meeting."

"It's part of what we gotta do. I'm a High Priestess. You're a Poet Laureate. We have to go to the Council Meetings." Stevie Rae let out a long puff of air and felt her shoulders slump. "Dang, I'll be glad when Z gets back here tomorrow."

"Yeah, yeah, I get that. What I don't get is what's got you so messed up in the head you seem turned inside out."

"My boyfriend has lost his dang mind and disappeared off the face of the earth. My best friend almost died in the Otherworld. The red fledglings—the other ones—are still out there somewhere doin' Bubba-knows-what, which I'm pretty sure means eating people. And to top it all off I'm supposed to be a High Priestess, even though I'm not even sure what all that means. I think that's enough to mess up anyone's head."

"Yeah, it is. But it ain't enough to keep givin' me weird-assed poems that all have the same freaky theme. They about you *and* beasts, and I want to know why."

"Kramisha, I do not know what you're talkin' 'bout."

Stevie Rae started to stand up, but Kramisha reached into her huge bag and pulled out a piece of violet-colored paper that had her bold writing scrawled across it. With another heavy exhale of breath, Stevie Rae sat down and held out her hand.

"Fine. Let me see."

"I wrote 'em both on this paper. The old one and the new one. Somethin' told me you might need your memory refreshed."

Stevie Rae didn't say anything. Her eyes went to the first poem on the paper. She took her time reading it. Not because she needed her memory refreshed. She didn't. Every line of the poem had been burned into her mind.

> *The Red One steps into the Light*
> *girded loins for her part in*
> *the apocalyptic fight.*
>
> *Darkness hides in different forms*
> *See beyond shape, color, lies*
> *and emotional storms.*
>
> *Ally with him; pay with your heart*
> *though trust cannot be given*
> *unless the Darkness you part.*
>
> *See with the soul and not your eyes*
> *because to dance with beasts you*
> *must penetrate their disguise.*

Stevie Rae told herself she wouldn't cry, but her heart felt bruised and broken. The poem had been right. She'd seen Rephaim with her soul, not her eyes. She'd parted Darkness and trusted and accepted him—and because of that, because she'd allied herself with a beast, she had paid with her heart. She was still paying with her heart.

Reluctantly, Stevie Rae looked to the second poem on the page—the new one. Reminding herself not to react, not to let her face give away anything, she started reading:

> *Beasts can be beautiful*
> *Dreams become desires*
> *Reality changes with reason*
> *Trust your truth*
> *Man . . . monster . . . mystery . . . magick*

Hear with your heart
See without scorn
Love will not lose
Trust his truth
His promise is proof
The test is time
Faith frees
If there is courage to change.

Stevie Rae's mouth felt dry. "Sorry, I can't help you. I don't know what these things are about." She tried to hand the piece of paper back to Kramisha, but the poet's hands were folded across her chest.

"You ain't a good liar, Stevie Rae."

"It's not smart to call your High Priestess a liar." There was an edge of meanness to Stevie Rae's voice that had Kramisha shaking her head.

"What's happenin' to you? You dealing with somethin' that's eatin' you from the inside out. If you was yourself, you'd be talkin' to me. You'd be trying to figure this out."

"I can't figure out this poetry stuff! It's metaphor and symbolism and weird, confusing predictions."

"That's a damn lie," Kramisha said. "We been figuring this stuff out. Zoey has. You and I did, or at least we did enough to get word to Z in the Otherworld. And it helped. Stark said it did." Kramisha pointed at the first poem. "Some of this one came true. You met the beasts. Those bulls. You been different ever since. Now I been given another one of them beast poems. I know they for you. And I know you know more than you sayin'."

"Look, stay outta my business, Kramisha." Stevie Rae stood up, stepped out of the alcove, and as she walked right into Dragon

Lankford she yelled back at Kramisha, "I'm done talking 'bout this beast stuff!"

"Hey, whoa, what's this about?" Dragon's strong hand steadied Stevie Rae when she stumbled because of their collision. "Did you say *beast stuff*?"

"She did." Kramisha pointed at the notebook page in Stevie Rae's hand. "Two poems come to me, one the day Stevie Rae tangled with them bulls, and the second just a little while ago. She don't want to pay them no mind."

"I didn't say I wasn't going to pay them any mind. I just want to take care of my *own* business my *own* self without every dang body in the universe nosing around."

"Do you consider me every dang body?" Dragon asked.

Stevie Rae forced herself to meet his gaze. "No, 'course not."

"And you are in agreement with me that Kramisha's poems are important."

"Well, yeah."

"Then you can't just ignore them." Dragon rested his hand on Stevie Rae's shoulder. "I know how it feels to want to keep your life private, but you've stepped into a position where there are more important things than your privacy."

"I know that, but I can deal with this myself."

"You didn't deal with the bulls," Kramisha said. "They still happened."

"They're gone, aren't they? So I did deal with them just fine."

"I remember seeing you after your battle with the bull. You were gravely injured. Had you understood Kramisha's warning the cost to you might not have been so great. And then there is the fact that a Raven Mocker appeared, and he might even be the creature Rephaim. That monster is still out there somewhere and a danger to all of us. So, you must understand, young priestess, that a forewarning meant for you cannot be kept private because it touches the lives of others."

Stevie Rae stared into Dragon's eyes. His words were strong. His tone was kind. But was that suspicion and anger she saw in his expression, or was it just the grief that had been shadowing him since the death of his wife?

While she hesitated, Dragon continued, "A beast killed Anastasia. We cannot allow any other innocent to be touched by these creatures of Darkness if we can prevent it. You know I speak truth, Stevie Rae."

"I-I know," she stuttered, trying to order her words. *Rephaim killed Anastasia the night Darius shot him from the sky. No one will ever forget that—I can never forget that, especially now that things have changed. It's been weeks and I haven't seen him. At all. Our Imprint is still there. I can feel it, but I haven't felt anything from him.*

And that lack of feeling made the decision for Stevie Rae. "Okay, you're right. I need help with this." *Maybe this is the way it was meant to be,* she thought as she handed Dragon the poems. *Maybe Dragon will discover my secret, and when he does it will all be destroyed: Rephaim, our Imprint, and my heart. But at least it'll be over.*

As Dragon read the poetry Stevie Rae watched his expression get darker. When he finally looked from the page and into her eyes, there was no mistaking his worry.

"The second bull you conjured, the black one that vanquished the evil bull, what type of connection did you have with him?"

Stevie Rae tried not to show how relieved she was that Dragon was focusing on the bulls and not questioning her about Rephaim.

"I don't know if you could really call it a connection, but I thought he was beautiful. He was black, but there was no Darkness about him. He was incredible—like the night sky, or the earth."

"The earth . . ." Dragon seemed to be thinking aloud. "If the bull reminds you of your element, perhaps that is enough for the two of you to remain connected."

"But we know he's good," Kramisha said. "They's no mystery 'bout that. The poems can't be talkin' 'bout him."

"So?" Stevie Rae couldn't hide her irritation. Kramisha was like a dang dog with a soup bone. She just wouldn't leave it alone.

"So, the poem, 'specially the last one, is all about trusting the truth. We already know he's good. You can trust the black bull. Why do you need a poem to tell you that?"

"Kramisha, like I tried to tell you before, I do not know."

"I just don't think they's talkin' 'bout the black bull," Kramisha said.

"What else could they be talkin' about? I don't know any other beasts." Stevie Rae said the words fast, as if speed could take away the lie.

"You said Dallas has an unusual new affinity, and that he has seemed to go mad. Is that correct?" Dragon asked.

"Yeah, basically," Stevie Rae said.

"The beast reference could be symbolic of Dallas. The poem might mean that you need to trust the humanity that is still within him," Dragon said.

"I don't know about that," Stevie Rae said. "He was one hot mess and super crazy last time I saw him. I mean he was saying some seriously weird stuff about that Raven Mocker he saw."

"Council Meeting is being called to session!" Lenobia's voice drifted down the hallway from the open door to the Council Chamber.

"Do you mind if I keep this?" Dragon lifted the piece of paper as they started down the hall. "I'll copy it, and then return it to you, but I'd like a chance to study and consider the poetry more thoroughly."

"Yeah, that's okay with me," Stevie Rae said.

"Well, I'm glad we got your brain workin' on this, Dragon," Kramisha said.

"Me, too," Stevie Rae said, trying to sound like she was telling the truth.

Dragon paused. "I won't share this with everybody, only those vampyres I believe could help us understand the poetry's meaning. I understand your wish for privacy."

"I'll tell Zoey about it as soon as she gets back tomorrow," Stevie Rae said.

Dragon frowned. "I do think you should share the poetry with Zoey, but sadly, she will not be returning to the House of Night tomorrow."

"What? Why not?"

"Apparently Stark isn't well enough to travel, so Sgiach has given them permission to remain on Skye indefinitely."

"Did Zoey tell you that?" Stevie Rae couldn't believe her BFF had called Dragon and not her. What was Z thinking?

"No, she and Stark spoke with Jack."

"Oh, the Celebration Ritual." Stevie Rae nodded in understanding. Z hadn't been keeping anything from her. Jack had been uber-exuberant about the Ritual he'd appointed himself in charge of music, food, and decorations for—he'd probably called her with an entire list of questions like: *What's your favorite color?* and *Doritos or Ruffles?*

"Gay boy is majorly obsessed. I bet he lost his damn mind when he found out Z ain't comin' home tomorrow."

"Actually, he's using the extra time to keep practicing that song he wants to sing, and he's decorating," Dragon said.

"Goddess help us," Kramisha said. "If he tries to hang rainbows and unicorns everywhere and make all of us wear them feather boas—again—I'm just gonna say 'ah hell no.'"

"Origami swords," Dragon said.

"Excuse me?" Stevie Rae was sure she couldn't have heard him right.

Dragon chuckled. "Jack came by the Field House and borrowed a claymore so he could have a real example to work from. In honor of Stark, he's going to use origami swords hung with fishing line. He said they'll look like the song."

"'Cause they'll be *defying gravity*." Stevie Rae couldn't help giggling. She did heart her some Jack. He was just too cute for words.

"I hope he don't do them in pink paper. That just ain't right."

They'd reached the door to the Council Chamber, and before they entered the already full room, Stevie Rae heard Dragon say, "Not pink. Purple. I saw him carrying a ream of purple paper."

Stevie Rae was still grinning when Lenobia called the Council Meeting to order. In the days that followed, she would remember her grin and wish she could hold on to the image of Jack making purple swords out of paper and singing "Defying Gravity," eternally looking on the bright side of life, eternally sweet, eternally happy, and, most important, eternally safe.

CHAPTER SIX

Jack

"Duch, what is it, beautiful girl? Why are you acting so psycho today?" Jack pulled the pile of purple origami papers from under the blond Lab and put them up out of dog-butt reach on the wooden stool he was using as an outside table and sword stand. The big dog huffed, thumped her tail on the ground, and scooted closer to Jack. He sighed and gave her a loving but exasperated look. "You don't have to be attached to my side. Everything's fine. I'm just decorating."

"She is being more than a little codependent today," Damien said, folding his legs and sitting on the grass beside Jack.

Jack stopped working on the paper sword he'd been folding into shape and stroked Duchess's soft head. "Do you think she can sense that S-T-A-R-K is still not feeling one hundred percent? Do you think she knows he's not coming back tomorrow?"

"Well, maybe. She is extraordinarily intelligent, but my guess is she's more worried about you climbing up there than Stark being tired and tardy."

Jack fluttered his fingers at the eight-foot ladder that sat open and ready not far from them. "Oh, there's nothing for Duch or you to be worried about. That ladder is perfectly safe. It even has an extra hold-it-open latch that makes it totally steady."

"I don't know. It's awful high up there." Damien gave the top rungs of the ladder a wary look.

"Nah, it's not so bad. Plus, it's not like I'm climbing up to the top—or at least not much. This poor tree has limbs that are hangy-downy now. You know, ever since *he* burst up from under it." Jack said the last sentence in a stage whisper.

Damien cleared his throat and gave the big oak they were sitting under the same wary glance he'd shot the ladder. "Okay, don't get mad, but I really need to talk to you about choosing this particular spot for Zoey's Celebration Ritual."

Jack held up his hand, palm out, in the universal *stop* signal. "I already know people are going to have issues with this location. I've just decided that my reasons for it are better than the reasons against it."

"Honey, you always have the best intentions," Damien took Jack's hand and held it in both of his. "But I think this time you need to consider that you might be the only one who can see anything positive about this place. Professor Nolan and Loren Blake were killed here. Kalona escaped from the earth, ripped open the ground, and split the tree right here. It just doesn't feel very celebratory to me."

Jack's free hand covered Damien's. "This is a place of power, right?"

"Correct," Damien said.

"And power isn't negative or positive in its unused form. It only takes on those characteristics when outside forces take over and influence it. Right?"

Damien paused, considered, and then reluctantly nodded. "Yes, I suppose you're correct again."

"Well, I feel that the power in this place—this shattered tree and the area here by the east wall—has been misused. It needs a chance to be used for Light and goodness again. I want to give it that chance; I *have* to. Something inside me is telling me that I need to be here, getting Zoey's Celebration Ritual ready for her return, even if she and Stark are going to be late."

Damien sighed. "You know I wouldn't ever ask you to discount your feelings."

"So you'll support me in this? Even when everyone is saying your boyfriend is super crazy?"

Damien smiled at him. "Everyone isn't saying you're super crazy. They're saying your zealous need to decorate and organize has tainted your judgment."

Jack giggled. "I'll bet they didn't say *zealous* or *tainted*."

"Their words were synonymous, if inferior."

"That's my Damien—the wordsmith!"

"And that's my Jack—the optimist." Damien leaned into Jack and kissed him gently on the lips. "You do what you need to do here. I know Zoey will be appreciative, when she finally gets home." He paused, smiled sadly into Jack's trusting eyes, and added, "Honey, you do understand that Zoey might not be coming back for quite a while? I know what Stark said to you, and I haven't talked to Z herself yet, but Aphrodite says Zoey isn't herself—that she isn't really staying on Skye because of Stark. She's staying there because she's withdrawn from the world."

"I just don't believe that, Damien," Jack said firmly.

"I don't want to believe it, either, but the facts are that Zoey isn't coming back with Aphrodite and Darius, and she really isn't talking to anyone about when she is returning. Then there's the whole Heath issue. Zoey comes back to Tulsa, and you know she's going to have to face the fact that Heath isn't here—that he'll never be here again."

"It's terrible, isn't it?" Jack said.

Their eyes met in perfect understanding. "Losing someone you love that much would be awful. It has to have changed Zoey."

"Of course it has, but she's still our Z. I have a strong feeling that she's going to be home sooner than you think," Jack said.

Damien sighed. "I hope you're right."

"Hey, even you admit that I'm right a bunch. I'll be right about Zoey coming back soon, too. I just know it."

"Okay, well, I'm going to believe you, mostly because I love your positive attitude."

Jack grinned and gave him a quick kiss. "Thank you!"

"Well, whether Z comes back in a week or a month, I'm still not sure it's a one-hundred-percent good idea for you to hang paper swords outside from a tree when you don't know when you're going to need those decorations. What if it rains tomorrow?"

"Oh, I'm not going to put them all up, silly! I'm just doing a test run on a few of them to be sure I have the folds perfect so they'll hang right."

"Is that why you have the claymore here? It looks awfully sharp and, well, *exposed* leaning against the table like that. Shouldn't the pointed end be down?"

Jack's gaze followed Damien's over to where the long silver sword rested, hilt down on the ground, blade up and shining in the flickering gaslights that illuminated the school at night.

"Well, Dragon gave me strict instructions, which I mostly listened to even though I kept being distracted by how sad he looked. You know, I don't think he's doing very well." Jack said the last part of the sentence in a hushed voice as if he didn't want Duchess to overhear him.

Damien sighed and threaded his hand with Jack's. "I don't think he's doing very well, either."

"Yeah, he was telling me stuff about not sticking the pointy part of the sword into the ground 'cause it'd make it dull or something, and all I could think about was how dark the circles were under his eyes," Jack said.

"Honey, I don't think he's been sleeping," Damien said sadly.

"I shouldn't have bothered him about borrowing a sword, but I wanted to use a real example to create origami from and not just a picture."

"I don't think you were bothering Dragon. Anastasia's death is something he's going to have to work through. I'm sorry to say it, but there's nothing we can or can't do to change that. And anyway, you had an excellent idea. Your origami is looking very realistic."

Jack wriggled with pleasure. "Oooh! Do you really think so?"

Damien put his arm around him and held him close. "Absolutely. You're a gifted decorator, Jack."

Jack snuggled into him. "Thank you. You're the best boyfriend ever."

Damien laughed. "That's not hard to be with you. Hey, do you need some help with folding the swords?"

It was Jack's turn to laugh. "No. You're not even good at present wrapping, so I'm guessing origami is not one of your many talents. But I could use your help with something else." Jack shot Duchess a pointed look, then leaned closer to Damien and whispered into his ear. "You could take Duch for a walk. She won't leave me alone and she keeps messing up my paper."

"Okay, no problem. I was going to go for a jog. You know what they say: a chubby gay is not a happy gay. Duch can take some laps with me. She'll be too exhausted to obsess over you."

"It's so cute that you jog."

"You don't say that when I'm hot and sweaty afterward," Damien said as he stood up and fished Duchess's leash from the winter-browned grass.

"Hey, sometimes I like you hot and sweaty," Jack said, smiling up at him.

"Then maybe I won't take a shower afterward," Damien said.

"Maybe that's a really good idea," Jack said.

"Or maybe you should take the shower with me."

Jack's grin widened. "Now *that's* more than *maybe* a really good idea."

"Tart," Damien said, bending to kiss Jack deeply.

"Linguist," Jack said before kissing him back.

Duchess wriggled her way between them, huffing and wagging and licking both of them.

"Oh, pretty girl! We love you, too!" Jack said, kissing Duchess on her soft muzzle.

"Come on, let's go get some exercise so we stay properly svelte and attractive for Jack," Damien said, pulling on the big dog's leash. She followed him, but with obvious hesitance.

"It's okay. He'll bring you back soon," Jack said.

"Yep, we'll see Jack soon, Duch."

"Hey," Jack called after the two of them. "I love you two!"

Damien turned, picked up Duchess's paw, waved it at Jack, and yelled, "We love you, too!" Then they jogged away, Duchess barking excitedly as Damien pretended to chase her.

Jack watched them go. "They're the best, ever," he said softly.

The sword he'd just put the final fold on was the last of the five he'd made. *One for each of the elements,* Jack told himself. *I'll hang these five and let them be the testers.*

As he cut the fishing line and threaded it through the last of the five, Jack's eyes kept going upward, seeking the right spots from which to hang the decorations. But he didn't need to look long. The tree seemed to be showing him where he needed to go. The thick trunk had been split almost in two, causing the sides of the massive old oak to tilt so that the thick branches leaned precariously close to the ground. Where before Kalona had escaped from the earth, the lowest branches couldn't have been reached with a twenty-foot ladder, now his eight-foot ladder gave Jack more than enough height.

"Up there. Right up there is where the first one should go." Jack gazed straight up from where he'd been sitting beside the little table at one of the major limbs of the tree that hung directly above him like a sheltering arm. "It's perfect because it'll hang over where I made all of the swords." Jack dragged the ladder closer to the table and held the first of the five paper swords by the long length of fishing line he'd tied to its hilt. "Oh, oopsie. Almost forgot. Gotta practice," he said to himself, pausing to punch the controls on the portable iPhone dock he'd carried out there with the table.

> *Something has changed within me*
> *Something is not the same*
> *I'm through with playing by the rules*
> *Of someone else's game . . .*

Rachel's voice began the song, strong and clear. Jack paused with one foot on the bottom rung of the ladder, and when Kurt took over the lyrics he sang with him, matching his sweet tenor, note for note.

> *Too late for second-guessing*
> *Too late to go back to sleep . . .*

Jack moved up the ladder as he and Kurt sang, pretending he was climbing the steps of the Radio City Music Hall where the *Glee* cast had performed on tour last spring.

It's time to trust my instincts
Close my eyes: and leap!

He reached the top rung of the ladder, paused, and began the first chorus with Kurt and Rachel while he reached up and threaded the fishing lure through the bare winter branches.

He was humming along with Rachel's next lines, waiting for Kurt's part again, when movement at the split base of the tree caught his attention and his gaze shifted to the damaged trunk. Jack gasped. He was sure he saw, right there, an image of a beautiful woman. The image was dark and indistinct, but as Kurt sang about losing love he'd guessed he'd lost, the woman became clearer, larger, more distinct.

"Nyx?" Jack whispered, awestruck.

Like a veil lifting, the woman was suddenly fully visible. She raised her head and smiled up at Jack, as exquisitely lovely as she was evil.

"Yes, little Jack. You may call me Nyx."

"Neferet! What are you doing here?" The question burst from him before he could think.

"Actually, at this moment, I'm here because of you."

"M-me?"

"Yes, you see, I need your help. I know how much you like to help others. That's why I've come for you, Jack. Wouldn't you like to do something for me? I can promise you that I'll make it worth your while."

"Worth my while? What do you mean?" Jack hated that his voice sounded squeaky.

"I mean if you do a little thing for me, then I'll do a little thing for you, too. I've been away from the House of Night fledglings far too long. Perhaps I've lost touch with what makes their hearts beat. You could help me—guide me—show me. In return I would reward you. Think about your dreams, what it is you would want to do with your long life after you Change. I could make your dreams come true."

Jack smiled and threw his arms out wide. "But I'm already living my dream. I'm here, in this beautiful place, with friends who have become my family. What more could anyone want?"

Neferet's expression hardened. Her voice was stone. "What more could you want? How about dominion over this 'beautiful place'? Beauty doesn't last. Friends and family decay. Power is the only thing that goes on forever."

Jack answered with his gut. "No, love goes on forever."

Neferet's laughter was mocking. "Don't be such a child. I'm offering you much more than love."

Jack looked at Neferet—really looked at her. She'd changed, and in his heart he knew why. She'd accepted evil. Utterly, completely, totally. He'd understood it before without really knowing it. *There is nothing of Light or me left within her.* The voice in his mind was gentle and loving, and it gave him the courage to clear the dryness from his throat and look Neferet squarely in her cold, emerald eyes. "Not to be mean or anything, Neferet, but I don't want what you're offering. I can't help you. You and I, well, we're not on the same side." He started to climb down the ladder.

"Stay where you are!"

He didn't know how, but Neferet's words commanded his body. It felt like he was suddenly wrapped tightly, frozen in place by an invisible cage of ice.

"You impudent boy! You actually think you can defy me?"

Kiss me goodbye
I'm defying gravity . . .

"Yes," he said as Kurt's voice rang around him. "Because I'm on Nyx's side, not yours. So just let me go, Neferet. I really won't help you."

"That is where you're wrong, you incorruptible innocent. You've just proven that you're going to help me very, very much." Neferet lifted her hands, making a sifting movement in the air around her. "As I promised, here he is."

Jack had no idea who Neferet was talking to, but her words made his skin crawl. Helplessly, he watched her leave the shadows of the tree. She appeared to glide away from him and toward the sidewalk that would take her to the main House of Night building. With an oddly detached observation he realized her movements were more reptile than human.

For an instant he thought she really was leaving—thought he was safe. But when she reached the sidewalk she looked back at him, and she shook her head, laughing softly. "You've made this almost too easy for me, boy, with your honorable refusal of my offer." She made a throwing motion at the sword. Wide-eyed, Jack was sure he saw something black wrap around the hilt. The sword turned, turned, turned, until the upraised point was aimed directly at him.

"There is your sacrifice. He is one I have been unable to taint. Take him, and my debt to your Master has been fulfilled, but wait until the clock chimes twelve. Hold him until then." Without another look at Jack, Neferet slithered out of his sight and into the building.

It seemed a long time before midnight came, before the school clock began chiming, even though Jack closed his mind to the cold, invisible chains that bound him. He was glad he'd put "Defying Gravity" on a loop. It comforted him to hear Kurt and Rachel singing about overcoming fear.

When the clock began chiming, Jack knew what was going to

happen. He knew he couldn't stop it—knew his fate couldn't be changed. Instead of pointless struggle, last-minute regrets, useless tears, he closed his eyes, took a deep breath, and then—joyously—joined Rachel and Kurt in the chorus:

> *I'd sooner buy*
> *Defying gravity*
> *Kiss me goodbye*
> *I'm defying gravity*
> *I think I'll try*
> *Defying gravity*
> *And you won't bring me down!*

Jack's sweet tenor was ringing through the branches of the shattered oak when Neferet's lingering, waiting magic hurled him off the top of the ladder. He fell gruesomely, horribly, onto the waiting claymore, but as the blade pierced his neck, before pain and death and Darkness could touch him, his spirit exploded from his body.

He opened his eyes to find himself standing in an amazing meadow at the base of a tree that looked exactly like the one Kalona had shattered, only this tree was whole and green, and beside it was a woman dressed in glowing silver robes. She was so lovely Jack thought he could stare at her forever.

He knew her instantly. He'd always known her.

"Hello, Nyx," he said softly.

The Goddess smiled. "Hello, Jack."

"I'm dead, aren't I?"

Nyx's smile didn't waver. "You are, my wonderful, loving, untaintable child."

Jack hesitated, then said, "It doesn't seem so bad, this being dead thing."

"You'll find it isn't."

"I'll miss Damien."

"You'll be with him again. Some souls find each other again and again. Yours will; you have my oath on it."

"Did I do okay back there?"

"You were perfect, my son." Then Nyx, the Goddess of Night, opened her arms and enfolded Jack, and with her touch the last remnants of mortal pain and sadness and loss dissolved from his spirit, leaving love—only and always, love. And Jack knew perfect happiness.

CHAPTER SEVEN

Rephaim

The moment before his father appeared the consistency of the air changed.

He'd known Father had returned from the Otherworld the instant it had happened. How could he not have known it? He'd been with Stevie Rae. She'd felt Zoey become whole again just as the knowledge of his father had come to him.

Stevie Rae . . . It had been less than a fortnight since he'd been in her presence, spoken with her, touched her, but it seemed that their time together had been an eternity ago.

If Rephaim lived for another century he would not forget what had happened between them just before Father had returned to this realm. The human boy in the fountain had been him. It hadn't made rational sense, but that didn't make it any less true. He'd touched Stevie Rae and imagined, for just a heartbeat in time, what could have been.

He could have loved her.

He could have protected her.

He could have chosen Light over Darkness.

But what could have been was not reality—was not to be.

He'd been born of hate and lust, pain and Darkness. He was a monster. Not human. Not immortal. Not beast.

Monster.

Monsters didn't dream. Monsters didn't desire anything except blood and destruction. Monsters didn't—couldn't—know love or happiness: they weren't created with that ability.

How then was it possible that he missed her?

Why this terrible hollowness in his soul since Stevie Rae had been gone? Why did he feel only partially alive without her?

And why did he long to be better, stronger, wiser, and *good, truly good* for her?

Could he be going mad?

Rephaim paced back and forth across the rooftop balcony of the deserted Gilcrease mansion. It was past midnight and the museum grounds were quiet, but since the cleanup after the ice storm had begun in earnest, the place was becoming busier and busier during daylight hours.

I'm going to have to leave and find another place. A safer place. I should leave Tulsa and make a stronghold in the wilderness of this enormous country. He knew that was the wise thing to do, the rational thing to do, but something compelled him to stay.

Rephaim told himself it was simply that he hoped now that his father had returned to this realm, he would also return to Tulsa, and he was waiting here for him to come back—to give him a purpose and a direction. But in the deepest recesses of his heart he knew the truth. He didn't want to leave this place because Stevie Rae was here, and even though he couldn't allow himself to contact her, she was still near, reachable, if only he dared.

Then, in the middle of his pacing and his self-recriminations, the air around him became heavy, thick with an immortal power that Rephaim knew as well as his own name. Something tugged within him, as if the power that floated in the night had attached itself to him and was using him as an anchor to pull itself ever nearer.

Rephaim braced himself, physically and mentally, concentrated on the illusive immortal magick, and willingly accepted the connection, not minding that it was painful and draining and filled him with a suffocating wave of claustrophobia.

The night sky above him darkened. The wind increased, battering Rephaim.

The Raven Mocker stood his ground.

When the magnificent winged immortal, his father, Kalona, deposed Warrior of Nyx, swooped down from the heavens and landed before him, Rephaim automatically dropped to his knees, bowing in allegiance.

"I was surprised to feel that you remained here," Kalona said without giving his son permission to rise. "Why did you not follow me to Italy?"

Head still bowed, Rephaim answered. "I was mortally wounded. I have only just recovered. I thought it wise to await you here."

"Wounded? Yes, I recall. A gunshot and a fall from the sky. You may rise, Rephaim."

"Thank you, Father." Rephaim stood and faced his father, and then was glad his face didn't betray emotions easily. Kalona looked as if he had been ill! His bronze skin had a sallow tint to it. His unusual amber eyes were shadowed by dark circles. He even looked thin. "Are you well, Father?"

"Of course I am well; I am an immortal!" the winged being snapped. Then he sighed and brushed a hand wearily across his face. "She held me within the earth. I was already wounded, and being trapped by that element made my recovery before my release impossible—and since then it has been slow."

"So Neferet did entrap you." Carefully, Rephaim kept his tone neutral.

"She did, but I could not have been so easily imprisoned had Zoey Redbird not attacked my spirit," he said bitterly.

"Yet the fledgling lives," Rephaim said.

"She does!" Kalona roared, towering over his son and causing the Raven Mocker to stumble backward. But just as quickly as his rage exploded, it fizzled, leaving the immortal looking tired again. He blew out a long breath, and in a more reasonable voice repeated, "Yes, Zoey does live, though I believe she will be forever changed by her Otherworld experience." Kalona stared off into the night. "Everyone who spends time in Nyx's realm is altered by it."

"So Nyx did allow you to enter the Otherworld?" Rephaim couldn't stop from asking. He steeled himself for his father's reprimand, but when Kalona spoke, his voice was surprisingly introspective, almost gentle.

"She did. And I saw her. Once. Briefly. It was because of the Goddess's intervention that that gods-be-damned Stark is still breathing and walking the earth."

"Stark followed Zoey to the Otherworld, and he lives?"

"He lives, although he shouldn't." As Kalona spoke he absently rubbed a spot on his chest, over his heart. "I suspect those meddling bulls have something to do with his survival."

"The black and white bulls? Darkness and Light?" Rephaim tasted the bile of fear at the back of his throat as he remembered the slick, eerie coat of the white bull, the unending evil in his eyes, and the white-hot pain the creature had caused him.

"What is it?" Kalona's perceptive gaze skewered his son. "Why do you look thus?"

"They manifested here, in Tulsa, just over a week ago."

"What brought them here?"

Rephaim hesitated, his heart beating painfully in his chest. What could he admit? What could he say?

"Rephaim, speak!"

"It was the Red One—the young High Priestess. She invoked the presence of the bulls. It was the white bull who gave her the knowledge that helped Stark find the way to the Otherworld."

"How do you know this?" Kalona's voice was like death.

"I witnessed part of the invocation. I was wounded so badly that I did not believe I would recover, that I would ever fly again. When the white bull manifested, it strengthened me and drew me to its circle. That was where I observed the Red One getting her information from it."

"You were healed, but you didn't capture the Red One? Didn't stop her before she could return to the House of Night and aid Stark?"

"I could not stop her. The black bull manifested and Light banished Darkness, protecting the Red One," he said honestly. "I have been here since, regaining my strength and, when I felt that you had returned to this realm, I have been awaiting you."

Kalona stared at his son. Rephaim met his gaze steadily.

Kalona nodded slowly. "It is good that you awaited me here. There is much that is left undone in Tulsa. This House of Night will soon belong to the Tsi Sgili."

"Neferet has returned, too? Is the High Council not holding her?"

Kalona laughed. "The High Council is made up of naïve fools. The Tsi Sgili blamed me for recent events, and has punished me by publically lashing me and then banishing me from her side. The Council has been pacified."

Shocked, Rephaim shook his head. His father's tone was light, almost humorous, but his look was black—his body weakened and wounded. "Father, I do not understand. Lashed? You allowed Neferet to—"

With immortal speed, Kalona's hand was suddenly around his

son's throat. The huge Raven Mocker was lifted off the ground as if he weighed no more than one of his slim, black feathers.

"Do not make the mistake of believing that because I have been wounded I have also become weak."

"I would not do that." Rephaim's voice was little more than a choked hiss.

Their faces were close together. Kalona's amber eyes blazed with angry heat.

"Father," Rephaim gasped. "I meant you no disrespect."

Kalona dropped him, and his son crumpled at his feet. The immortal lifted his head and threw his arms wide as if he would take on the heavens. "She still imprisons me!" he shouted.

Rephaim drew in air and rubbed his throat, then his father's words penetrated the confusion in his mind and he looked up at him. The immortal's face was twisted as if in agony—his eyes were haunted. Rephaim slowly got to his feet, and approached him carefully. "What has she done?"

Kalona's arms fell to his sides, but his face remained open to the sky. "I pledged to her my oath that I would destroy Zoey Redbird. The fledgling lives. I broke my oath."

Rephaim's blood felt cold. "The oathbreaking held a penalty."

He didn't phrase it as a question, but Kalona nodded. "It did."

"What is it you owe Neferet?"

"She holds dominion over my spirit for as long as I am immortal."

"By all the gods and goddesses, we are both lost then!" Rephaim couldn't stop the escaping words.

Kalona turned to him and his son saw that a sly glint had replaced the rage in his eyes. "Neferet has been immortal for less than a breath of this world's time. I have been so for uncountable eons. If there is one lesson I have learned over several lifetimes, it is that there is nothing that is unbreakable. Nothing. Not the strongest heart, not the purest soul—not even the most binding of oaths."

"You know how to break her dominion over you?"

"No, but I do know that if I give her what she most desires, she will be distracted while I discover how to break the oath I made her."

"Father," Rephaim said hesitantly, "there are always consequences for an oathbreaking. Will you not simply incur another if you break this second oath?"

"I cannot think of a consequence I would not gladly pay to rid myself of Neferet's domination."

The cold, deadly anger in Kalona's voice caused Rephaim's throat to go dry. He knew when his father got like this, the only thing he could do was to agree with him, to aid him in whatever he sought, to ride the storm silently, mindlessly, at Kalona's side. He was used to Kalona's volatile emotions.

What Rephaim was not used to was feeling resentful of them.

Rephaim could sense the immortal's gaze studying him. The Raven Mocker cleared his throat and said what he knew his father expected to hear. "What is it that Neferet most desires and how do we give it to her?"

Kalona's expression relaxed a little. "The Tsi Sgili most desires lording power over humans. We give it to her by helping her begin a war between vampyres and humans. She means to use the war as an excuse for the destruction of the High Council. With them gone, vampyre society will be in disarray and Neferet, using the title of Nyx Incarnate, will rule."

"But vampyres have become too rational, too civilized, to war with humans. I think they would withdraw from society before they would fight."

"True enough for most vampyres, but you're forgetting the

new breed of bloodsucker the Tsi Sgili created. They do not seem to have the same scruples."

"The red fledglings," Rephaim said.

"Ah, but they aren't all fledglings, are they? I hear another of the boys has Changed. And then there is the new High Priestess, the Red One. I am not so sure she is as dedicated to Light as is her friend Zoey."

Rephaim felt like a giant fist was closing around his heart. "The Red One evoked the black bull—the manifestation of Light. I do not think she can be swayed from the Goddess's path."

"You said she also conjured the bull of Darkness, did you not?"

"I did, but from what I observed she did not call upon Darkness intentionally."

Kalona laughed. "Neferet has told me that Stevie Rae was quite different when she first was resurrected. The Red One reveled in Darkness!"

"And then she Changed, like Stark. They're both committed to Nyx now."

"No, what Stark is committed to is Zoey Redbird. I do not believe the Red One has formed any such attachment."

Carefully, Rephaim remained silent.

"The more I think on it, the more I like the idea. Neferet gains power if we use the Red One, and Zoey loses someone close to her. Yes, that pleases me. Very much."

Rephaim was trying to sift through the mixture of panic and fear and chaos in his mind and conjure a response that might distract Kalona from his pursuit of Stevie Rae when the air around them rippled and changed. Shadows within shadows appeared to quiver briefly but ecstatically. His questioning eyes went from the Darkness lurking in the corners of the rooftop, to his father.

Kalona nodded and smiled grimly. "The Tsi Sgili has paid her debt to Darkness; she has sacrificed the life of an innocent who could not be tainted."

Rephaim's blood pounded in his ears, and for an instant he was savagely, incredibly afraid for Stevie Rae. And then he realized *No, it could not be Stevie Rae Neferet has sacrificed. Stevie Rae has been tainted by Darkness. For now, from this one threat, she is safe.*

"Who is it Neferet has killed?" Rephaim was so distracted by relief, he spoke the words without thinking.

"What possible difference could it make to you who the Tsi Sgili sacrificed?"

Rephaim's mind refocused on the here and now swiftly. "I am simply curious."

"I feel a change in you, my son."

Rephaim met his father's gaze steadily. "I came close to death, Father. It was a sobering experience. You must remember that I only share a measure of your immortality. The rest of me is human and, therefore, mortal."

Kalona nodded briefly in acknowledgment. "I do forget that you are weakened by the humanity within you."

"Mortality, not humanity. I am not humane," he said bitterly.

Kalona studied him. "How did you manage to survive your wounds?"

Rephaim looked away from his father and answered as truthfully as possible. "I am not entirely sure how or even why I survived." *I will never understand why Stevie Rae saved me,* his mind added silently. "Much of that time remains a blur for me."

"The how is not important. The why is obvious—you survived to serve me, as you have done your entire life."

"Yes, Father," he said automatically. Then, to cover the hopelessness even he could hear in his voice, he added, "And in serving you I must tell you that you and I cannot remain here."

Kalona raised his brow questioningly. "What is it you are saying?"

"This place," his arm swept around them to take in Gilcrease grounds. "There are too many humans present since the ice has gone. We cannot stay here." Rephaim drew a deep breath and continued. "Perhaps it would be wisest for you and me to leave Tulsa for a time."

"Of course we cannot leave Tulsa. I have already explained to you that I must distract the Tsi Sgili so that I can free myself from her bondage. That is best done here, using the Red One and her fledglings. But you are correct to note that this place is not adequate for us."

"Then would it not behoove us to leave the city until we can discover a better location?"

"Why do you continue this insistence that we depart here when I have made it clear to you that we must remain?"

Rephaim drew a deep breath and said only, "I grow weary of the city."

"Then draw on the reserves of strength you have within you as legacy from my blood!" Kalona commanded, clearly annoyed. "We remain in Tulsa for as long as it takes to achieve my objective. Neferet has already considered where I should stay. She demands that I am close, but she knows I must not be seen, at least not right away." Kalona paused, grimacing in obvious anger at being so thoroughly controlled by the Tsi Sgili. "We will move, tonight, to the building Neferet has acquired. Soon we will begin hunting the red fledglings, and their High Priestess." Kalona's gaze shifted to his son's wings. "You are able to fly again, are you not?"

"I am, Father."

"Then, enough of this useless talk. Let us take to the sky and begin climbing toward our future, and our freedom."

The immortal spread his massive wings and leaped from the roof of the deserted Gilcrease Manor. Rephaim hesitated, trying to think—to breathe—to understand what he was going to do. From the corner of the rooftop an image flickered and the little blond spirit that had been haunting him since he'd arrived, broken and bleeding, manifested.

"You can't let your father hurt her. You know that, right?"

"For the last time, begone, apparition," Rephaim said as he unfurled his wings and prepared to follow his father.

"You have to help Stevie Rae."

Rephaim rounded on her. "Why do I have to? I'm a monster—she can be nothing to me."

The child smiled. *"Too late, she already means something to you. Plus there's another reason you have to help her."*

"Why?" Rephaim asked wearily.

"Because you're not all monster. You're part boy and that means someday you'll die. When you die, there's only one thing you take with you into forever."

"And what is that?"

Her grin was radiant. *"Love, silly! You get to take love with you. So you see, you have to save her or you'll regret it forever and ever."*

Rephaim stared at the girl. "Thank you," he said softly just before he vaulted into darkness.

CHAPTER EIGHT

Stevie Rae

"I think y'all should give Zoey a break. After what she's been through she could use a vacation," Stevie Rae said.

"If that's all it is," Erik said.

"What's that supposed to mean?"

"Word is she isn't planning on coming back. At all."

"That's just plain silly."

"Have you talked to her?" Erik asked.

"No, have you?" she countered.

"No."

"Actually, Erik brings up a valid point," Lenobia said. "No one has talked with Zoey. Jack said that she's not returning. I've spoken with Aphrodite. She and Darius are, indeed, arriving soon. Zoey is not making or taking calls."

"Zoey is tired. Stark is still messed up. Isn't that what Jack reported?" Stevie Rae said.

"Yes," Dragon Lankford said. "But the truth is, we have barely spoken to Zoey since her return from the Otherworld."

"Okay, seriously, why is this such a big deal? You're acting like Z is some truant bad kid, and not a kick-ass High Priestess."

"Well, for one thing, it concerns us because she does have so much power. With power comes responsibility. You know that," Lenobia said. "And then there is the issue of Neferet and Kalona."

"Here I must speak," Professor Penthasilea said. "I am not the only one of us to have received the High Council's most recent message. There is no Neferet *and* Kalona. Neferet has broken with her Consort since his spirit returned to his body and he regained consciousness. Neferet had him publically lashed, and then banished from her side, and from vampyre society for one century. Neferet spearheaded his punishment for the crime of killing the human boy. The High Council ruled that Kalona, and not Neferet, was responsible for the crime."

"Yes, we know that, but—," Lenobia began.

"What are y'all talkin' about?" Stevie Rae interrupted, feeling like her head was going to explode.

"Looks like we ain't on the email list," Kramisha said, looking every bit as freaked out as Stevie Rae.

As the clock outside began to chime midnight, Neferet stepped from within the hidden door that was the High Priestess's entrance to the Tulsa Council Chamber. She moved with purpose to the huge round table. Her voice was whip-like and full of confidence and command.

"I see I have returned none too soon. Would someone please explain to me why we have begun allowing fledglings access to our Council Meetings?"

"Kramisha is more than just a fledgling. She's a Poet Laureate and a Prophetess. Add to that the fact that *I'm* a High Priestess and I've invited her—all that gives her the right to be in this Council Meeting." Stevie Rae swallowed the sick fear that came with confronting Neferet and was incredibly relieved that her voice sounded steady when she finally freed the words from the back of her throat. "And why aren't you in jail for Heath's murder?"

"Jail?" Neferet's laughter was cruel. "What impudence! I am a High Priestess, one who has earned that title and not simply been given it by default."

"And yet you avoid the question of your culpability in the human's murder," Dragon said. "I, too, did not receive communication from the Vampyre High Council. I would like an explanation of your presence, and why you were not held responsible for the behavior of your Consort."

Stevie Rae expected Neferet to explode at Dragon's questioning, but instead her expression softened and her green eyes filled with pity. Neferet's voice was warm and understanding when she answered the Sword Master. "I imagine the High Council is holding your communication because they are cognizant that you are still grieving deeply for your lost mate."

Dragon's face paled, but his blue eyes hardened. "I did not lose Anastasia. She was taken from me. Murdered by a creature who was the creation of your Consort, acting under his command."

"I understand how your grief can taint judgment, but you need to know that Rephaim and the other Raven Mockers were not under orders to harm anyone. On the contrary, they were commanded to *protect*. When Zoey and her friends set the House of Night afire and stole our horses, they took that as an attack. They simply reacted."

Stevie Rae and Lenobia shared a quick look that telegraphed *don't let them know who was in on what,* and Stevie Rae kept her mouth shut, refusing to give up Lenobia's part in Zoey's "escape."

"They killed my mate," Dragon said, pulling everyone's attention to him.

"And for that I will be eternally sorry," Neferet said. "Anastasia was a good friend to me."

"You chased Zoey and Darius and the rest of the gang," Stevie Rae said. "You threatened us. You commanded Stark to shoot Zoey. How do you excuse all of that?"

Neferet's beautiful face seemed to crumple. She leaned on the table, and sobbed softly. "I know . . . I know. I was weak. I let the winged immortal taint my mind. He said Zoey had to be destroyed, and because I believed he was Erebus Incarnate, I also believed him."

"Oh, that's just a bunch of bull," Stevie Rae said.

Neferet's emerald eyes skewered her. "Have you never cared for someone, only to find out later that he was truly a monster in disguise?"

Stevie Rae felt all the blood drain from her face. She answered the only way she knew how—with the truth. "In my life, monsters don't disguise themselves."

"You did not answer my question, young Priestess."

Stevie Rae lifted her chin. "I'll answer your question. No, I've never cared for someone and not known what he was from the beginning. And if you're talkin' 'bout Dallas, I knew he might have issues, but I never expected him to turn to Darkness and go all crazy."

Neferet's smile was sly. "Yes, I heard about Dallas. So sad . . . so sad."

"Neferet, I still need to understand the ruling of the High Council. As Sword Master and Leader of the Sons of Erebus at this House of Night, I am entitled to be kept informed regarding anything that might compromise the security of our school, whether I am in mourning or not," Dragon said, looking pale but determined.

"You are quite right, Sword Master. It is really very simple. When the immortal's soul returned to his body, he confessed to me that he killed the human boy because he thought Heath's hatred for me was a threat." Neferet shook her head, looking sad and contrite. "The poor child had somehow convinced himself that I was to blame for the deaths of Professor Nolan and Loren Blake. Kalona believed that by executing Heath, he was protecting me." She shook her head. "He had been apart from this world for too long. He truly did not understand the human could pose no threat to me. His action in executing Heath was simply a misguided Warrior protecting his High Priestess, which is why the High Council and I have been so merciful in his punishment. As some of you are already aware, Kalona was flogged one hundred strokes and then banished from vampyre society and my side for one full century."

There was a long stretch of silence, then Penthasilea said, "It seems like this entire debacle has been one tragic misunderstanding after another, but surely we have all paid enough for what has happened in the past. What is important now is that the school reconvene and we all get on with our lives."

"I bow to your wisdom and experience, Professor Penthasilea," Neferet said, inclining her head respectfully. Then she turned to face Dragon. "This has, indeed, been a difficult time for many of us, but you have paid the greatest price, Sword Master. So it is you I must look to for absolution for my mistakes, both personal and professional. Can you possibly lead the House of Night into a new era, creating a Phoenix from the ashes of our heartache?"

Stevie Rae wanted to scream at Dragon that Neferet was fooling them all—that what had happened at the House of Night wasn't a tragic mistake, it was a tragic misuse of power by Neferet and Kalona. But her heart sank as she watched Dragon bow his head and in an utterly heartbroken and defeated voice say, "I would like us all to move on, for if we do not, I'm afraid I will not survive the loss of my mate."

Lenobia looked like she wanted to speak up, but when Dragon began to sob brokenly, she kept silent and moved to his side to comfort him.

That leaves me to stand up to Neferet, Stevie Rae thought, and glanced at Kramisha, who was watching Neferet with a barely veiled what-the-fuck look. *Okay, so that leaves me and Kramisha to stand up to Neferet,* Stevie Rae corrected inside her head. She squared her shoulders and readied herself for the epic confrontation that was sure to come when she called bullshit on the fallen High Priestess.

At that moment a weird noise drifted into the Council Chamber from the window that had been left open to the crisp night air. It was a horrible, mournful sound, and it caused the small hairs on Stevie Rae's arms to lift.

"What is that?" Stevie Rae said, her head turned—along with everyone else's—to the open window.

"I never heard nothin' like it," Kramisha said. "And it gives me the creeps."

"It's an animal. And it's in pain." Dragon instantly pulled himself together, his expression shifted, and he was, once again, a Warrior and not a heartbroken mate. He got to his feet and crossed the Council Chamber to the window.

"A cat?" Penthasilea said, looking distressed.

"I can't see it from here. It's coming from the east side of campus," Dragon said, turning from the window and heading to the door purposefully.

"Oh, Goddess! I think I know the sound." Tragic and broken, Neferet's voice had them all turning their attention back to her. "It's the howling of a dog, and the only canine on this campus is Stark's Labrador, Duchess. Has something happened to Stark?"

Stevie Rae watched Neferet press one slim hand against her throat, as if to hold back the pounding of her heart at the terrible thought that something could have happened to Stark.

Stevie Rae wanted to slap her. Neferet could have received a dang Academy Award for Best Fake Tragic Performance by a Lead Bitch. *That's it.* She wasn't going to let her get away with this crap.

But Stevie Rae didn't get a chance to confront Neferet. The moment Dragon opened the door to the hallway a cacophony of sound flooded everyone. Fledglings were rushing toward the Council Chamber. Most of them were crying and shouting, but above all of the noise—above even the horrible howling—one sound became distinctly recognizable: that of a person keening in grief.

Within the grief, Stevie Rae recognized the voice.

"Oh, no," she said, rushing down the hallway. "That's Damien."

Stevie Rae was ahead of even Dragon, and when she wrenched open the outside door of the school, she barreled into Drew Partain with such force that both of them tumbled to the ground. "Jeeze Louise, Drew! Get outta my—"

"Jack's dead!" Drew shouted, scrambling to his feet and pulling her up with him. "Over there by the broken tree at the east wall. It's bad. Really bad. Hurry—Damien needs you!"

Stevie Rae felt a surge of nausea as she processed what Drew was saying. And then she was swept with Drew in a tide of vampyres and fledglings as they all rushed across campus.

When Stevie Rae got to the tree she had a terrible moment of déjà vu. The blood. There was so much blood everywhere! She flashed back to the night Stark's arrow had opened her body and drained practically all of her life's blood out of it at this very spot.

Only this time it wasn't her. This time it was kind, sweet Jack and he really was dead, so it was terrible times ten. For a second the scene didn't seem to make sense to her because no one moved—no one spoke. There were no sounds except Duchess's howling and Damien's keening. The boy and the dog were crouched beside Jack, who lay, facedown, on the blood-soaked grass, with the point of a long sword protruding several feet from the back of his neck. It had run through him with such force that it had almost severed his head from his body.

"Oh, Goddess! What has happened here?" It was Neferet who unfroze everyone. She hurried up to Jack, bending to rest her hand gently on his body. "The fledgling is dead," she said solemnly.

Damien looked up. Stevie Rae saw his eyes. They were filled with pain and horror and maybe, just maybe, even a shadow of madness. As he stared at Neferet she watched his already pale face blanch almost colorless, and that jolted her.

"I'm thinkin' you should leave him alone," Stevie Rae said, moving so that she stood between Neferet and Jack and Damien.

"I am High Priestess here. It is my place to deal with this tragedy. What's best for Damien is for you to step aside and let adults sort all of this out," Neferet said. Her tone was reasonable, but Stevie Rae was looking into her emerald eyes and she saw something stir there that made her skin crawl.

Stevie Rae could feel everyone watching her. She knew there was some rightness in what Neferet was saying—she hadn't been a High Priestess long enough to know how to deal with something as horrible as what had happened tonight. Heck, she was really only a High Priestess because there weren't any other red fledgling girls who had Changed. Did she have any right to speak up as Damien's "High Priestess"?

Stevie Rae stood there, silent and struggling with her own insecurities. Neferet ignored her and crouched beside Damien, taking his hand and forcing him to look at her. "Damien, I know you are in shock, but you must get control of yourself and tell us how this happened to Jack."

Damien blinked blindly at Neferet, and then Stevie Rae saw his vision clear and he focused on her. He snatched his hand from hers. Shaking his head back and forth, back and forth, he started sobbing, "No! No! No!"

That was it. Stevie Rae had had enough. She didn't care if the whole damn universe couldn't see through Neferet's bullshit. She wasn't gonna let her terrorize poor Damien.

"What happened? *You're* asking what happened? Like it's just a coincidence that Jack is murdered at the same time you show up back here at school?" Stevie moved back to Damien's side, taking his hand. "You can trick-or-treat the blind-as-bats High Council. You can even talk some of these good folks into believin' you're still on our side, but Damien and Zoey and"—she paused when she heard two very similar gasps of horror as the Twins ran up. "—and Shaunee and Erin and Stark and I. We do not effing believe you're a good guy. So why don't *you* explain what happened here?"

Neferet shook her head, looking sad and tragically beautiful. "I feel sorry for you, Stevie Rae. You used to be such a sweet, loving fledgling. I do not know what happened to you."

Stevie Rae felt rage rush through her. Her body trembled with the force of it. "You know better than anyone on this earth what happened to me." She couldn't help herself. The anger was too much. Stevie Rae started to move toward Neferet. At that moment she wanted nothing so much as to wrap her hands around the vampyre's throat and press and press and press until she no longer breathed—was no longer a threat.

But Damien didn't loosen his hold on her hand. That link of touch and trust between them, as well as Damien's broken whisper, held her back. "She didn't do it. I saw it happen and she didn't do it."

Stevie Rae hesitated, glancing down at Damien. "What do you mean, honey?"

"I was way over there. Just outside the field house door. Duchess wouldn't let me jog. She kept pulling me back toward here. I finally gave in to her." Damien's voice was rough and he spoke in sharp bursts of words. "She made me worried. So I was looking. I saw it." He started to sob again. "I saw Jack fall from the top of the ladder and land on the sword. There was no one around him. No one at all."

Stevie Rae turned to Damien and pulled him into her arms. As she did so she felt two more pairs of arms enfolding them as the Twins joined their circle, holding them tightly.

"Neferet was with us in the Council Chamber when this horrible accident happened," Dragon said solemnly, touching Jack's hair gently. "She was not responsible for this death."

Stevie Rae couldn't look at Jack's poor broken body, so she was watching Neferet when Dragon spoke. Only she saw the flash of smug victory that passed over her face, quickly replaced by a practiced look of sadness and concern.

She killed him. I don't know how, and I can't prove it right now, but she did. Then, as quickly as that thought formed, another came on its heels: *Zoey would believe me. She'd help me figure out how to expose Neferet.*

Zoey has to come back.

CHAPTER NINE

Zoey

So, Stark and I had done *it*.

"I don't feel any different," I told the nearest tree. "I mean, except for feeling closer to Stark and kinda sore in unmentionable places, that is." I walked over to a little stream that bubbled cheerily through the grove and peered down. The sun was in the process of setting, but it had been an unusually clear, cold day on the island and the sky still held enough of its dramatic coral and gold light that I could see my reflection. I studied myself. I looked like, well, *me*. "Okay, so technically I'd done *it* once before, but that had been a whole different thing." I sighed. Loren Blake had been a giant mistake. James Stark was totally different, as was the commitment we'd made to each other. "So, shouldn't I look different now that I am in a Real Relationship?" I squinted at my reflection. Didn't I look older? More experienced? Wiser?

Actually, no. The squint just made me look nearsighted. "And Aphrodite would probably say it'll give me wrinkles, too."

A little pang went through me as I remembered saying bye to Aphrodite and Darius the night before. She'd been predictably sarcastic, and more than a little bitchy about me not going back to Tulsa with her, but our hug had been tight and genuine, and I knew I'd miss her. I already missed her. I missed Stevie Rae and Damien, Jack and the Twins, too.

"And Nala," I told my reflection.

But did I miss them enough to go back to the real world? Enough to face everything from resuming school to possibly fighting Darkness and Neferet?

"No. No, you don't." Saying it made it even truer. I could feel some of the *I miss them* being diluted by the serenity of Sgiach's island. "It's magick here. If I could send for my cat, I swear I'd stay forever."

Sgiach's laughter was soft and musical. "Why is it we tend to miss our pets more than we miss people?" She was smiling as she joined me at the stream.

"I think it's 'cause we can't Skype them. I mean, I know I can go back to the castle and talk to Stevie Rae, but I've tried doing the computer video thing with Nala. She just looks confused and even more disgruntled than she usually does, which is pretty darn disgruntled."

"If cats understood technology and had opposable thumbs, they'd rule the world," said the queen.

I laughed. "Don't let Nala hear you say that. She *does* rule her world."

"You're right. Mab believes she rules her world, as well."

Mab was Sgiach's giant, long-haired black and white tuxedo cat who I was just getting to know. I think she was possibly, like, a thousand years old and mostly stayed only semi-conscious and barely moving on the end of the queen's bed. Stark and I had started calling her Dead Cat, but not within Sgiach's hearing.

"By world you mean your bedroom?"

"Exactly," Sgiach said.

Both of us laughed, and then the queen walked over to a large moss-covered boulder not far from the stream. She sat gracefully and patted the chair-sized area next to her. I joined her, wondering vaguely if my movements would ever be graceful and regal like hers—and doubting it.

"You could send for your Nala. Vampyre familiars fly as companion animals. It would only be a matter of showing her vaccination record to get her into Skye."

"Wow, seriously?"

"Seriously. Of course that means you would need to commit yourself to staying here for at least several months. Cats don't travel particularly well—and moving them from one time zone to another, and then back again, really isn't good for them."

I looked into Sgiach's eyes and said exactly what I was thinking, "The longer I stay here the more I'm sure that I don't want to leave, but I know it's probably irresponsible of me to hide from the real world like that. I mean"—I hurried on when I saw the concern grow in her gaze—"it's not like Skye isn't real and all. And I know I've been through a bunch of bad stuff lately, so it's okay for me to take a break. But I am still in school. I suppose I do have to go back. Eventually."

"Would you feel that way if school came to you?"

"What do you mean?"

"Since you've come into my life I've begun to reflect on the world—or rather on how disassociated I've become from it. Yes, I have the internet. Yes, I have satellite TV. But I don't have new followers. I don't have student Warriors and young Guardians. Or at least I didn't until you and Stark arrived. I find that I've missed the energy and input from young minds." Sgiach looked away from me and deeper into the grove. "Your arrival here has awakened something that was sleeping on my island. I feel a change coming in the world, greater than the influence of modern science or technology. I can ignore it and let my island go back to sleep, perhaps to become completely separate from the world and its problems, perhaps even to be lost to the mists of time—like Avalon and the Amazons. Or I can open myself to it, meeting the challenges it might bring." The queen met my gaze again. "I choose to allow my island to awaken. It is time Skye's House of Night accepted new blood."

"You're going to take down the protective spell?"

Her smile was wry. "No, as long as I live and, hopefully, as long as my successor and, eventually her successors, live, Skye will remain protected and separate from the modern world. But I did think I would put out a Warrior's Call. At one time Skye trained the best and brightest of the Sons of Erebus."

"But then you broke from the Vampyre High Council, right?"

"Correct. Perhaps I could begin, slowly, to mend that break, especially if I had a young High Priestess as one of my trainees."

I felt a stirring of excitement. "Me? You mean me?"

"I do, indeed. You and your Guardian have a connection to this Isle. I'd like to see where that connection takes us."

"Wow, I'm seriously honored. Thank you so much." My mind was whirring! If Skye became an active House of Night it wouldn't be like I'd be hiding from everyone here. It would be more like I'd transferred to another school. I thought about Damien and the rest of the gang and wondered if they'd think about coming to Skye, too.

"Would there be a place here for fledglings who aren't Warriors in training?" I asked.

"We could discuss that." Sgiach paused, seemed to come to a decision, and added, "You do know, don't you, that this island is rich in magickal tradition that encompasses more than just Warrior training and my Guardians?"

"No. I mean, yes. Like it's obvious that *you're* magick, and you're basically this island."

"I've been here so long that many do see me as the island, but I am more the caretaker of its magick than the possessor of it."

"What do you mean?"

"Find out for yourself, young queen. You have an affinity for each of the elements. Reach out and see what the island has to teach you."

When uncertainty had me hesitating, Sgiach coaxed, "Try the first element, air. Simply call it to you and observe."

"Okay. Well, here goes." I stood up and moved a couple of feet from Sgiach, into a mossy area that was kinda clear of rocks. I took three deep, cleansing breaths, settling into the familiar feeling of being centered. Instinctively, I turned my face to the east and called: "Air, please come to me."

I was used to the element responding. I was used to it stirring the breeze around me like an eager puppy, but all of my experience with my affinities didn't prepare me for what happened next. Air didn't just respond—it engulfed me. It swirled around me powerfully, feeling strangely tangible, which should have really been crazy because air isn't tangible. It's unseen yet everywhere. And then I gasped because I realized *air had become tangible!* Wafting around me, in the midst of the blustering wind that had sprung to me at my call, were the forms of beautiful beings. They were bright and ethereal, a little see-through. As I gawked at them they changed form—sometimes looking like lovely women, sometimes looking like butterflies, and then they'd change and look more like gorgeous fall leaves drifting in a wind of their own.

"What are they?" I asked in a hushed voice. Of its own accord, I lifted my hand and watched the leaves change to brilliantly colored hummingbirds, which settled on my outstretched palm.

"Air sprites. They used to be everywhere, but they've left the modern world. They prefer the ancient groves and the old ways. And this island has both." Sgiach smiled and opened her own hand to a sprite that took on the form of a tiny woman with dragonfly wings and danced, weaving in and out of her fingers. "It's good to see them come to you. There are rarely so many of them in one place, even here in the grove. Try another element."

This time she didn't need to coax me further. I turned to the south and called, "Fire, please come to me!"

Like brilliant fireworks, sprites burst into being all around me, tickling my body with the controlled warmth of their flames and making me giggle. "They remind me of Fourth of July sparklers!"

Sgiach's smile matched mine. "I rarely see the flame sprites. I'm much closer to water and air—flame almost never shows itself to me."

"Shame on you," I scolded. "You guys should let Sgiach see you—she's one of the good guys!"

Instantly the sprites around me started to flutter crazily. I could feel the distress radiating from them.

"Oh, no! Tell them you're teasing them. Flame is terribly sensitive and volatile. I don't want them to cause an accident," Sgiach said.

"Hey, guys, sorry! I was just kidding. Everything's fine, really." I breathed a sigh of relief as the flame sprites settled back into less frantic flickering and fluttering. I glanced at Sgiach. "Is it safe to call the other elements?"

"Of course, just be careful what you say. Your affinity is powerful, even without being in a place rich in old magick like this grove."

"Will do." I drew three more cleansing breaths and was sure I recentered myself. Then I turned clockwise to face the west. "Water, please come to me." And found myself washed in the element. Cool, slick sprites brushed against my skin, shimmering with aqua iridescence. They frolicked around, making me think of mermaids and dolphins, jellyfish and seahorses. "This is seriously super cool!"

"Water sprites are especially strong on Skye," Sgiach said, caressing a little starfish-shaped creature that swam around her.

I turned to the north. "Earth, come to me!" The grove came alive. The trees glowed with glee, and from their gnarled, ancient trunks emerged woodland beings that reminded me of things that should be in Rivendell with Tolkien's elves—or maybe even *Avatar*'s 3-D jungle.

I pulled my attention to the center of my impromptu circle and called the final element, "Spirit, please come to me, too."

This time Sgiach gasped. "I have never seen all five groups of sprites together like this. It is magnificent."

"Ohmygoddess! It's incredible!"

The air around me, already alive with gossamer beings, was filled with such radiance that it suddenly brought Nyx to mind, and the brilliance of her smile.

"Do you want to experience more?" Sgiach asked me.

"Of course," I said without hesitation.

"Come here, then. Give me your hand." Surrounded by the ancient sprites that personified the elements, I approached Sgiach and held my hand out to her.

She took my right hand in her left and turned it so that my palm faced up. "Do you trust me?"

"Yes. I trust you," I said.

"Good. It will only hurt for a moment."

With a blindingly fast motion, she slashed the hard, sharp nail of her right pointer finger across the meaty pad of my palm. I didn't flinch. Didn't move. But I did suck in a bunch of air. Though she was right—it hurt only for a moment.

Sgiach turned my palm over and the blood began dripping from my hand, but before it could touch the mossy ground beneath us, the queen caught the scarlet drops. Cupping them in her own palm, she let them pool and then, speaking words that I felt more than heard but did not understand at all, she flung the blood, scattering it in a circle around us.

Then something truly amazing happened.

Each sprite that my blood drops touched, for an instant, became flesh. They were no longer ethereal elementals, only wisps and trails of air, fire, water, earth, and spirit. What my blood touched became reality—living, breathing birds and fairies, mer-folk and forest nymphs.

And they danced and celebrated. Their laughter painted the darkening sky with joy and magick.

"It is the ancient magick. You've touched things here that have been sleeping for ages. None other has awakened the fey. None other had the ability," Sgiach spoke and then slowly, majestically, she bowed her head in homage to me.

Absolutely engulfed in the wonder of the five elements, I took the Queen of Skye's hand, noticing that my blood had stopped running the instant she'd flung it around us. "Can I share this with other fledglings? If you allow them to come in, can I teach a new generation how to reach the old magick?"

She smiled at me through tears that I hoped were from happiness. "Yes, Zoey. Because if you can't bridge the gap between the ancient and the modern worlds, I don't know who can. But for now, take this moment. The reality your blood has created will soon fade. Dance with them, young queen. Let them know there is hope that today's world has not completely forgotten the past."

Her words worked on me like a goad and, in time to the sound of bells and pipes and cymbals that I suddenly heard, I began to dance with the creatures my blood had solidified.

Looking back on it, I should have paid more attention to the sharp profile of horns that I glimpsed as I twirled and jumped, arm in arm with the fey. I should have noticed the color of the bull's coat and the gleam in his eye. I should have mentioned his presence to Sgiach. A lot might have been avoided, or at least anticipated, had I known better.

But that night I danced in innocence and the newness of ancient magick revealed, oblivious to any consequences more dire than me feeling tired and drained and needing a big dinner and a good eight hours of sleep.

"You were right. It didn't last very long," I said, breathing heavily as I plopped down next to Sgiach on her moss boulder. "Can't we do something to make them stay longer? They seemed so happy to be real."

"The fey are elusive beings. They only owe allegiance to their element, or those who wield it."

I blinked in surprise. "You mean they're loyal to me?"

"I believe they are, though I cannot tell you for certain as I have no true affinity to an element, though I am an ally to water and wind, as I am protector and queen of this island."

"Huh. So, can I call them to me, even if I leave Skye?"

Sgiach smiled. "And why would you ever want to do that?"

I laughed with her, at that moment not understanding why in the world I would ever want to leave this magickal, mystical island.

"Aye, if I followed the sound of wummen's chattering, I knew I'd be finding yous two."

Sgiach's smile grew and turned warm. Seoras joined us in the grove, moving to his queen's side. She touched him just for a moment on his strong forearm, but that touch was filled with several lifetimes of love and trust and intimacy.

"Hello, my Guardian. Did you bring the bow and arrows for her?"

Seoras's lips twisted. "Aye, of course I did." The old Warrior turned and I could see that he held an intricately carved bow made of dark wood. The matching leather quiver filled with red-feathered arrows was slung across his shoulder.

"Good." She smiled appreciation at him before turning her gaze to me. "Zoey, you've learned much today. Your Guardian needs a lesson in believing in magick and Goddess-given gifts, too." Sgiach took the bow and arrows from Seoras and held them out to me. "Take these to Stark. He has too long been without them."

"You really think that's a good idea?" I asked Sgiach, glancing askance at the bow and arrows.

"What I think is that your Stark will not be complete unless he accepts his Goddess-given gifts."

"He had a claymore in the Otherworld. Couldn't that be his weapon here, too?"

Sgiach just looked at me, the shadow of the magick we'd both just experienced still reflected in her green eyes.

I sighed.

And, reluctantly, held out my hand to take the bow and quiver of arrows from her.

"He's not really comfortable with this," I said.

"Aye, but he should be," Seoras said.

"You wouldn't say that if you knew everything that went along with this thing," I said.

"If it's that he cannae miss his mark that yur meanin', then, aye, I know that, as well as the guilt he carries about the death of his mentor," Seoras said.

"He told you all about it."

"He did."

"And you still think he should get back into using his bow?"

"It's not so much Seoras *thinking* it as the fact that he *knows*, from centuries of experience, what happens when a Guardian's Goddess-given gifts are ignored," Sgiach said.

"What happens?"

"The same thing as happens if a High Priestess tries to turn from the path her Goddess has paved before her," Seoras said.

"Like Neferet," I whispered.

"Aye," he said. "Like the fallen High Priestess who tainted yur House of Night and caused the death of yur Consort."

"Though in all truthfulness you should know that it's not necessarily such a dire choice between good and evil when a Guardian, or a Warrior, ignores his gifts from his Goddess and turns from her appointed path. Sometimes that simply means a life unfulfilled and as mundane as is possible for a vampyre," Sgiach explained.

"But if 'tis a Warrior whose gifts are powerful, or one who has faced Darkness, been touched by the fight against evil—well, that Warrior cannae fade so easily into obscurity," Seoras said.

"And Stark is both," I said.

"He is indeed. Continue to trust me, Zoey. It is better for your Guardian to walk the path meant for him than to slink around and, perhaps, get caught in the shadows," Sgiach said.

"I see your point, but getting him to use his bow again isn't going to be easy."

"Ach, well, yu have the magick of the ancients to call upon while yur here on our isle, don't you now?"

I looked from Seoras to Sgiach. They were right. I felt it in my gut. Stark couldn't hide from the gifts Nyx had given him any more than I could deny my connection to the five elements. "Okay, I'll convince him. Where is he anyway?"

"The laddie is restless," Seoras said. "I saw him walkin' by the shore side of the castle."

My heart squeezed. We'd just decided the day before that we were going to stay here on Skye, indefinitely. And after what had just happened with Sgiach and me, I could hardly bear thinking about leaving. "But he seemed fine with staying," I spoke my thoughts aloud.

"What's wrong with him isna so much where he is, but who he is," Seoras said.

"Huh?" I said brilliantly.

"Zoey, what Seoras means is that you'll find your Guardian's restlessness much improved when he is a whole Warrior again," Sgiach said.

"And a whole Warrior uses all of his gifts," Seoras said with finality.

"Go to him and help him become whole again," Sgiach said.

"How?" I asked.

"Ach, wumman, use yur Goddess-given brains and figure that oot for yurself."

With a gentle push and a shooing motion, the queen and her Guardian sent me from the grove. I sighed, mentally scratched my head, and started toward the shoreline wondering just what the heck kind of word *ach* was.

CHAPTER TEN

Zoey

Distracted by thinking about Stark, I made my way down the slippery stone stairway that wound around the base of the castle, emptying out on the rocky shore from which Sgiach's edifice had been built straight up, so that it was cliff-like and totally imposing.

The sun was beginning to set, allowing the sky to retain some of its illumination, but I was glad for the rows of torches that jutted from the stone base of the castle's foundation.

Stark was alone. His back was to me and I got to watch him as I picked my way across the shore to him. He held a large leather shield in one hand, and a long claymore in the other, and he was practicing thrusts and parries as if he were facing a dangerous, but invisible, enemy. I moved quietly, taking my time and enjoying the view.

Had he gotten taller all of a sudden? And more muscular? He was sweating and breathing hard, and he looked strong and very, very male and dangerous-ancient-Warrior-like in his kilt. I remembered how his body had felt against mine the night before, and how we'd slept all pressed together, and my stomach gave a weird little lurch.

He makes me feel safe, and I love him.

I could stay here with him, away from the rest of the world, forever.

A chill passed over me with the thought and I shivered. At that moment Stark dropped his guard and turned. I saw the alert concern in his eyes that only faded when I smiled and waved at him. Then his gaze went to what I was holding in the hand I was waving, and his welcoming smile faded, even though he opened his arms to me, hugged me, and gave me a lingering kiss.

"Hey, you look hot when you do that sword stuff," I said.

"It's called training. And I'm not supposed to look hot, Z. I'm supposed to look intimidating."

"Oh, you do, you do. I was practically scared to death." I put on my best bad, fake–Southern belle accent and pressed the back of my hand to my forehead like I was gonna swoon.

"You're really not very good at accents, ma'am," he said in a seriously good fake-Southern accent. Then he took my hand and held it against his chest right over his heart, moving close to me. "But if you want, Miss Zoey, I could try to teach you."

Okay, I know it's silly, but his Southern gentleman accent made my knees feel all weak—and then his words actually got through the lust fog I was brewing for him, and suddenly I knew how to start getting him comfortable with his bow again.

"Hey, I am hopeless at accents, but there is something you could teach me."

"Aye, wumman, there's lots I could be teachin' yu the now," he leered, sounding totally like Seoras.

I smacked him. "Be good. I'm talking about this." I raised the bow. "I've always thought archery was cool, but I really don't know much about it. Could you teach me? Please?"

Stark took a step away from me, giving the bow a wary glance. "Zoey, you know I shouldn't shoot that."

"No. What you shouldn't do is aim for something that's alive. Well, that is unless the alive thing needs to be un-alive. But I'm not asking you to shoot it. I'm asking you to teach *me* how to shoot it."

"Why do you all of a sudden want to learn?"

"Well, it makes sense. We're going to be staying here, right?"

"Right."

"And Warriors have been trained here for, like, zillions of years. Right?"

"Right again."

I grinned at him, trying to lighten things up. "I really like it when you admit that I'm right. Again. Anyway, you're a Warrior. We're here. I'd like to learn some kind of Warrior skill. That's too darn heavy for me." I pointed at the claymore. "Plus, this is pretty." I lifted the elegant-looking bow.

"No matter how pretty it is, you need to remember it's a weapon. It can kill, especially if I fire it."

"If you fire it *and* aim to kill," I said.

"Sometimes mistakes happen," he said, looking haunted by memories from his past.

I rested my hand on his arm. "You're older now. Smarter. You won't make the same mistakes again." He just stared at me without speaking, so I lifted the bow again and went on. "Okay, show me how this works."

"We don't have a target."

"Sure we do." I thumped the worn leather shield he'd laid on the ground when I'd joined him. "Prop this between a couple rocks down the beach a little way. I'll try to shoot it—*after* you prop it up and get back here out of my line of fire, of course."

"Oh, of course," he said.

Looking resigned and miserable, he walked a few paces away from us, hefted some rocks around until he had the shield held semi-steady between two of them, then came back to me.

Reluctantly, he took the bow and set the quiver of arrows at our feet.

"This is how you hold it." He demonstrated gripping the grip-thingie while I watched. "And the arrow goes here." He rested it across the side of the bow, point down and away from us. "You nock it like this. These arrows make it easy to know which way to do it because the black ones should be turned like this, with the one red one up this way." As he talked Stark began to relax. His hands knew the bow, and knew the arrow. It was obvious that he could do what he was showing me with his eyes shut—do it quickly and well. "Plant your legs firmly, about hip-width apart, like this." He demonstrated and I checked out his excellent legs, which was one of the many reasons I liked the fact that he'd started wearing the kilt all the time.

"And then you lift the bow and, holding the arrow between your first two fingers, pull the string back, taut." He explained what I was supposed to do, but he'd stopped demonstrating. "Sight down the arrow, but aim a little low. That will help adjust for distance and the breeze. When you're ready, let loose. Be careful to bow your left arm or you'll smack it and give yourself a nasty bruise." He held the bow out to me. "Go ahead. Try it."

"Show me," I said simply.

"Zoey, I don't think I should."

"Stark, the target is a leather shield. It's not alive. There's nothing alive even vaguely attached to it. Just aim for the center of the shield and show me how it's done." He hesitated. I rested my hand on his chest and leaned forward. He met me halfway. Our kiss was sweet, but I could feel the tension in his body. "Hey," I said softly, still touching his chest. "Try to trust yourself as much as I trust you. You're my Warrior, my Guardian. You need to use the bow because it's your Goddess-given gift. I know you'll use it wisely. I know it because I know *you*. You're good. You've fought to be good, and you've won."

"But I'm not all good, Z," he said, looking totally frustrated. "I've seen the bad part of me. It was there—real—in the Otherworld."

"And you defeated it," I said.

"Forever? I don't think so. I don't think that's possible."

"Hey, no one's all good. Not even me. I mean, if some smart kid left his test out in geometry, I'm telling you—I'd look."

He smiled for a breath of a moment, then the tension was back in his face. "You joke about it, but it's different for me. I think it's different for all of the red fledglings and even Stevie Rae. Once you've known Darkness, real Darkness, there's always a shadow on your soul."

"No," I said firmly. "Not a shadow. Just a different kind of experience. You and the rest of the red fledglings have experienced something we haven't. It doesn't make you part of the shadow of Darkness—it makes you experienced with it. That could be a good thing if you use your extra knowledge to fight for good, and you do."

"Sometimes I worry that it might be more than that," he said slowly, staring into my eyes like he was looking for a hidden truth.

"What do you mean?"

"Darkness is territorial, possessive. Once it's had a piece of you, it doesn't like to let go."

"Darkness doesn't have any choice if you choose the path of the Goddess, and you have. It can't beat Light."

"But I'm not sure Light can ever really beat Darkness, either. There's a balance to things, Z."

"Which doesn't mean you can't choose sides. And you've chosen. Trust yourself. I trust you. Completely," I repeated.

Stark kept staring into my eyes like he was grabbing on to a lifeline. "As long as you see me as good—as long as you believe in me—I can trust myself because I trust you, Zoey. And I love you."

"I love you, too, Guardian," I said.

He kissed me and then, in a movement that was fast and graceful and lethal, Stark pulled back the bow and let the arrow fly. It thunked with finality into the absolute center of the target.

"Wow," I said. "That was amazing. *You're* amazing."

He blew out a long breath, and with it the tension that had been so obvious in his body seemed to be blown away, too. Stark smiled his cute, cocky grin. "Center of the target, Z. I hit it dead-on."

"Of course you did, silly. You can't miss."

"Yeah, that's right. And it's just a target."

"Are you gonna teach me or not? And this time don't go so darn fast. Slow down. Show me."

"Yeah, yeah, sure. Okay, here." He aimed and shot more slowly, giving me time to follow his movements.

And the second arrow split the first one down the middle.

"Oh, woops. I forgot about doing that. I used to waste a lot of arrows that way."

"Here, my turn. I'll bet I don't have that problem."

I tried to do what Stark had done, but ended up shooting my arrow short and watching it skitter off the smooth, wet rocks.

"Well, crap. It's definitely harder than it looks," I said.

"Here. I'll show you. You're not standing right." He came up behind me, fitting his arms over mine and snuggling against my backside. "Think of yourself as an ancient warrior queen. Stand strong and proud. Shoulders back! Chin up!" I did as he said and inside the powerful circle of his arms I felt myself transform into someone powerful and majestic. His hands guided mine to pulling the bow taut. "Stay steady and strong—focus," he whispered. Together we sighted the target, and as we let loose the arrow, I could feet the jolt that rippled through his body and mine and guided the arrow to the dead center of the target again, splintering the two before it.

I turned and smiled up at my Guardian. "What you have is magick. It's special. You have to use it, Stark. You have to."

"I've missed it," he said, speaking so softly I had to strain to hear him. "I don't really feel right if I don't stay connected to my bow."

"It's because through it you're connected to Nyx. She gave you your gift."

"Maybe I can start again here. This place feels different to me. Somehow I feel like I belong here—like *we* belong here."

"I feel it, too. And it seems like it's been forever since I've felt this safe and this happy." I stepped into his arms. "Sgiach just told me that she's going to start opening the island up to Warriors again—and also to other gifted fledglings." I smiled up at Stark. "You know, like fledglings with special affinities."

"Oh, you mean like affinities for the elements?"

"Yep, that's exactly what I mean." I hugged him, and spoke into his chest. "I want to stay here. I really do."

Stark stroked my hair and kissed the top of my head. "I know you do, Z. And I'm with you. I'll always be with you."

"Maybe here we can get rid of the Darkness Neferet and Kalona have tried to bring to us," I said.

Stark held me tightly. "I hope so, Z. I really do hope so."

"Do you think it might be enough to just have one piece of the world that's safe from Darkness? Is it still walking the path of the Goddess even if I'm just walking it here?"

"Well, I'm no expert, but it makes sense to me that what's important is that you're trying your best to stay true to Nyx. I can't see that where you're doing it is such a big deal."

"I understand why Sgiach doesn't leave this place," I said.

"So do I, Z."

Stark held me then, and I felt the bruised, battered places inside of me begin to warm and, slowly, I started to heal.

Stark

Zoey felt damn good in his arms. When Stark thought back to how close he'd come to losing her, it could still scare him so badly that it made his stomach sick. *I did it. I got to her in the Otherworld and made sure she came back to me. She's safe now and I'm gonna always keep her that way.*

"Hey, you're thinking awful hard," Zoey said. Curled up with him in the big bed they shared, she nuzzled his neck and kissed his cheek. "I can practically hear the wheels turning inside your head."

"I'm the one who's supposed to have the super psychic abilities." He said it with a kidding tone, but at the same time Stark gave a little mental push and slipped around just on the outskirts of her psyche—not close enough to her real thoughts to piss her off with his eavesdropping, but just near enough to be sure that she really did feel safe and happy.

"Want to know something?" she asked, with a hesitant tone to her voice.

Stark propped himself up on his elbow and grinned down at her. "Are you kidding, Z? I want to know *everything*."

"Stop it—I'm being serious."

"Me, too!" She gave him a *look* and he kissed her on the forehead. "Okay, fine. I'm being serious. What is it?"

"I, um, really like it when you touch me."

Stark's brows went up and he had to struggle not to break into a giant grin. "Well, that's good." He watched her cheeks get pink and a little grin slipped through. "I'm guessing that's *real* good."

Zoey chewed her lip. "Do you like it?"

Stark couldn't help laughing then. "You're kidding, right?"

"No. Dead. Serious. I mean, how am I supposed to know? I'm not exactly experienced—not like you are."

Her cheeks were flaming by that time and he thought she looked mega uncomfortable, which put a damper on his laughter. The last thing he wanted to do was to embarrass her or make her feel weird about what was happening between them.

"Hey." He cupped her flushed cheek. "Being with you is beyond awesome. And, Zoey, you're wrong. You're *more* experienced than me about love." When she started to speak he pressed his finger against her lips. "No, let me say this. Yeah, I've had sex before. But I've never been in love. Never until you. You're my first, and you're going to be my last."

She smiled up at him with such love and trust that he thought his heart would beat out of his chest. It was only Zoey—it would always be only Zoey for him.

"Would you make love to me again?" she whispered.

As her answer Stark held her even closer and began a long, slow kiss. His last thought before everything went wrong was, *I've never been this happy in my life . . .*

CHAPTER ELEVEN

Kalona

He could feel Neferet getting near and he steeled himself, schooling his expression and cloaking the hatred he had begun to feel for her with a careful demeanor of expectation and accommodation.

Kalona would bide his time. If there was one thing the immortal understood, it was the power of patience.

"Neferet approaches," he told Rephaim. His son was standing before one of the several large sets of glass doors that opened onto the huge balcony that was the predominate feature of the penthouse loft the Tsi Sgili had purchased. Penthouse meant all the opulence Neferet craved and the privacy and rooftop access he required.

"Has she Imprinted with you?"

Rephaim's question brought Kalona's thoughts up short. "Imprinted? Neferet and I? What an odd question for you to ask me."

Rephaim turned from the downtown Tulsa panorama to look at his father. "You can sense her approach. I assume she's tasted of your blood and you've Imprinted."

"No one tastes of an immortal's blood."

The elevator doors chimed just before they opened and Kalona turned in time to see Neferet stride across the gleaming marble floor. She moved gracefully, with a sweeping glide those who were less informed would believe vampyric. Kalona knew differently. He understood her movement had changed, shifted, evolved—just as she had changed, shifted, and finally evolved into a being much more than vampyre.

"My Queen," he said, bowing respectfully to her.

Neferet's smile was dangerously beautiful. Serpentine, she wrapped one arm around his shoulder and exerted more pressure than was necessary. Obediently, Kalona bent so that she could press her lips to his. He let his mind go blank. His body alone responded, deepening the kiss, letting her tongue slither into his mouth.

As abruptly as she had begun it, Neferet ended the embrace. Glancing over his shoulder she said, "Rephaim, I thought you were dead."

"Wounded, not dead. I healed and awaited my father's return," Rephaim said.

Kalona thought that though his son's words were proper and respectful, there was something about his tone that was off, though it had always been difficult to read Rephaim as the visage of a beast tended to mask any human emotion he had. If, indeed, he had *any* emotion that could be classified as human.

"I learned that you have allowed yourself to be spotted by fledglings from Tulsa's House of Night."

"Darkness called. I responded. That there were fledglings there was inconsequential to me," Rephaim said.

"Not just fledglings—Stevie Rae was there, too. She saw you."

"As I said before, those beings are inconsequential to me."

"Still, it was a mistake for you to allow anyone to know you're here, and I do not tolerate mistakes," Neferet said.

Kalona saw her eyes begin to take on a reddish hue. Anger stirred within him. That he was in bondage to Neferet was bad enough—that his favorite son could be chastised and harangued by her was intolerable.

"Actually, my Queen, it could work in our favor that they are aware Rephaim remained in Tulsa. I am supposed to be banished from your side, so I cannot be seen here. If the local House of Night rabble hears rumors of a winged being, they will assume a Raven Mocker stalks the night and there will be no thought of me."

Neferet raised an arched amber brow. "A point well taken, my winged love, especially as the two of you work to bring the rogue red fledglings back to me."

"As you say, my Queen," Kalona said smoothly.

"I want Zoey to return to Tulsa." Neferet abruptly changed the subject. "Those fools at the House of Night tell me she refuses to leave Skye. She is not within my reach there—and I very much want her within my reach."

"The death of the innocent should cause her to return," Rephaim said.

Neferet's green eyes narrowed. "And how do you know about this death?"

"We felt it," Kalona said. "Darkness reveled in it."

Neferet's smile was feral. "How lovely that you felt it. That ridiculous boy's death was pleasing. Though I am worried that it might have the opposite effect on Zoey. Instead of making her come rushing back to her weak, whining group of friends, it could fuel her decision to stay hidden away on that island."

"Perhaps you should harm one closer to Zoey. The Red One is like a sister to her," Kalona said.

"True, and that wretched Aphrodite has become close to her as well," Neferet said, tapping her chin, considering.

An odd noise coming from his son drew Kalona's attention to Rephaim. "Did you have something to add, my son?"

"Zoey is hiding on Skye. She believes you cannot reach her there, is that not true?" Rephaim asked.

"We cannot," Neferet said, irritation making her voice hard and cold. "No one can breach the boundaries of Sgiach's kingdom."

"You mean like no one was supposed to be able to breach the boundaries of Nyx's Realm?" Rephaim said.

Neferet skewered him with her emerald eyes. "Do you dare to be impertinent?"

"Make your point, Rephaim," Kalona said.

"Father, you already breached a seemingly impossible boundary by entering Nyx's Otherworld, even after the Goddess herself banished you. Use your connection to Zoey. Reach her through her dreams. Let her understand she cannot hide from you. That, the death of her friend, and Neferet's return to her House of Night should be enough to coax the young High Priestess out of seclusion."

"She is *not* a High Priestess. She is a fledgling! And the Tulsa House of Night is *mine,* not hers!" Neferet practically shrieked. "No. I have had enough of your father's *connection* to her. It didn't bring about her death, so I want it severed. If Zoey is to be lured from Sgiach, I will do it by using Stevie Rae or Aphrodite—or perhaps both of them. They need a lesson in showing me the proper respect."

"As you wish, my Queen," Kalona said, sending his son a pointed look. Rephaim met his gaze, hesitated, and then he, too, bowed his head and said softly, "As you wish . . ."

"Good, then that is that. Rephaim, local news reports say that there has been gang violence near Will Rogers High School. The gang is cutting throats and draining blood. I believe if we follow that *gang* we'll find the rogue red fledglings. Do that. Discreetly."

Rephaim didn't speak, but he bowed his head in acknowledgment.

"And now I'm going to luxuriate in that lovely marble bathtub in the other room. Kalona, my love, I will join you in our bed very soon."

"My Queen, did you not wish me to search for the red fledglings with Rephaim?"

"Not tonight. Tonight I need a more *personal* service from you. We have too long been apart." She ran one red nail down Kalona's chest and he had to force himself not to flinch away from her.

She must have seen something of his desire to avoid her touch, though, because her next words were cold and hard. "Do I displease you?"

"Of course not. How could you possibly displease me? I will be ready and willing for you, as always."

"And you will be in my bed, awaiting my pleasure," she said. With a cruel smile she spun around and glided into the huge bedchamber that took up half of the palatial penthouse, closing the double doors to the bathroom with a dramatic slam that Kalona thought sounded much like a gaoler closing a prison door.

He and Rephaim remained still and silent for almost one full minute. When the immortal finally spoke his voice was rough with repressed anger.

"There is no price too great to pay to break the hold she has over me." Kalona swiped his hand down his chest as if he could wipe away her touch.

"She treats you as if you are her servant."

"Not for all of eternity, she will not," Kalona said grimly.

"For now she does, though. She even commands you to stay

away from Zoey, and you've been bound to the Cherokee maiden that shares her soul for centuries!"

The disgust in his son's voice was mirrored by Kalona's own thoughts. "No," he said quietly, speaking more to himself than his son. "The Tsi Sgili may believe she commands my every move, but though she thinks herself a goddess, she is not omniscient. She cannot know everything. She will not see everything." Kalona's massive wings moved restlessly, mirroring his agitation. "I believe you were correct, my son. It may prod Zoey to leave the ancient Isle of Skye if she understands that even there she cannot escape her connection with me."

"It seems logical," Rephaim said. "The girl hides there to avoid you. Show her your powers are too great for that, whether the Tsi Sgili approves or not."

"I do not require that creature's approval."

"Exactly," Rephaim said.

"My son, take to the night's sky and track the rogue fledglings. That will pacify Neferet. What I *truly* wish you to do is to find and watch Stevie Rae. Observe her carefully. Note where she goes and what she does, but do not capture her yet. I believe her powers are linked to Darkness. I believe she can be of use to us, but first her continuing friendship with Zoey and the House of Night has to be corroded. She must have a weakness. If we watch her long enough we will discover it." Kalona paused, then he chuckled, though the sound was utterly humorless. "Weaknesses can be so beguiling."

"Beguiling, Father?"

Kalona looked at his son, wondering at his odd expression. "Beguiling, indeed. Perhaps you have been so long apart from the world that you do not remember the power of a single human weakness."

"I . . . I am not human, Father. Their weaknesses are difficult for me to understand."

"Of course . . . of course, just find and observe the Red One. I will consider what to do with her from there," Kalona said dismissively. "And while I await Neferet's next *command*"—he spoke the word as a sneer, like the very voicing of it was distasteful— "I will search the realm of dreams and give Zoey—as well as Neferet—a lesson in hide-and-seek."

"Yes, Father," Rephaim said.

Kalona watched him open the double doors and step out onto the stone roof. Rephaim strode across the balcony to the balustrade-like wall that ringed the edge, leaped up on its flat ledge, and then opened his huge ebony wings and dropped silently, gracefully, into the night, gliding black and almost invisible against the Tulsa skyline.

Kalona envied Rephaim for a moment, wishing he, too, could leap from the rooftop of the majestic building called Mayo and glide the black, predator's sky, hunting, searching, finding.

But no. This night there was another hunting job he would complete. It would not take him to the sky, but it would also, in its own way, be satisfying.

Terror could be satisfying.

For an instant he remembered the last time he'd seen Zoey. It was the same moment his spirit had been torn from the Otherworld and returned to his body. The terror then had been his, caused by his failure to keep Zoey's soul in the Otherworld, thereby killing her. Darkness, under the direction of Neferet's oath, sealed by her blood and his acceptance, had been able to control him—to seize his soul.

Kalona shuddered. He'd long trafficked with Darkness, but he had never given it dominion over his immortal soul.

The experience had not been pleasant. It hadn't been the pain that had been so unbearable, though it had, indeed, been great. It hadn't been the helplessness he'd known as the tendrils of the Beast had encased him. His terror had been caused by Nyx's rejection.

"Will you ever forgive me?" he'd asked her.

The Goddess's response had cut him more deeply than had Stark's Guardian claymore: *"If you are ever worthy of forgiving you may ask it of me. Not until then."* But the most terrible blow had been delivered with her next words. *"You will pay my daughter the debt you owe her, and then you will return to the world and the consequences awaiting you there, knowing this, my fallen Warrior, your spirit, as well as your body, is forbidden entrance to my realm."*

Then she had abandoned him to the clutches of Darkness, banishing him again without a second glance. It was worse than the first time. When he'd fallen it had been his choice, and Nyx had not been cold and uncaring. It had been different the second time. The terror the finality of that banishment caused would haunt him for an eternity, just as would that last, bittersweet glimpse he'd had of his Goddess.

"No. I will not think of it. This has long been my path. Nyx has not been my Goddess for centuries, nor would I want to return to my life as her Warrior, forever second to Erebus in her eyes." Kalona spoke to the night sky, staring after his son, and then he closed the door on the cold January night and with it, once again, closed his heart to Nyx.

With renewed purpose the immortal strode through the penthouse, past the stained glass windows, gleaming wood bar, the dangling light fixtures, and the velvet furnishings, and into the lush bedchamber. He glanced at the closed double doors to the bathing room, through which he could hear water running, filling the huge tub in which Neferet so loved to luxuriate. He could smell the scent she always added to the steaming water, oil that was a mixture of night-blooming jasmine and clove made especially for her at the Paris House of Night. The scent seemed to slither under the door and fill the air around him like a smothering blanket.

Disgusted, Kalona turned and retraced his steps through the penthouse. With no hesitation he went to the closest set of glass doors that led to the rooftop, opened them, and gulped in the clean, cold night air.

She would have to come to him, seek him out, find him here, under the open sky, when she deigned to stoop so low as to actually look for him. She would punish him for not being in her bed, awaiting her pleasure as if he were her whore.

Kalona growled.

It was not so long ago that, drawn by his power, she had been enthralled with him.

He wondered briefly if he would decide to enslave her to him when he broke her hold over his soul.

The thought gave him some pleasure. Later. He would consider it later. Now time was short and he had much to accomplish before he had to, once again, placate Neferet.

Kalona walked to the thick stone railing that was ornate as well as strong. He spread his huge, dark wings, but instead of leaping from the rooftop and tasting the night air, the immortal lay on the stone floor, closing his wings over him, cocoon-like.

He ignored the coldness of the stone beneath him and felt only the strength of the limitless sky above and the ancient magicks that floated free and alluring within the night.

Kalona closed his eyes and slowly . . . slowly . . . breathed in and then out. As the breath left him Kalona also released all thoughts of Neferet. When he drew in his next breath he pulled, within his lungs his body and his spirit, the invisible power that filled the night over which his immortal blood gave him author-ity. And then he drew to him thoughts of Zoey.

Her eyes—the color of onyx.

Her lush mouth.

The strong stamp of her Cherokee foremothers that informed her features and so reminded him of that other maiden whose soul she shared and whose body had once captured and comforted him.

"Find Zoey Redbird." The fact that Kalona pitched his voice low made it no less commanding as he conjured from his blood and the night a power so ancient it made the world seem young. "Take my spirit to her. Follow our connection. If she is in the Realm of Dreams, she cannot hide from me. Our spirits know each other too well. Now go!"

This leave-taking of his spirit was nothing like what had be-fallen him when Darkness, bidden by Neferet, had stolen his soul. This was a gentle lifting—a pleasurable sensation of flight that was familiar and enjoyable. It wasn't sticky tentacles of Darkness he followed, but instead the swirling energy that hid in the folds between the currents of the sky.

Kalona's released spirit moved swiftly and with purpose to the east at a speed not comprehensible by the mortal mind.

He hesitated briefly when he reached the Isle of Skye, sur-prised that the protective spell Sgiach had laid on the island so long ago could give even him pause. She was, indeed, a powerful vampyre. He thought what a pity it was that she had not an-swered his call instead of Neferet.

Then he wasted no more time on idle thoughts and his spirit swatted away Sgiach's barrier and let himself float down, slowly but resolutely, toward the vampyre queen's castle.

His spirit was given pause once more as it passed the grove that grew lush and deep and close to the castle of the Great Taker of Heads and her Guardians.

The Goddess's fingerprint was all over it. It made his soul quiver with a pain that transcended the physical realm. The grove didn't stop him. It didn't forbid him from passing. It simply caused him an agonizing moment of remembrance.

So like Nyx's grove that I will never again see . . .

Kalona turned from the verdant proof of Nyx's blessing on someone else and allowed his spirit to be drawn to Sgiach's castle. He would find Zoey there. If she was sleeping, he would follow their connection and enter the mystical Realm of Dreams.

As he passed over its grounds he glanced with approval at the human heads and the obvious battle-ready state of the ancient place. Sinking down through the thick gray stone that was speckled with the sparkling marble of the isle, Kalona considered how much he'd rather be living there instead of the gilded cage of the Mayo's penthouse in Tulsa.

He needed to complete this task and force Zoey back to the House of Night. Like moves in an intricate game of chess, this was just one more queen that had to be captured so that he could be free.

His spirit sank lower and lower. Using his soul sight, the power through which his immortal blood made visible to him the layers of reality that lifted and shifted, roiled and surged all around the mortal world, he focused on the Realm of Dreams, that fantastical sliver of reality that wasn't completely corporeal, nor was it only spirit, and pulled taut the thread of connection he'd been following, knowing that when the cacophony of colors shifting realities caused cleared, he would be joined to Zoey there.

Kalona was relaxed and confident and therefore utterly unprepared for what happened next. He felt an unfamiliar tug, as if his spirit had become grains of sand being forced through the narrow funnel of an hourglass.

Sight first, his senses began to stabilize. What he saw shocked him so badly he almost lost the thread of the spirit journey altogether and was jolted back to his body. Zoey smiled up at him with an expression filled with warmth and trust.

By the shades of reality surrounding him, Kalona knew immediately he hadn't entered the Realm of Dreams. He stared down at Zoey, hardly daring to breathe.

And the sense of touch returned to him. She was wrapped in his arms, her naked body, pliant and warm, pressed against him. She touched his face, letting her fingers linger over his lips. His hips automatically lifted to her and she made a small sound of pleasure as her eyes fluttered closed and she raised her lips to his.

Just before she kissed him and he settled deeply within her body, Kalona's sense of hearing returned.

"I love you, too, Stark," she said, and began to make love to him.

The pleasure was so unexpected—the shock so intense—that the connection was severed. Breath ragged, Kalona pulled himself to his feet and leaned against the rooftop balustrade. Blood pumped hot and fast through his body. He shook his head in disbelief.

"Stark." Kalona spoke the name to the night, reasoning aloud. "The connection I followed wasn't to Zoey at all. The connection was to Stark." He understood, and then felt a fool for not anticipating what had happened. "In the Otherworld I breathed the spirit of my immortal soul within him. Some of that spirit has, obviously, remained." The smile that broke over the immortal's face was as fierce as his raging blood. "And now I have access to Zoey Redbird's Guardian and Oath Sworn Warrior." Kalona spread his wings, threw back his head, and let his triumphant laughter ring into the night.

"What is so amusing and why are you not awaiting me in my bed?"

Kalona turned to see Neferet standing naked in the doorway to the suite, a look of irritation on her haughty face. But that look quickly changed as she gazed at his fully aroused body.

"I am not amused, I am joyous. And I am here because I wish to take you on the roof with the open sky stretching above us." He strode to Neferet, lifted her, carried her back to the balcony railing, closed his eyes, and imagined dark hair and eyes as he made her cry out in pleasure over and over again.

Stark

The first time it happened so quickly Stark couldn't be sure, totally, absolutely sure, it had happened at all.

But he should have listened to his instincts. His gut told him something had gone wrong, very wrong, even if it was only for a few minutes.

He'd been in bed with Zoey. They'd talked and laughed and basically just been having a good time being alone. The castle was awesome. Sgiach and Seoras and the rest of the Warriors were great, but Stark was really a loner. Here on Skye, no matter how cool it was, someone was always around. Just because the place was withdrawn from the "real" world didn't make it any less busy. There was shit going on constantly—training and castle maintenance, trading with the locals and such. And that's not even taking into account that he'd been teamed with Seoras, which meant he was more or less the old dude's slave/errand boy/fodder for comedy.

Then there were the garrons. He'd never really been a horse

guy, but the highland garrons were amazing animals, even if they did seem to produce an amount of horse crap that was totally out of proportion with their size. Stark should know. He'd spent most of that evening shoveling it, and when he'd made a couple offhanded comments that, sure, might have sounded like complaining, Seoras and some other old Warrior with an Irish accent, bald head, and a ginger-colored beard had started calling him *Ach, poor wee Mary with the sweet, smooth hands of a lassie.*

Needless to say he was seriously glad to be alone with Z. She smelled so damn good and felt so damn good that he had to keep reminding himself it wasn't a dream. They weren't still in the Otherworld. This was real and Zoey was his.

It had happened between deep, hot make-out kisses that made him feel like he was going to explode. He'd just told her he loved her, and Z had been smiling up at him. All of a sudden something inside him had changed. He'd felt heavier yet weirdly stronger. And there was a strange sense of shock that jolted all along his nerve endings. She'd kissed him then and, as usual when Z kissed him, it'd been more than kinda hard for him to think, but he'd known something was off.

He'd felt shocked.

And that was bizarre as hell because he and Z had been kissing and more—lots more—for a while. It was like somewhere inside him, but apart from him, there was a guy who was totally blown away by what was going on between him and Z.

Then he'd started making love to Z and there was a sizzling sense of utter astonishment. It had felt strange, but everything was intensified when he touched Zoey. And it had gone away almost as quickly as it had started, leaving Z in his arms, melting into him so that the only thing filling his heart, mind, body, and soul was her . . . only her.

Afterward Stark tried to remember what it had been that had seemed so weird—what bothered him so much. But by that time the sun was rising, he was drifting into a happily exhausted sleep, and it just didn't seem so important anymore.

After all, why should he worry? Zoey was tucked away safely in his arms.

CHAPTER TWELVE

Rephaim

The Raven Mocker let himself fall from the seventeenth-story rooftop of the Mayo building. Wings outstretched, he soared over the city center, his dark plumage making him almost invisible.

As if humans ever looked up—poor, earthbound creatures. Odd that even though Stevie Rae was earthbound, he never thought of her as one of the rest of the unwinged, pathetic horde.

Stevie Rae . . . His flight faltered. His speed slowed. *No. Don't think of her now. I have to get well away first and be certain my thoughts are my own. Father must not guess anything is amiss. And Neferet can never, ever know.*

Rephaim closed his mind to everything except the night sky and purposefully made a long, slow circle, assuring himself Kalona had not changed his mind and defied Neferet to join him. When he knew he had the night to himself, he positioned himself so that he was headed northeast on a flight path that would take him first to the old Tulsa depot and then to Will Rogers High School and the scene of supposed gang violence that had recently been plaguing that part of the city.

He agreed with Neferet that the cause of the attacks was most likely the rogue red fledglings. That was all he agreed with Neferet on, though.

Rephaim flew soundlessly and quickly to the abandoned depot building. Circling it, he used his sharp vision to look for even a breath of movement that might betray the presence of any vampyre or fledgling, red or blue. He studied the building with an odd mixture of anticipation and reluctance. What would he do if Stevie Rae had come back and reclaimed the basement and the labyrinthine series of tunnels below it for her fledglings?

Would he be able to remain silent and invisible in the night sky, or would he let himself be known to her?

Before he could formulate an answer a truth came to him: he wouldn't have to make that decision. Stevie Rae wasn't there at the depot. He would know if she was near. The knowledge settled over him like a shroud, and with a long exhalation of breath Rephaim dropped to the roof of the depot.

Finally completely alone, he allowed himself to think of the terrible avalanche of events that had begun that day. Rephaim folded his wings tightly to his back and paced.

The Tsi Sgili was weaving a web of fate that could unravel Rephaim's world. Father was going to use Stevie Rae in his war with Neferet for dominion over his spirit. *Father would use anyone to win that war.* The moment after Rephaim had the thought he instantly rejected it, automatically reacting as he would have before Stevie Rae had entered his life.

"Entered my life?" Rephaim laughed humorlessly. "It's more like she entered my soul and my body." He paused in his pacing, remembering how it'd felt to have the beautiful, clean power of the earth flow into and heal him. He shook his head. "Not for me," he told the night. "My place is not with her; it is impossible. My place is as it has always been, with my father in the Darkness."

Rephaim stared down at his hand, resting on the rusted edge of a metal grate. He wasn't man or vampyre, immortal or human. He was monster.

But did that mean he could look idly on as Stevie Rae was used by his father and abused by the Tsi Sgili? Or worse, could he take part in her capture?

She wouldn't betray me. Even if I captured her, Stevie Rae wouldn't betray our connection.

Still staring at his hand, Rephaim realized where it was he was standing, on which grate his hand was resting, and he jerked back. It was here that the rogue red fledglings had entrapped them—here that Stevie Rae had almost lost her life—and here that she'd been so mortally wounded he had allowed her to drink from him . . . Imprint with him . . .

"By all the gods, if only I could take it back!" he shouted to the sky. The words echoed around him, repeating, mocking. His shoulders slumped and his head bowed as his hand smoothed over the surface of the rough iron grate. "What am I supposed to do?" Rephaim whispered the question.

No answer came, but he didn't expect one. Instead he withdrew his touch from the unforgiving iron and collected himself.

"I will do what I have always done. I will follow the commands of my father. If I can do that and, at least by some small measure, protect Stevie Rae, then so be it. If I cannot protect her, then so be it. My path was chosen at my conception. I cannot deviate from it now." His words sounded as cold as the January night, but his heart felt hot, as if what he had said made his blood boil at the core of his body.

With no more hesitation, Rephaim leaped from the roof of the depot and continued on his easterly route, flying the short miles from downtown to Will Rogers High School. The main building was set on a little rise beside an open field space. It was large and rectangular and made of light-colored brick that looked like sand in the moonlight. He was drawn to the centralmost part of the structure, the first of two large, ornately carved square towers lifting from it. That was where he landed. That was also where he immediately assumed a defensive crouch.

He could smell them. The scent of the rogue fledglings was everywhere. Moving stealthily, Rephaim positioned himself so he could peer down at the front grounds of the school. He saw a few trees, large and small, a long expanse of lawn, and nothing else.

Rephaim waited. It wasn't long. He knew it wouldn't be. Dawn was too close. So he'd expected to see the fledglings—he just hadn't expected to see them walk boldly up to the front door of the school, reeking of fresh blood and led by the newly Changed Dallas.

Nicole was wrapped around him. That big, dumb Kurtis obviously thought he was some kind of bodyguard because while Dallas pressed his hand against one of the rust-colored steel doors, the oversized fledgling stood at the edge of the concrete steps, looking out and holding a gun as if he thought he knew what to do with it.

Rephaim shook his head in disgust. Kurtis didn't look up. None of the fledglings, or even Dallas, looked up. He was no longer the broken creature they'd captured and used; they had no idea how pathetically vulnerable they were to his attack.

But Rephaim didn't attack. He waited and watched.

There was a sizzling sound and Nicole ground briefly against Dallas. "Oh, yeah, baby! Work your magic." Her voice lifted in the night as Dallas laughed and pulled the no longer locked or alarmed door open.

"Let's go," Dallas told Nicole, sounding older and harder than Rephaim remembered. "Dawn's close and there's somethin' you got to take care of before the sun rises."

Nicole rubbed her hand down the front of his pants while the rest of the red fledglings laughed. "Then let's get us down to those basement tunnels so I can get going on it."

She led the fledglings inside the school. Dallas waited outside until they were all in, then followed them, closing the door. In another moment Rephaim heard a sizzling sound like before and then all was quiet. And when, in the next moment, the security guard drove lazily by, all was still quiet. He, too, didn't look up to see the enormous Raven Mocker crouched on the top of the school's tower.

When the guard drove away Rephaim leaped into the night, his mind whirring in time with the beating of his wings.

Dallas was leading the rogue red fledglings.

He was controlling the modern magick of this world and it somehow allowed him access to buildings.

Will Rogers High School was where they were making their nest.

Stevie Rae would want to know that. She would need to know that. She still felt responsible for them, even though they had tried to kill her. And Dallas, what did she still feel for him?

Just thinking about seeing her in Dallas's arms made him angry. But she'd chosen *him* over Dallas. Clearly and completely.

Not that that made any difference now.

It was then that Rephaim realized the direction he'd been flying was too far south to take him back to the downtown Mayo. Instead he was gliding over midtown Tulsa, passing the dimly lit abbey of the Benedictine nuns, cutting over Utica Square, and silently approaching the stone wall–protected campus. His flight faltered.

Vampyres would look up.

Rephaim beat against the night air, lifting up and up. Then, too high to be easily seen, he skirted the campus, diving soundlessly outside the east wall into a pool of shadow between streetlights. From there he moved from shadow to shadow, using the darkness of his feathers to blend with the night.

He heard the eerie howling before he reached the wall. It was a sound so filled with despair and heartbreak that it cut even him to the bone. *What is making that terrible howl?*

He knew the answer almost as quickly as he'd formulated the thought. The dog. Stark's dog. During one of her sessions of non-stop talking, Stevie Rae had told him how one of her friends, the boy named Jack, had more or less taken ownership of Stark's dog when he'd turned into a red fledgling, and how close the boy and the dog had become and what a good thing she thought that was for both of them because the dog was so smart and Jack was so sweet. As he remembered Stevie Rae's words, everything slid into place. By the time he reached the school's boundary and heard the crying that accompanied the terrible howling, Rephaim knew what he'd see when he carefully and quietly scaled the wall and peered down at the scene of devastation before him.

He looked. He couldn't stop himself. He wanted to see Stevie Rae—just see her. After all, he couldn't do anything except look—Rephaim definitely couldn't allow any of the vampyres to see him.

He'd been correct; the innocent whose blood had fulfilled Neferet's debt to Darkness had been Stevie Rae's friend Jack.

Under the shattered tree through which Kalona had escaped his earthen prison, a boy knelt, sobbing "Jack!" over and over beside a howling dog in the middle of bloodstained grass. The body wasn't still there, but the bloodstain was. Rephaim wondered if anyone else would be able to detect the fact that there was a lot less blood than there should have been. Darkness had fed deeply from Neferet's gift.

Beside the weeping boy the school's Sword Master, Dragon Lankford, stood silently, his hand on his shoulder. The three of them were alone. Stevie Rae wasn't there. Rephaim was trying to convince himself that was for the best. It really was a good thing that she hadn't been there—maybe hadn't seen him—when a wave of feelings slammed into him: sadness, worry, and hurt foremost among them. Then, arms filled with a big wheat-colored cat, Stevie Rae rushed up to the mourning trio. It was so good to see her that Rephaim almost forgot to breathe.

"Duchess, you gotta stop this now." Her distinctly accented voice washed over him like a spring rain in the desert. He watched her crouch beside the big dog, depositing the cat between her legs. The feline instantly started rubbing against the dog, as if he were trying to wipe away her pain. Rephaim blinked in surprise when the dog actually quieted and began licking the cat. "There's a good girl. Let Cameron help you." Stevie Rae looked up at the Sword Master. Rephaim saw him nod almost imperceptibly. She turned her attention to the sobbing boy. Digging into the pocket of her jeans, she pulled out a wad of tissues, and handed it to him. "Damien, sweetie, you gotta stop this now, too. You're gonna make yourself sick."

Damien took the tissue and wiped quickly across his face. In a shaking voice he said, "I d-don't care."

Stevie Rae touched his cheek. "I know you don't, but your cat needs you, and so does Duchess. Plus, honey, Jack would be real upset if he saw you like this."

"Jack won't ever see me again." Damien had stopped crying, but his voice sounded terrible. It seemed to Rephaim that he could hear the boy's heart breaking within it.

"I do not believe that for one hot second," Stevie Rae said firmly. "And if you really think about it, neither do you."

Damien looked at her with haunted eyes. "I can't think right now, Stevie Rae. All I can do is feel."

"Some of the sadness will pass," Dragon said in a voice that sounded as heartbroken as Damien's. "Enough so that you will be able to think again."

"That's right. Listen to Dragon. When you can think again, you can find a thread of the Goddess inside you. Follow that thread. Remember there is an Otherworld we can all share. Jack's there now. Someday you'll see him again there."

Damien looked from Stevie Rae to the Sword Master. "Have you been able to do that? Does it make losing Anastasia any easier?"

"Nothing makes her loss easier. Right now I am still searching for the thread to our Goddess."

Rephaim felt a horribly sick jolt within him as he realized *he* had caused the pain the Sword Master was feeling. He had killed the spells and rituals professor, Anastasia Lankford. She had been Dragon's mate. He had done it so coldly, with an absolute lack of any feeling except, perhaps, annoyance at being detained for the short time it had taken him to overpower and destroy her.

I killed her with no thought for anything or anyone except my need to follow Father, to do his bidding. I am a monster.

Rephaim couldn't stop looking at the Sword Master. He carried his pain like a cloak around him. He could almost literally see the empty hole his mate's absence had left in his life. And Rephaim, for the first time in his centuries-long life, felt remorse for his actions.

He didn't think he'd made any sound, any movement, but he knew when Stevie Rae's gaze found him. Slowly, he looked from Dragon to the vampyre with whom he was Imprinted. Their eyes met; their gazes locked. Her emotions engulfed him as if she'd purposely directed them to him. First, he felt her shock at seeing him. It left him flushed and almost embarrassed. Then he felt sadness—deep, jagged, painful. He tried to telegraph his own sorrow to her, hoping that somehow she would be able to understand how much he missed her and how sorry he was for having any part in the grief she was experiencing. Anger hit him then with such a force Rephaim almost lost his grip on the stone wall. He shook his head back and forth, back and forth, not sure whether it was in denial of her anger, or the reason for it.

"I want you and Duchess to come with me, Damien. Y'all need to get away from this place. Bad things have happened here. Bad things are still lurkin' 'round here. I can feel it. Let's go. Now." She spoke to the kneeling boy, but her gaze never left Rephaim's.

The Sword Master's response was swift. His eyes swept the area and Rephaim froze, willing the shadows and the night to cloak him.

"What is it? What's here?" Dragon asked.

"Darkness." Stevie Rae was still staring at him when she spoke that single word as if throwing a dagger into his heart. "Tainted, unredeemable Darkness." Then she turned her back on him dismissively. "My gut says it's not anything worth raisin' your sword against, but let's get outta here just the same."

"Agreed," Dragon said, though Rephaim heard reluctance in his voice.

He will be a force to be reckoned with in the future, Rephaim acknowledged to himself. And what about Stevie Rae? *His* Stevie Rae. What will she be? *Could she really hate me? Could she utterly reject me?* He sifted through her feelings as he watched her take Damien's hand and help him to his feet, and then lead him, the dog, cat, and Dragon away toward the dormitories. He certainly felt her anger and her sorrow, and he understood those feelings. But hatred? Did she really hate him? He didn't know for sure, but Rephaim believed, deep in his heart, that he deserved her hatred. No, he hadn't killed Jack, but he was allied with the forces that had.

I am my father's son. It's all I know how to be. It is my only choice.

After Stevie Rae was gone Rephaim pulled himself up to the top of the wall. He took a running start and leaped into the sky. Beating against the night with his massive wings, he circled around the watchful campus and headed back to the roof of the Mayo building.

I deserve her hatred . . . I deserve her hatred . . . I deserve her hatred . . .

The litany pounded through his mind in time with his wing strokes. His own despair and grief joined with the echo of Stevie Rae's sadness and anger. The dampness of the cool night sky mixed with his tears as Rephaim's face was bathed in moonlight and loss.

CHAPTER THIRTEEN

Stevie Rae

"Oh, for shit's sake! Are you telling me no one has called Zoey?" Aphrodite said.

Stevie Rae took Aphrodite by the elbow and, with a grip that was maybe firmer than technically necessary, guided her to the door in Damien's dorm room. At the doorway she paused and both girls looked back at the bed, where Damien was curled up with Duchess and his cat, Cameron. Boy, dog, and cat had finally, just minutes before, fallen into a sleep induced by grief and exhaustion.

Silently, Stevie Rae pointed her finger from Aphrodite to the hallway. Aphrodite sneered. Stevie Rae crossed her arms and planted herself. *"Outside,"* she mouthed, *"now."* Then she followed her out of the room and closed the door softly behind them. "And keep your dang voice down out here, too," Stevie Rae whispered fiercely.

"Fine. I'll keep it down. Jack is dead and no one has called Z?" she repeated her question, much less loudly.

"No. I haven't exactly had time. Damien has been hysterical. Duchess has been hysterical. The school's in a dang uproar. I'm the only effing High Priestess who isn't, supposedly, locked away in her room praying or *whatever,* so I've been busy handling the shit storm out here and the fact that a really nice boy just died."

"Yeah, I understand that and I'm sad, too, and all, but Zoey needs to get here and get here now. If you were too busy to do it, then you should have let one of the professors call her. The sooner she knows the sooner she'll be on her way here."

Darius hurried up to them and took Aphrodite's hand.

"It was Neferet, right? That bitch killed Jack," Aphrodite asked him.

"Not possible," Darius and Stevie Rae said together. Stevie Rae flashed Aphrodite an annoyed *I told you so* look as Darius went on to explain. "Neferet was, indeed, in the school Council Meeting when Jack fell from the ladder. Not only did Damien see Jack fall, but another witness corroborates the time. Drew Partain was crossing the grounds when he heard the music Jack was singing to. He said he only heard part of the song because the bell clock on Nyx's Temple began chiming midnight, or at least that was why he thought he didn't hear any more of Jack's voice."

"But really that's when Jack died," Stevie Rae said, her voice gone hard and flat because that was the only way she could keep from sounding as shaky as she felt.

"Yes, the timing is right," Darius said.

"And you're sure Neferet was in the meeting then?" Aphrodite said.

"I heard the clock gonging while she was talking," Stevie Rae said.

"I still don't believe for an instant she's not behind his death," Aphrodite said.

"I'm not disagreein' with you, Aphrodite. Neferet is slicker than hen crap on a tin roof, but facts are facts. She was in front of all of us when Jack fell off that ladder."

"Okay, seriously, eew with your bumpkin analogies. And how

about the whole sword thing? How the hell could it have 'accidentally' "—she air quoted—"almost sliced his head off?"

"Swords should be positioned hilt down, point up. Dragon
explained that to Jack. As the boy fell on the blade, the hilt was
driven into the ground, impaling him. Technically, it could have
been an accident."

Aphrodite wiped a shaking hand across her face. "That's horrible. Really horrible. But it was no damn accident."

"I don't think any of us believe Neferet is innocent of the boy's
death, but what we believe and what we can prove are two different things. The High Council has already ruled once in Neferet's
favor and, basically, against us. If we go to them with more sup-
position and no proof of her wrongdoings, we will only discredit
ourselves more," Darius said.

"I get that, but it pisses me off," Aphrodite said.

"It pisses us all off," Stevie Rae said. "Bad. Real bad."

Picking up on the unusually hard edge in Stevie Rae's voice,
Aphrodite lifted an eyebrow at her. "Yeah, and let's use some of
that *pissed off* to kick that cow the hell outta here once and for all."

"What's your idea?" Stevie Rae said.

"First, get Zoey's vacationing butt back here. Neferet hates Z.
She'll come against her—she always does. Only this time we'll
all be watching and waiting and we'll get proof not even the
Neferet-loving High Council will be able to ignore." Without
waiting for a response from either of them, Aphrodite pulled her
iPhone from her metallic Coach clutch, punched in her code,
and said, "Call Zoey."

"I was gonna do that," Stevie Rae said.

Aphrodite rolled her eyes. "Whatever. You're too. Damn.
Late. Plus, you're too damn nice. What Z needs is a big dose of
get-your-shit-together-and-do-the-right-thing. I'm the girl to

feed it to her." She paused, listened, and rolled her eyes again. "It's her revolting Disney Channel–sounding *Hey guys! Leave me a message and have an awesome day* voice mail," Aphrodite quoted in an uber-bubbly voice. She drew a breath, waiting for the beep.

And Stevie Rae grabbed the phone from her hand, speaking quickly into it. "Z, it's me, not Aphrodite. I need you to call me the second you get this. It's important." She hit the *end* button to hang up and squared off against Aphrodite. "Okay, let's get somethin' real straight. Just because I try to be a decent human being, it does not mean I'm *too* nice. It's bad enough what happened to Jack. Learnin' 'bout it in a message is super, super bad. Plus, I don't think it's a good idea to freak Zoey out like that, 'specially so soon after her soul being shattered."

Aphrodite snatched the iPhone from Stevie Rae. "Look. We do not have time to tiptoe around Zoey's feelings. She needs to put on her big-girl High Priestess panties and deal."

"No, you look." Stevie Rae stepped forward and into Aphrodite's personal space, making Darius automatically move closer to her. "Z doesn't need to put on High Priestess panties. She is one. But she's been through losin' someone she loves. That's somethin' you obviously just don't get. Watchin' out for her feelings right now isn't about babyin' her. It's about bein' her friend. Sometimes all of us just need a little protection from our friends." She glanced at Darius, shaking her head. "No, that doesn't mean you need to protect Aphrodite from me. Jeeze, Darius, what's wrong with you?"

Darius caught and held her gaze. "For a moment your eyes flashed red."

Stevie Rae made sure her expression didn't change. "Yeah, well, I'm not surprised. Watchin' Neferet walk away without paying any consequences for what happened to Jack has been pretty hard for me to take. You'd feel the same way if you'd been here and saw it go down."

"I imagine I would, but my eyes would not glow red," Darius said.

"Die and un-die and then talk to me 'bout that," Stevie Rae said. She turned to Aphrodite. "I have stuff I gotta do while Damien is sleepin'. Are you and Darius gonna stay here and keep an eye on him? Not for one hot second do I believe Neferet is really locked away in her room praying to Nyx for the rest of the night like she wants everyone to believe."

"Yeah, we'll stay," Aphrodite said.

"If he wakes up, be nice," Stevie Rae said.

"Don't be a jerk. Of course I'll be nice."

"Good. I'll be back pretty soon, but if you need a break, call the Twins and they'll relieve you."

"Whatever. Goodbye."

"Bye." Stevie Rae hurried down the hallway, feeling Darius's questioning gaze following her with an intensity that was a physical weight. *I have to stop letting Darius make me feel guilty!* she told herself roughly. *I haven't done anything wrong. So what if my eyes glow red when I'm pissed? It doesn't have anything to do with the fact that I've Imprinted with Rephaim. I left him. Tonight I ignored him. Yeah, I have to find him and ask what the hell he knows about what happened to Jack, but not because I want to. Because I have to.* She told that big ol' lie silently to herself, and was so distracted by her thoughts that she almost ran smack into Erik.

"Hey, uh, Stevie Rae. Is Damien okay?"

"Well, what do you think, Erik? His boyfriend who he loved just died in a real horrible way. No, he's not okay. But he is sleepin'. Finally."

"You know, you don't have to be like that. I really am worried about him, and I cared about Jack, too."

Stevie Rae took a good look at Erik. He did look like crap, which was totally unusual for pretty-boy Erik. And he'd obviously been crying. Then she remembered that he'd been Jack's roommate, and also had been real sweet about standing up for Jack when that asshole Thor tried to pick on him for being gay. "Sorry," she said, touching Erik's arm. "I'm just upset 'bout all this, too. I got no reason to be a B to you. Here, I'll start over." She took a breath and smiled sadly. "Damien's sleepin' right now, but he's not okay. He'll be needin' friends like you when he wakes up. Thanks for askin' and thanks for bein' here for him."

Erik nodded and squeezed her hand briefly. "Thanks back at you. I know you don't like me much, what with the stuff that went down between Zoey and me, but I really am Damien's friend. Let me know if there's anything I can do to help." Erik paused, glancing up and down the hallway, as if to be sure they were alone, and then he took a step closer to Stevie Rae and lowered his voice. "Neferet had something to do with this, didn't she?"

Stevie Rae's eyes widened in surprise. "What makes you say that?"

"I know she's not what she pretends to be. I've seen her be her real self, and it's not pretty."

"Yeah, well, you're right. Neferet's real self isn't pretty. But just like me you saw that she was right in front of us when Jack died."

"Still, you think she's behind this."

It wasn't a question, but Stevie Rae nodded a silent *yes* answer.

"I knew it. This House of Night sucks. I was right to say yes to the L.A. House of Night."

Stevie Rae shook her head. "So that's it? That's what you do when you know somethin' evil is happening? You run away."

"What can one vampyre do against Neferet? The High Council reinstated her; they're on her side."

"*One* vampyre can't do much. A whole bunch of us joining together can."

"A few kids and a vamp here and there? Against a powerful High Priestess and the High Council? That's insanity."

"No, what's insanity is steppin' aside and lettin' the bad guys win."

"Hey, I have a life waiting for me—a good one, with a kick-ass acting career, fame, fortune, all that stuff. How can you blame me for not wanting to get mixed up in the Neferet mess?"

"You know what, Erik? All I'm gonna say to you is this: evil wins when good folks do nothing," Stevie Rae said.

"Well, I'm technically doing something. I'm leaving. Hey, did you ever think about this—what if all the good folks leave and evil gets bored playing all by itself and goes home, too?"

"I used to think you were the coolest guy I'd ever met," she said sadly.

Erik's blue eyes glinted with humor and he beamed his one-hundred-watt smile at her. "And now you *know* I am?"

"Nope. Now I know you're a weak, selfish boy who's gotten almost everything he ever wanted just 'cause of his looks. And that's not cool at all." She shook her head at his stunned look and began walking away. Over her shoulder she called back, "Maybe someday you'll find somethin' you care about enough to stand up for."

"Yeah, and maybe someday you and Zoey will figure out it's not really your job to save the world!" he shouted after her.

Stevie Rae didn't so much as glance back at him. Erik was a tool. The Tulsa House of Night would be better without his weak butt dragging them down. The going was going to get really tough, and that meant the tough needed to get going—and the sissies needed to get gone. Just like John Wayne, it was time to rally the troops.

"And, hell no, it's not weird that my troops include a Raven Mocker," Stevie Rae muttered to herself as she hurried out to the parking lot and Z's Bug. "I'm not really gonna rally him. I'm just gonna get info from him. Again." Purposefully, she shut her mind to what had happened between her and Rephaim last time she'd "just needed information from him."

"Hey, Stevie Rae, you and me gotta—"

Not pausing in her rush to the car, Stevie Rae held up a hand and cut Kramisha off. "Not now. I don't have time."

"I'm just sayin' that—"

"No!" Stevie Rae shouted her frustration at Kramisha, who stopped and stared at her. "Whatever it is you want to be sayin' to me, it can keep. I don't like soundin' mean to you, but I have things I have to do and exactly two hours and five minutes until the sun comes up to do them in." Then she left Kramisha standing in her dust as she jogged the final few feet to the Bug, started it, put it into gear, and practically peeled out of the student parking lot.

It took her exactly seven minutes to get to the Gilcrease grounds. She didn't drive the car up there. The ice storm had been cleaned up and the electric gate was working again, so everything was shut up tightly. Stevie Rae pulled the Bug off the side of the road behind a big tree. Automatically cloaking herself with the power she filtered from the earth, she went directly to the ramshackle mansion.

The door was no problem. No one had bothered to relock it yet. Actually, as she made her way through the old house and up to the rooftop, she detected very little change from the last time she'd been there.

"Rephaim?" she called his name. Her voice sounded eerie and too loud in the cold, empty night.

The door to the closet where he'd made his nest was open, but he wasn't crouched within.

She went out onto the rooftop balcony. That, too, was empty.

The entire place was deserted. But she'd known he wasn't here since she'd stepped onto the museum grounds. Had Rephaim been here she would have felt him, just like she'd felt him earlier when he'd been at the House of Night, watching her. Their Imprint connected them—as long as it was there, unbroken, it would tie them together.

"Rephaim, where are you now?" she asked the silent sky. And then Stevie Rae's thoughts slowed and rearranged themselves, and she had the answer; she'd had it all along. All she'd had to do was to get her pride and her hurt and her anger out of the way and the answer was there, waiting. *Their Imprint connected them—as long as it was there, unbroken, it would tie them together.* She didn't have to find him. Rephaim would find her.

Stevie Rae sat down in the middle of the roof and faced north. She drew a long, deep breath and let it out. With her next breath she concentrated on drawing in all of the scents of the earth surrounding her. She could smell the cold dampness of the winter-bare boughs, the crispness of the frozen ground, the richness of the Oklahoma sandstone that littered the grounds. Drawing the earth's strength with her breath, Stevie Rae said, "Find Rephaim. Tell him to come to me. Tell him I need him." Then she released the earth power with her exhalation. Had her eyes been open, Stevie Rae would have seen the green glow that hovered around her. She would have also seen that as it rushed off into the night to do her bidding, it was shadowed by a scarlet glow.

CHAPTER FOURTEEN

Rephaim

He'd been circling the Mayo building, dreading landing and facing Kalona and Neferet, when he felt Stevie Rae's call. He knew it was her instantly. He recognized the feel of the earth as the power lifted from the ground below and wrapped itself around the air currents to find him.

She calls you . . .

It was all the prompting Rephaim needed. No matter how angry she was at him. No matter how much she hated him—she was calling him. And if she called, he would answer. In his heart he knew, no matter what, he would always try to answer.

He remembered Stevie Rae's last words to him. *. . . When you decide your heart matters as much to you as it does to me, come find me again. It should be easy. Just follow your heart . . .*

Rephaim shut off the part of his mind that told him he couldn't be with her—couldn't care about her. They'd been apart more than a week. He'd felt every day of that week as if it had been an eon in itself. How had he ever thought he could stay completely away from her? His very blood cried to be with her. Even facing her anger was better than nothing. And he needed to see her. Needed to find a way to warn her about Neferet. *And about Father, too.*

"No!" he shouted into the wind. He couldn't betray his father.

But I can't betray Stevie Rae, either, he thought frantically. *I'll find a balance. I'll find a way. I must.* Not sure exactly what he was going to do, Rephaim stilled his seething thoughts and concentrated on following the ribbon of glowing green back to Stevie Rae as if it were his lifeline.

Stevie Rae

She was waiting for him with such concentrated intensity that Stevie Rae had no trouble sensing when Rephaim drew near the Gilcrease. When he dropped gracefully from the sky she was standing, looking up, watching for him. She'd meant to be totally cool. He was the enemy. She was supposed to remember that. But the instant he landed their eyes locked and, breathlessly, he said, "I heard your call. I came."

That was all it took. Just the sound of his wonderful, familiar voice. Stevie Rae hurled herself into his arms and buried her face in the feathers at his shoulder. "Ohmygood*ness*, I've missed you so much!"

"I've missed you, too," he said, holding her tightly to him.

They stood there like that, trembling in each other's arms, for what seemed to her a very long time. Stevie Rae drank in the scent of him—that amazing mixture of immortal and mortal blood that beat through his body—that linked them in Imprint and, therefore, also beat throughout her own body.

And then, quite suddenly, like it had occurred to each of them at once that they couldn't do what they were doing, Stevie Rae and Rephaim broke the embrace and took a step away from each other.

"So, uh, you've been okay?" she asked him.

He nodded. "I have. And you? You're safe? You weren't hurt when Jack was killed today?"

"How did you know Jack was killed?" Her voice was sharp.

"I felt your sadness. I came to the House of Night to be sure you were okay. That's when I saw you with your friends. I-I heard the boy crying for Jack." He hesitated over the words, trying to choose them carefully, honestly. "That and your sadness told me he was dead."

"Do you know anything about his death?"

"Maybe. What kind of boy was Jack?"

"Jack was good and sweet, and might have been the best of all of us. What do you know, Rephaim?"

"I know why he died."

"Tell me."

"Neferet owed Darkness a life debt in payment for entrapping my father's immortal soul. The debt had to be paid by the sacrifice of someone who was an innocent, incorruptible by Darkness."

"That was Jack; she killed him. It's frustrating as all get-out 'cause it looks like Neferet didn't! She was talkin' to the school's High Council, right in front of me, when Jack's accident happened."

"The Tsi Sgili fed him to Darkness. She need not have been present. She needed only to have marked him as her sacrifice and then let loose the threads of Darkness to follow through with the actual killing. She didn't have to witness the death."

"How do I prove she was responsible?"

"You cannot. The deed is over. Her debt is paid."

"Damn it! I'm so dang mad I could spit nails! Neferet keeps gettin' away with all of this awful crap. She keeps winnin'. I don't understand why. It's not right, Rephaim. It's just not right." Stevie Rae blinked hard, forcing back tears of frustration.

For a moment, Rephaim touched her shoulder and she allowed herself to lean into his hand, to take comfort in the contact with him. Then he pulled back from her and said, "All that anger. All that frustration and sadness. I felt it from you earlier tonight, too, and I thought—" He hesitated, obviously trying to decide whether to keep speaking.

"What?" she asked softly. "You thought what?"

He met her eyes again. "I thought it was me you hated. Me you were so angry at. I heard you, too. You told the Sword Master tainted, unredeemable Darkness lurked outside. You were looking straight at me when you said it."

Stevie Rae nodded. "Yeah, I saw you, and I knew if I didn't say somethin' to get Dragon and Damien outta there, they were gonna see you, too."

"Then you were not talking about me?"

It was Stevie Rae's turn to hesitate. She sighed. "I was seriously pissed and scared and upset. I wasn't thinkin' 'bout my words. I was just reacting 'cause I was freaked." She paused again and then added, "I didn't mean nothin' against you, but Rephaim, I do need to know what's goin' on with Kalona and Neferet."

Rephaim turned and walked slowly to the edge of the rooftop. She followed him and stood beside him as they stared out at the quiet night.

"It's almost dawn," Rephaim said.

Stevie Rae shrugged. "I got about half an hour before the sun rises. It'll only take ten minutes or so to get back to the school."

"You should leave now and not take any chances. The sun can cause you too much damage, even with my blood inside you."

"I know. I'll go pretty soon." Stevie Rae sighed. "So, you're not gonna tell me what's up with your daddy, are you?"

He turned to look at her again. "What would you think of me if you knew I betrayed my father?"

"He's not a good guy, Rephaim. He's not worth your protection."

"But he *is* my father," Rephaim said.

Stevie Rae thought Rephaim sounded exhausted. She wanted to take his hand, to tell him it'd be okay. But she couldn't. How the heck was it going to be okay with him on one side and her on the other? "I can't fight against that," she finally said. "You're gonna have to come to terms with what Kalona is and isn't yourself. But you need to understand that I have to keep my people safe, and I know he's workin' right beside Neferet, no matter what she says."

"My father is bound to her!" Rephaim blurted.

"What do you mean?"

"He didn't kill Zoey, so he didn't fulfill his oath to Neferet, and now the Tsi Sgili holds dominion over his immortal soul."

"Oh, great! So Kalona is like a loaded gun Neferet is holding."

Rephaim shook his head. "He should be, but my father does not serve others well. He chafes uneasily under her command. I believe the analogy would be more accurate if you said that Father is like a *misfiring* loaded gun Neferet is holding."

"You're gonna have to be more specific than that. Give me an example—what do you mean?" She tried to keep the excitement from her voice, but by the way his eyes closed off from her, Stevie Rae knew she'd been unsuccessful.

"I will not betray him."

"Okay, fine. I get that. But does that mean you can't help me?"

Rephaim stared at her silently so long she thought he wasn't going to answer, and she was trying to formulate another question in her head when he finally said, "I want to help you, and I will as long as it doesn't mean betraying my father."

"That's a lot like the first deal you and I made, and that didn't end up so bad, did it?" she asked, smiling up at him.

"No, not so bad."

"And, really, aren't we all basically against Neferet?"

"I am," he said firmly.

"And your daddy?"

"He wants to be rid of her control."

"Well, that's practically the same thing as bein' on our side."

"I can't be on your side, Stevie Rae. You have to remember that."

"So you'd fight against me?" She met his gaze squarely.

"I could not hurt you."

"Well, then—"

"No," he interrupted. "Not being able to hurt you is different than fighting for you."

"You'd fight for me. You already have."

Rephaim grabbed her hand, squeezing it as if through touch he could make her understand him. "I've never fought my father for you."

"Rephaim, do you remember that boy we saw in the fountain?" She changed his grip on her hand and threaded her fingers with his.

He didn't speak. He only nodded.

"You know he's inside you, don't you?"

Again, Rephaim nodded, this time slowly and hesitantly.

"That boy inside you is your mama's son. Not Kalona's. Don't forget about her. And don't forget about that boy and what he'd fight for, too. Okay?"

Before Rephaim could reply, Stevie Rae's phone rang with Miranda Lambert's "Only Prettier." She dropped Rephaim's hand and groped in her pocket for it, saying "That's Z's ringtone! I have to talk to her. She doesn't know about Jack yet."

Before she could press the answer button, Rephaim's hand caught hers. "Zoey needs to return to Tulsa. That's one way all of us can fight Neferet. The Tsi Sgili hates Zoey, and her presence here will be a distraction."

"A distraction from what?" Stevie Rae asked just before she hit the answer button and spoke quickly into the phone, saying, "Z, hang on. I gotta tell you something important but I need a sec."

Zoey's voice came through the line sounding like she was talking from the bottom of a well. "No problem, but call me back, 'kay? I'm seriously roaming."

"Will do in two shakes of a dead cat's tail," Stevie Rae said.

"Do you know how gross that sounds?"

Stevie Rae smiled into the phone. "Yep and bye."

"You mean yuck and bye. Talk to you in a sec."

The line disconnected and Stevie Rae looked up at Rephaim. "So explain about Neferet."

"My father wishes to discover a way to sever the bonds that tie him to Neferet. To do so, he'll need her to be distracted. Her obsession with Zoey is an excellent distraction, as is her desire to use the rogue red fledglings in her war with humans."

Stevie Rae's brows went up. "There isn't any war going on between vampyres and humans."

"If Neferet's will is done, there will be."

"Okay, well, we'll have to be sure that doesn't happen. Looks like Z really does need to get home."

"They want to use you, too," Rephaim blurted.

"Huh? Who's they? Me? For what?"

Rephaim looked away from her and spoke very quickly. "Neferet and Father. They don't believe you've firmly chosen the way of the Goddess. They think you could be persuaded to move to the side of Darkness."

"Rephaim, there is not even one tiny small chance of that. I'm not perfect. I have my issues. But I chose Nyx and Light when I regained my humanity. I'm never gonna change that choice."

"I have never doubted that, Stevie Rae, but they do not know you as I do."

"And Neferet and Kalona can never find out about us, either, can they?"

"It would be very bad if they did."

"Very bad for you or for me?"

"For both of us."

Stevie Rae sighed. "Okay, so I'll be careful." She touched his arm. "You be careful, too."

He nodded. "You should start back. Call Zoey as you drive. Dawn is too close."

"Yeah, yeah, I know," she said, but neither of them moved.

"And I must get back," he said, as if trying to convince himself.

"Wait, you aren't staying here anymore?"

"No. The ice storm has passed and there are too many humans about the grounds now."

"Well, where are you?"

"Stevie Rae, I cannot tell you that!"

"Because you're with your daddy, right?" When he didn't speak she continued. "Hey, it's not like I didn't already know it was totally b.s. when Neferet announced the whole hundred-lashes-and-banish-Kalona-for-a-century punishment."

"She did have him lashed. The threads of Darkness cut him one hundred times."

Stevie Rae shivered, remembered how awful just the touch of one of those threads had been. "Well, I wouldn't wish that on anyone." She met Rephaim's eyes. "But the part about him being banished from Neferet's side for a century is b.s., right?"

Rephaim gave a quick, almost imperceptible nod.

"And you won't tell me where you're stayin' because that's where your Kalona's stayin', too?"

He gave another slight nod.

She sighed again. "So if I need to see you I gotta go lurk around some scary old building somewhere or somethin'?"

"No! You stay safe and in public places. Stevie Rae, if you need me come here and call me as you did tonight. Promise me that you won't go out trying to find me," he said, giving her arm a little shake.

"Okay, okay. I promise. But this worried-about-you thing goes both ways. Rephaim, I know he's your daddy, but he's also into some bad stuff. I just don't want him to take you down with him. So be careful, 'kay?"

"I will be careful," he said. "Stevie Rae, tonight I saw the rogue red fledglings. They are making their nest at Will Rogers High School. Dallas has joined them."

"Rephaim, please don't tell Kalona and Neferet."

"Why, so you can show them kindness and humanity and they can have another opportunity to kill you?" he shouted at her.

"No! Just 'cause I try to be nice doesn't mean I'm stupid *or* weak. Jeeze, what is it with you and Aphrodite? I wouldn't run off to talk to them all alone. Heck, Rephaim, I wouldn't try to reason with them at all. I already proved that won't work. Whatever I'd do would be with Lenobia and Dragon and Z, at the very least. Basically, I just don't want them joining Neferet, so I don't want her to know 'bout them."

"It is too late. It was Neferet who put me on their trail tonight. Stevie Rae, I'm asking you to stay away from the rogue reds. They mean nothing but doom for you."

"I'll be careful. I already told you I would. But I'm a High Priestess and the red fledglings are my responsibility."

"The ones who have chosen Darkness are not your responsibility. And Dallas is no longer a fledgling. He is not your responsibility."

Stevie Rae's smile was crooked. "Are you jealous of Dallas?"

"Do not be ridiculous. I simply don't want to see you hurt again. Stop changing the subject."

"Hey, Dallas isn't my boyfriend anymore," she said.

"I know that."

"Are ya sure?"

"Yes. Of course." He shook himself and his wings unfurled. Stevie Rae's breath caught as she watched him. "Call your Zoey as you drive back to the safety of the school. I will see you again soon."

"Stay safe, 'kay?"

He turned to her and cupped her face in his hand. Stevie Rae closed her eyes and stood there, taking comfort and strength from his touch. Too soon it was gone. Too soon he was gone. She opened her eyes to watch his majestic wings beat against the night air and lift him higher, higher, until he disappeared into the barely discernable lightening of the eastern sky.

Rephaim had been right. It was too close to dawn for comfort. Stevie Rae hit redial as she hurried through the deserted mansion and back to the Bug.

"Hey, Z. It's me. I got some hard stuff to tell you, so brace yourself . . ."

CHAPTER FIFTEEN

Zoey

"Z? Are you still there? Are you okay? Say somethin'."

The worry in Stevie Rae's voice made me wipe the snot and tears from my face with the sleeve of my shirt and kinda sorta pull myself together. "I'm here. N-not okay, though," I said with a little hiccup.

"I know, I know. It's terrible."

"And there's no chance of a mistake? Jack's really dead?" I knew in my heart it was ridiculous to cross my fingers and close my eyes when I asked, but I had to give it one silly little-girl try. *Please, please don't let it be true . . .*

"He's really dead," Stevie Rae said through her own tears. "There's no mistake, Z."

"It's so hard to believe, and it's just not fair!" It felt good to get mad, better than breaking down in completely useless snot and tears. "Jack was the sweetest guy in the world. He didn't deserve what happened to him."

"No," Stevie Rae said in a shaky voice. "He didn't deserve it. I-I wanna believe Nyx has him and is takin' care of him real good. You've been there—to the Otherworld, I mean. Is it true that it's wonderful there?"

Her question tugged at my heart. "I know we've never talked about it, but didn't you go there, *before,* you know, when you—"

"No!" she said as if she wanted to cut off my words. "I don't re-member much from that time, but I do know I wasn't anywhere nice. And I didn't see Nyx."

The words came to me as I began to speak and I knew in my soul that Nyx was talking through me. "Stevie Rae, when you died Nyx was with you. You're her daughter. You have to re-member that always. I don't know why you and the other kids died and un-died, but I can tell you that I am one hundred per-cent sure Nyx never abandoned you. You just took a different path than Jack. He is in the Otherworld with the Goddess, and he's happier than he's ever been in his life. It's hard for those of us back here to understand, but I saw it with Heath. For what-ever reason, it was Heath's time to die this go-round, and he be-longed there, with Nyx. Just like Jack belongs there, too, now. I know in my heart that they are both completely at peace."

"Promise?"

"Absolutely. We have to be strong for each other back here, though, and believe we'll see them again someday."

"If you say it, then I'll believe it, Z," she said, her voice sound-ing better. "You really need to come home. It's not just me who needs to hear your High Priestess everything's-gonna-be-okay speech."

"Damien's pretty bad, huh?"

"Yeah, I'm worried 'bout him, and the Twins, and the rest of the kids. Heck, Z, I'm even worried 'bout Dragon. It's like the whole world is drownin' in sadness."

I didn't know what to say. No, that's not true. I did know what I wanted to say: I wanted to shriek, *If the whole world's drowning in sadness why do I want to come back to it?* But I knew that was weak and wrong on many different levels. So instead I said, kinda lamely, "We'll make it through this. We really will."

"Yeah, we will!" she said firmly. "Okay, look, together you and me, we gotta be able to figure out a way to expose Neferet's evil to the High Council once and for all."

"I still can't believe they bought that load of bullpoopie she shoveled at them," I said.

"Me neither. I guess it basically came down to a High Priestess's word against a dead human kid. Heath lost."

"Neferet isn't a High Priestess anymore! Jeesh, it pisses me off! And now it's not just Heath, but Jack. She's going to pay for what she did, Stevie Rae. I'm gonna make sure she does."

"She's gotta be stopped."

"Yeah, she does." I knew we were right—that we had to fight to get Neferet out of power, but just the thought overwhelmed me. Even I heard the exhaustion in my voice. I was tired all the way down to my soul, truly sick and tired of fighting against Neferet's evil. It seemed like for every one step forward I won I was somehow, eventually, no matter what, knocked two steps back.

"Hey, you're not in this alone."

"Thanks, Stevie Rae. I know I'm not. And anyway, this really isn't about me. It's *really* about doing what's right for Heath and Jack and Anastasia and whoever else Neferet and her evil horde decide to mow down next."

"Yeah, you can say that, but evil has taken a pretty dang big toll on you lately."

"That's true, but I'm still standing. A bunch of other folks aren't." I wiped my face with my sleeve again, wishing I had a Kleenex. "Speaking of evil and death and whatnot: have you seen Kalona? No way did Neferet really have him whipped and banished. He's gotta be all into everything with her. That means if she's in Tulsa, he's in Tulsa."

"Well, rumor has it she really did have him whipped," Stevie Rae said.

I snorted. "That figures. He's supposed to be her Consort, so she has him beaten. Wow. I kinda knew he liked pain, but even I'm surprised that he agreed to that."

"Well, uh, rumor has it he didn't exactly agree to it."

"Oh, please. Neferet is scary, but she can't order around an immortal."

"Looks like she can order around this one. She has some kinda hold over him because he failed in his, uh, dastardly mission to annihilate you."

I could hear the humor that Stevie Rae was trying to add to her voice and I attempted a little laugh for her benefit, but I think both of us knew the funny didn't begin to overcome the horrible.

"Well, ya know, being bossed around by Neferet is something Kalona isn't gonna like, and it's about time he got a big old dose of not liking something," I said.

"I hear you. I think Kalona's probably here somewhere lurkin' around all in her nasty shadow, and by that I mean her crotch," said Stevie Rae.

"Eeeew!" That did make me laugh, and Stevie Rae's giggle joined mine. For a moment we were BFFs again, being cracked up by the proliferation of skank in our world. Sadly, too soon the less amusing parts of our world intruded and our laughter dried up way faster than it used to. I sighed and said, "So, during all this rumor listening and stuff you didn't actually happen to see Kalona, did you?"

"Nope, but I'm keepin' my eyes open."

"Good, 'cause catching that jerk with Neferet after she's told the High Council she's banished him for a hundred years would definitely be a step toward proving she's not what everyone thinks," I said. "Oh, while you're keeping your eyes open, remember to have them pointed up. Wherever Kalona is, those gross birdboys of his will eventually show, too. No way do I think they've all suddenly disappeared."

"Okay. Yeah. Got it."

"And didn't Stark tell me that there actually was a Raven Mocker spotted in Tulsa?" I paused, trying to remember what he had said.

"Yeah, there was one seen once, but not since then."

Stevie Rae's voice sounded weird, all tight like she was having trouble talking. Hell, who could blame her? I'd basically left her holding the ball there at my House of Night. Just thinking about what she'd gone through with Jack and Damien made me feel sick.

"Hey, be careful, 'kay? I couldn't stand it if anything happened to you," I said.

"Don't worry. I'll be careful."

"Good. So, sunset is in just a little over two hours. As soon as Stark's up we'll get our stuff together and be on the first plane home," I heard myself say, even though it made my stomach feel sick.

"Oh, Z! I'm so glad! Besides needin' you back here, I've missed you so much."

I smiled into the phone. "I've missed you, too. And it'll be good to be home," I lied.

"So text me when you know what time y'all will get in. If I'm not in my coffin I'll be there to meet ya."

"Stevie Rae, you do not sleep in a coffin," I said.

"I might as well 'cause I'm seriously dead to the world when the sun's up."

"Yeah, Stark, too."

"Hey, how is your boy? Feelin' better?"

"He's good." I paused and added, "*Real* good, actually."

True to form, Stevie Rae's BFF radar heard between the lines. "Oh, nuh uh. Y'all did *not*?"

"What if I said we *did*?" I could feel my cheeks getting warm.

"Then I'd say a big ol' Oklahoma *yee haw*!"

"Well yee haw away then."

"Details. I want some serious details," she said, and then gave a giant yawn.

"You'll get details," I said. "Almost dawn there?"

"A little past, actually. I'm fadin' fast, Z."

"No problem. Get some sleep. I'll see ya soon, Stevie Rae."

"Later, 'gator," she said around another yawn.

I ended the call and went over to stare at Stark where he slept like a dead guy in our canopied bed. That I was totally in love with Stark wasn't in question, but just then I would really, *really* have liked it if I could shake his shoulder and have him wake up like a normal guy. But I knew it would be useless to even try to get him up early. Today the sun was unusually shiny on Skye—I mean, super bright with not one speck of clouds. No way Stark would be able to communicate decently with me for—I glanced at the clock—two and a half more hours. Well, at least that gave me time to pack and also to find the queen and break the news to her—that I was gonna leave this place that felt so right, so much like a home to me, this place that Sgiach had decided to bring back into the real world again, at least kinda sorta, because of what I'd brought back into her life. And now I was going to take off and leave it all behind because . . .

My brain caught up with the babbling chaos of my thoughts and everything clicked into place.

"Because this isn't my home," I whispered. "Home is Tulsa. It's where I belong." I smiled sadly at my sleeping Guardian. "It's where *we* belong." I felt the rightness of it even as I understood all that was waiting for me there—and all that I was losing leaving here.

"It's time I went home," I said firmly.

* * *

"Say something. Anything. Please." I'd just blurted my guts out to Sgiach and Seoras. Naturally, telling the story of Jack's horrible death had made me bawl and snot. Again. And then I'd babbled about having to go home and be a proper High Priestess even though I wasn't one hundred percent sure what that really meant, while both of them watched me silently with expressions that looked wise and unreadable at the same time.

"The death of a friend is always difficult to bear. It is doubly difficult if it comes too soon—too young," Sgiach said. "I am sorry for your loss."

"Thank you," I said. "It doesn't seem real yet."

"Aye, well, it will, lass," Seoras said gently. "You should be rememberin', though, that a queen puts aside grieving fur duty. You cannae have a clear head if 'tis filled with grief."

"I don't think I'm old enough for all of this," I said.

"No one is, child," Sgiach said. "I would have you consider something before you take your leave of us. When you asked if you could remain here on Skye I said that you should stay here until your conscience bade you leave. Is it your conscience talking to you now, telling you the time is right for you to leave, or is it the machination of others that is—"

"Okay, stop," I said. "Neferet probably believes she's manipulating me into coming back, but the truth is that I have to go back to Tulsa because it's my home." I met Sgiach's eyes as I continued speaking, hoping that she would understand. "I love it here. On lots of levels it feels right to be here—so right that it'd be easy for me to stay. But, like you've said, the path of the Goddess isn't easy—doing right isn't easy. If I stayed here and ignored my home I wouldn't just be ignoring my conscience, I'd be turning my back on it."

Sgiach nodded, looking pleased. "So your return comes from a place of power, not one of manipulation, though Neferet will not know that. She will believe that it only took one simple death to make you do her bidding."

"Jack's death isn't a simple thing," I said angrily.

"No, 'tisnae simple for you, but a creature of Darkness kills quickly, easily, and with nae thought beside her own gain," Seoras said.

"And because of that Neferet will not understand that you return to Tulsa because it was your choice to follow the path of Light and Nyx. She will underestimate you because of that," Sgiach said.

"Thank you. I'll remember that." I met Sgiach's clear, strong gaze. "You and Seoras and any of the rest of the Guardians who want to could come with me, you know. With you guys beside me there's no way Neferet could win."

Sgiach's response was instantaneous. "If I left my isle the consequences of that would ripple through the High Council. We have coexisted with them peacefully for centuries because I chose to absent myself from the politics and restrictions of vampyre society. Were I to join the modern world they would not be able to continue to pretend I do not exist."

"What if that's a good thing? I mean, it seems to me it's time the High Council was shaken up, and vamp society with it. *They believe Neferet and let her get away with killing people—innocent people.*" My voice was strong and sharp and for a moment I thought I sounded almost like a real queen.

"'Tis not our battle, lassie," Seoras said.

"Why not? Why isn't fighting against evil your battle, too?" I rounded on Sgiach's Guardian.

"What makes you think we're not fighting evil here?" It was Sgiach who answered me. "You've been touched by the old magick since you've been here. Tell me honestly, before then had you ever felt anything like it out there in your world?"

"No, I hadn't." I shook my head slowly.

"It's fighting to keep the old ways alive we've been doing," Seoras said. "And that cannae been done in Tulsa."

"How can you be so sure?" I asked.

"Because there is no old magick left there!" Sgiach said, almost shouting in frustration. She turned her back and paced over to the huge picture window that looked out on the sun setting into the gray-blue water that surrounded Skye. Her back was stiff with tension, her voice thick with sadness. "Out there in that world of yours, the mystical, wonderful magick of old, where the black bull was revered along with the Goddess, where the balance of male and female was respected, and where even the rocks and trees had souls, had names, has been destroyed by civilization and intolerance and forgetfulness. People today, vampyres and humans alike, believe the earth is just a dead thing that they live on—that it is somehow wrong or evil or barbaric to listen to the voices of the souls of the world, and so the heart and the nobility of an entire way of life dried up and withered away . . ."

"And found sanctuary here," Seoras continued when Sgiach's voice faded. He'd moved to her side. Her back was turned to me, but he faced me. Lightly, Seoras touched her shoulder and then let his fingers trail down her arm to take his queen's hand. I could see her body react to his touch. It was like through him she'd found her center. Before she turned to me, I saw her squeeze and then release his hand, and when our eyes met again she was, once more, noble and strong and calm.

"We are the last bastion of the old ways. It has been my charge for centuries to protect the ancient magicks. The land here is still sacred. By revering the black bull, and respecting his counterpart, the white bull, the old balance is maintained and there is one small place left in this world that remembers."

"Remembers?"

"Aye, remembers a time when honor meant more than self, and loyalty wasnae an option or an afterthought," Seoras said solemnly.

"But I see some of that in Tulsa. There's honor and loyalty there, too, and many of my grandma's people, the Cherokee, still respect the land."

"To some extent that might be true, but think of the grove—how you felt within it. Think of how this land speaks to you," Sgiach said. "I know you hear it. I see it in you. Have you felt anything truly like that outside my isle?"

"Yes," I said before actually thinking. "The grove in the Otherworld feels a lot like the grove across the street from the castle." Then I realized what I was saying, and Sgiach all of a sudden made sense. "That's it, isn't it? You literally have a piece of Nyx's magick here."

"In a way. What I really have is even older than the Goddess. You see, Zoey, Nyx hasn't been lost to the world. Yet. Her masculine balance has, and I'm afraid because of that the balance between good and evil, Light and Darkness, has been lost, too."

"Aye, we *know* it has been," Seoras corrected her gently.

"Kalona. He's part of this out-of-balance thing," I said. "It's true that he used to be Nyx's Warrior. Somehow that got out of whack, along with a bunch of other stuff when he turned up in our world, 'cause that's not where he belongs." Knowing it didn't make me feel sorry for him, or bad for him, but it did make me begin to understand the air of desperation I'd sensed so many times around him. And it was knowledge. With knowledge came power.

"So you see why it's important that I not leave my isle," Sgiach said.

"I do," I said reluctantly. "But I still think you could be wrong about there being no old magick left in the outside world. The black bull did materialize in Tulsa, remember?"

"Aye, but not until after the white bull appeared first," Seoras said.

"Zoey, I would very much like to believe that the outside world hasn't entirely destroyed the magick of old, and because of that there's something I want you to have."

Sgiach reached up and untwined a long length of silver from the mass of twinkling necklaces that dangled from around her neck. She lifted the delicate chain over her head and held it up at my eye level. Hanging from the silver was a perfectly round milk-colored stone that was smooth and soft and reminded me of a coconut-flavor Life Saver. The torches that the Warriors had begun to light flickered against the stone's surface, making it glisten, and I recognized the rock.

"It's a piece of Skye marble," I said.

"It is—a special piece of Skye marble called a seer stone. It was found more than five centuries ago by a Warrior on his Shamanic quest as he ran the Cuillin Ridge on this very island," Sgiach said.

"A Warrior on a Shamanic quest? That doesn't happen very often," I said.

Sgiach smiled and her gaze went from the piece of dangling marble to Seoras. "About once every five hundred years it does."

"Aye, that's about right," Seoras said, returning her smile with an intimacy that made me feel like I should look away.

"In my opinion, once every five hundred years is more than enough for some poor Warrior dude to do the Shaman thing."

My stomach give a silly little flip-flop of pleasure at the sound of his voice and I looked from the queen and her Guardian to see Stark standing in the shadows behind the arched doorway, rumpled and squinting at what was left of the fading light in the picture window. He was wearing jeans and a T-shirt, and he looked so much like his old self that a pang of homesickness—the first real one I'd felt since I'd returned to myself—speared through me. *I'm going home.* The thought had me smiling as I hurried toward Stark. Sgiach made a gesture with her hand. The heavy drapes were drawn over the last of the sunlight, allowing Stark to step from the shadows and take me into his arms.

"Hey, I didn't think you'd be up for an hour or so," I said, hugging him tightly.

"You were upset, and that woke me up," he whispered into my ear. "Plus, I was having some majorly weird dreams."

I pulled back so I could look into his eyes. "Jack's dead."

Stark started to shake his head in denial, and then stopped, touched my cheek, and blew out a long breath. "That's what I felt. Your sadness. Z, I'm so sorry. What the hell happened?"

"Officially an accident. Really it was Neferet, but no one can prove it," I said.

"When do we leave for Tulsa?"

I smiled my thanks at him as Sgiach said, "Tonight. We can arrange for you to leave as soon as you have your bags packed and ready."

"So, what's with this stone?" Stark asked, taking my hand.

Sgiach lifted it again. I was thinking how pretty it looked when it twisted gently on the chain and my gaze was pulled to the perfect circle in the center. The world narrowed and faded away around me as my entire being became focused on the hole in the stone because for an instant I caught a glimpse of the room through the hole.

The room was gone!

Fighting a wave of nauseating vertigo, I stared through the seer stone at what had looked like an undersea world. Figures floated and flitted around, all in hues of turquoise and topaz, crystal and sapphire. I thought I saw wings and fins and long, swirling cascades of drifting hair. *Mermaids? Or are they sea monkeys? I have utterly lost my mind,* was my last thought before I lost my battle with dizziness and ended up flat on my back on the floor.

"Zoey! Look at me! Say something!"

Stark, looking completely freaked, was bent over me. He'd grabbed me by the shoulders and was currently shaking the be-jeezus outta me.

"Hey, stop," I said weakly, trying unsuccessfully to shove him away.

"Just let her breathe. She'll be fine in a moment," came Sgiach's uber-calm voice.

"She fainted. That's not normal," Stark said. He was still grip-ping my shoulders, but he had stopped rattling my brains around.

"I'm conscious and I'm right here," I said. "Help me sit up."

Stark's frown said he'd rather not, but he did as I asked.

"Drink this," Sgiach held a goblet of wine under my nose that I could smell was laced heavily with blood. I grabbed it and drank deeply while she said, "And it is normal for a High Priest-ess to faint the first time she uses the power of a seer stone, espe-cially if she is unprepared for it."

Feeling much better after the bloody wine (eesh, but yum), I raised my brows at her and stood up. "Couldn't you have pre-pared me for it?"

"Aye, but then a seer stone only works for some High Priest-esses, and if it hadnae worked for yu, yu'd have had yer feelins hurt, now wouldn't ya?" Seoras said.

I rubbed my backside. "I think I'd rather have risked the hurt feelings instead of the hurt butt. Okay, what the heck did I see?"

"What did it look like?" Sgiach asked.

"A weird undersea fishbowl through that little hole." I pointed in the direction of the stone, but was careful not to look at it.

Sgiach smiled. "Yes, and where have you seen beings like that before?"

I blinked in understanding, "The grove! They're water sprites."

"Indeed," Sgiach nodded.

"So it's like a magick finder?" Stark asked, giving the stone a sideways glance.

"It is, when used by a High Priestess with the right kind of power." Sgiach lifted the chain and placed it around my neck. The seer stone settled between my breasts, feeling warm like it was alive.

"This really finds magick?" I put my hand reverently over the stone.

"Only one kind," Sgiach said.

"Water magick?" I asked, confused.

"It isnea the element that matters. 'Tis the magick itself," Seoras said.

Before I could say the *huh* that was obviously all over my face, Sgiach explained, "A seer stone is in tune with only the most ancient of magicks: the kind I protect on my isle. I am gifting you with it so that you might, indeed, recognize the Old Ones if any still exist in the outside world."

"If she finds any of that kind of magick, what should she do?" Stark asked, still giving the stone leery looks.

"Rejoice or run, depending on what you discover," Sgiach said with a wry smile.

"Mind, lass, it was the old magick that sent yur Warrior to the Otherworld, and the old magick that made him yur Guardian," Seoras said. "It hasnea been watered down by civilization."

I closed my hand around the seer stone, the memory of Seoras standing over Stark, trance-like, cutting him over and over again so that his blood ran down the ancient knotwork in the stone they called the Seol ne Gigh, the Seat of the Spirit. Suddenly I realized I was trembling.

Then Stark's warm, strong hand covered mine and I looked up into his steady gaze.

"Don't worry. I'll be with you, and whether it's time to run or rejoice, we'll be together. I'll always have your back, Z."

Then, for at least that moment, I felt safe.

CHAPTER SIXTEEN

Stevie Rae

"She's really coming home?"

Damien's voice was so soft and shaky that Stevie Rae had to lean down over the bed to hear him. His eyes were glassy and more than a little vacant, and she couldn't tell if that was because the drug/blood cocktail the vamps in the infirmary had come up with was actually working, or whether he was still in shock.

"Are you kiddin'? Z got on the first plane outta there. She'll be home in, like, three hours. If you want, you can come to the airport with me to pick her and Stark up." Stevie Rae was sitting on the edge of Damien's bed, so it was easy for her to give Duchess's head a rub—since the dog was curled around Damien. When he didn't make any response except to stare blankly at the wall in front of him, she gave Duchess another pat. In return the Lab thumped her tail weakly once, twice. "You're a dang good dog and that's all there is to it," Stevie Rae told the blond Lab. Duchess opened her eyes and gave Stevie Rae a soulful look, but her tail didn't thump again and she didn't make her usual happy huffing dog noise. Stevie Rae frowned. Did she look thin? "Damien, honey, has Duch had anything to eat recently?"

He blinked at her, looked confused, looked at the dog curled around him, and then his eyes actually began to clear, but before he could say anything Neferet's voice came from behind Stevie Rae, though she had no way heard the vamp enter the room.

"Stevie Rae, Damien is in a very fragile emotional state right now. He should not have to be concerned about such trivialities as feeding a dog or acting like a common butler and going to the airport to collect a fledgling."

Neferet swept past her. Full of motherly concern, she bent over Damien. Stevie Rae automatically stood up and backed several feel away. She could have sworn that something in the shadows that lapped around the hem of Neferet's long, silky dress had begun to slither toward her.

In a similar reaction, Duchess moved off Damien's lap and curled up morosely at the end of his bed, joining his still sleeping cat, all the while keeping her unblinking gaze trained on Damien.

"Since when is picking a friend up from the airport the butler's job? And believe me—I know what's what with a butler's job."

Stevie Rae glanced over at the doorway where Aphrodite seemed to have just materialized.

Well, slap me and call me a baby—am I so out of it I can't hear nothing anymore? Stevie Rae thought.

"Aphrodite, I have something to say to you that applies to everyone in this room," Neferet said, sounding regal and super-incharge.

Aphrodite put a hand on her slim hip, and said, "Yeah? What?"

"I have decided that Jack's funeral should be in the manner of a fully Changed vampyre. His funeral pyre will be lit tonight, as soon as Zoey arrives at the House of Night."

"You're waitin' for Zoey? Why?" Stevie Rae asked.

"Because she was Jack's good friend, of course. But more important, because of the confusion that reigned here when I was under Kalona's influence, Zoey served as Jack's High Priestess. That unfortunate time is, thankfully, behind us, but it is only right that Zoey light Jack's pyre."

Stevie Rae thought how terrible it was that Neferet's beautiful emerald eyes could look so perfectly guileless, even when she was weaving a web of deceit and lies. She wanted so badly to scream at the Tsi Sgili that she knew her secret; Kalona was here and she was controlling him, and not the other way around. She'd never been under his influence. Neferet had known from the start exactly who and what Kalona was, and what she was doing now was lying her butt off.

But Stevie Rae's own terrible secret stopped the words in her throat. She heard Aphrodite draw in a breath, like she was getting ready to launch into a major ass-chewing, but at that moment Damien drew everyone's attention to him when he put his head in his hands and began to sob, saying brokenly, "I-I just c-can't understand how he can be gone."

Stevie Rae pushed around Neferet and pulled Damien into her arms. She was happy to see Aphrodite stride over to the other side of the bed and rest her hand on Damien's heaving shoulder. Both girls gave Neferet narrow-eyed looks of distrust and dislike.

Neferet's face remained sad but impassive, like she knew Damien's grief but she let it wash around her and not into her. "Damien, I'll leave you to the comfort of your friends. Zoey's plane lands at Tulsa International at 9:58 tonight. I've set the funeral pyre for midnight exactly, as that is an auspicious time. I shall see all of you then." Neferet left the room, closing the door behind her with an almost inaudible click.

"Fucking lying bitch," Aphrodite said under her breath. "Why is she playing nice?"

"She's seriously up to somethin'," Stevie Rae said while Damien cried into her shoulder.

"I can't do this." Damien suddenly pulled back and away from both of them. He shook his head back and forth, back and forth. The heaving sobs had stopped, but tears continued to leak down his cheeks. Duchess crawled up to him and lay across his lap, with her nose pointed up near his cheek. Cammy curled up tightly against his side. Damien wrapped one arm around the big blond dog, and another around his cat. "I can't say goodbye to Jack and deal with Neferet's drama." He looked from Stevie Rae to Aphrodite. "I understand why Zoey's soul shattered."

"No no no no." Aphrodite bent over and put her finger in Damien's face. "I am *not* dealing with that stress again. Jack being dead is bad. Really bad. But you gotta keep yourself together."

"For us," Stevie Rae added in a much softer tone, giving Aphrodite a *be nice!* look. "You gotta keep yourself together for your friends. We almost lost Zoey. We lost Jack and Heath. We can't lose you, too."

"I can't fight her anymore," Damien said. "I don't have any heart left."

"It's still there," Stevie Rae said softly. "It's just broken."

"It'll fix," Aphrodite added, not unkindly.

Damien's eyes were bright with tears when he looked at her. "How do you know? Your heart's never been broken." He turned his gaze to Stevie Rae. "Neither has yours." As Damien continued to speak, the tears fell faster and faster down his cheeks. "Don't let your hearts be broken. It hurts too much."

Stevie Rae swallowed hard. She couldn't tell him—she couldn't tell any of them, but the more she cared about Rephaim, the more her heart broke every single day.

"Zoey's going to make it, and she lost her Heath," Aphrodite said. "If she can do it, you can do it, too, Damien."

"And she's really coming home?" Damien repeated the question he'd started with.

"Yes," Aphrodite and Stevie Rae said together.

"Okay. Good. Yeah. It'll be better when Zoey's here," Damien said, still hugging Duchess, with Cameron pressed close to his side.

"Hey, Duchess and Cammy look like they could use some dinner," Aphrodite said. Stevie Rae was surprised to see her reach out and, tentatively, pat the big dog's head. "I don't see any dog food in here, and all Cammy has is that wretched dry stuff. Quite frankly Maleficent won't even look at anything that doesn't appear to be fresh catch. How about I have Darius help me bring some food up for them? Unless you'd rather be alone. If so, I can take Cammy and Duchess with me and feed them for you."

Damien's eyes got all big and round. "No! Don't take them. I want them to stay here with me."

"Okay, okay, no problem. Darius can get Duchess's dog food," Stevie Rae spoke up, wondering what the heck Aphrodite was thinking. No way did Damien need to be without those two animals.

"Duch's food and stuff is in Jack's room," Damien said, ending on a little sob.

"Would you like us to bring all her stuff in here for you?" Stevie Rae asked, taking Damien's hand.

"Yes," he whispered. Then his body jerked and his face blanched even whiter than it had been. "And don't let them throw away Jack's stuff! I have to see it! I have to go through it!"

"I'm already ahead of you on that. No way was I letting those vamps get their claws into Jack's cool collections. I delegated the responsibility of boxing up his stuff and sneaking it out to the Twins," Aprodite said, looking smug.

Damien, clearly forgetting for just an instant that his world was filled with tragedy, almost smiled. "*You* got the Twins to do something?"

"Damn right," Aphrodite said.

"What'd it cost you?" Stevie Rae asked.

Aphrodite scowled. "Two shirts from Hale Bob's new collection."

"But I didn't think his spring stuff was out yet," Damien said.

"*A:* Hello—*gay* that you know that, and *b:* collections are always out early if you're filthy rich and your mom 'knows' someone," she said, air-quoting the word.

"Who's Hale Bob?" Stevie Rae asked.

"Oh, for shit's sake," Aphrodite said. "Just come with me. You can help me carry the dog accoutrements."

"And by that you mean I'm carryin' them, right?"

"Right." Aphrodite bent and, like she did it every day, kissed Damien on the top of his head. "I'll be right back with the dog and cat crap. Oh, want me to bring Maleficent? She—"

"No!" Damien and Stevie Rae said together with twin tones of horror.

Aphrodite lifted her chin indignantly. "It's so typical that no one understands that magnificent creature except me."

"See you soon," Stevie Rae told Damien, and kissed him on the cheek.

Out in the hall Stevie Rae frowned at Aphrodite. "Seriously, even you couldn't have thought taking those animals away from him would be a good idea."

Aphrodite rolled her eyes and flipped her hair back. "Of course not, moron. I knew it would horrify him and start to snap him out of his non-thinking-super-depressed state, which it did. Darius and I will bring animal food back for the dog and cat zoo up there and, just coincidentally, we'll stop by the dining hall and get some to-go stuff for our dinner, bring enough for him, and Damien is too much of a lady to kick us out or make us eat by ourselves. *Et voilà!* Damien has something in his stomach before he has to go through the whole funeral pyre horribleness."

"Neferet is up to something really, *really* bad," Stevie Rae said.

"Count on it," Aphrodite said.

"Well, at least it's gonna happen in front of everybody, so she can't, like, kill her."

Aphrodite raised her brow disdainfully at Stevie Rae. "In front of everybody Neferet broke loose Kalona, killed Shekinah, and tried to order Stark, who cannot miss what the hell he shoots at, to fire an arrow at you once and at Z another time. Seriously, bumpkin, get a clue."

"Well, there were extenuatin' circumstances with me, and Neferet didn't order Stark to shoot Z in front of the whole school, just in front of us and a bunch of nuns. Of course now she's saying Kalona made her do it for both things. Plus, it's still our word against hers. No one listens to teenagers, or nuns, for that matter."

"Do you doubt for one single instant that Neferet can make whatever she does tonight look like she's as innocent as an infant?" Aphrodite paused to grimace. "Goddess, I can't stand babies—ugh, all that puking and eating and pooping and stuff. Plus, they stretch out your—"

"Really?" Stevie Rae interrupted her tirade. "I'm not talkin' 'bout girl parts and babies with you."

"I was just using an analogy, stupid. Basically, we're in for some shit in just a few hours. So get Z ready while I try to prop up Damien so he won't dissolve into a puddle of tears and snot and angst tonight."

"You know, you can't pretend to be all 'I don't care about Damien' with me after I saw you *kiss him on the top of his head.*"

"Which I will deny for the rest of my very long and attractive life," Aphrodite said.

"Aphrodite, is you ever gonna get un-obsessed with your own self?"

Stevie Rae and Aphrodite came to a sudden stop when Kramisha stood up from the shadows at the edge of the porch of the girl's dorm.

"I'm gonna have to get my eyes checked. I can't see crap until it's right in front of me," Stevie Rae said.

"It's not you," Aphrodite said in a deadpan voice. "It's Kramisha. She's black. Shadows are black—hence the reason we didn't see her."

Kramisha stood up and looked down her nose at Aphrodite. "No, you did not just—"

"Oh, please, save it." Aphrodite breezed past her to the door of the dorm. "Prejudice, oppression, the Man, blah, blah, yawn, blah. I'm the biggest minority here, so don't even try to pull that on me."

Kramisha blinked twice and looked as stunned as Stevie Rae felt.

"Uh, Aphrodite," Stevie Rae said. "You look like Barbie. How in the heck can you be a minority?"

Aphrodite pointed to her forehead, which was completely blank and unMarked. "*Human* in a school full of fledglings and vamps equals mi-nor-i-ty." She opened the door and twitched into the building.

"That girl ain't no human," Kramisha said. "I'd say she more like a mad dog, but I don't want to offend no dogs."

Stevie Rae let out a long-suffering sigh. "I know. You're right. She's really not nice, even when she's bein' nice. For her. If that makes any sense."

"It don't, but you ain't been makin' a whole lot of sense in general lately, Stevie Rae," Kramisha said.

"You know what? I do not need this right now *and* I do not know what you mean *and* at this second I do not care. I'll see you later, Kramisha." Stevie Rae started to walk by her, but Kramisha stepped firmly in her way. She smoothed back the outside flip edge of her yellow bob wig and said, "You got no call to have that hateful tone of voice with me."

"My tone's not hateful. My tone's annoyed and tired."

"Nope. It be hateful and you know it. You shouldn't lie much. You ain't very good at it."

"Fine. I won't lie much." Stevie Rae cleared her throat, gave herself a little shake like a cat caught in a springtime shower, planted a big, fake grin on her face, and started again in a super bright tone of voice. "Hey there, girlfriend, nice to see ya, but I gotta be goin' now!"

Kramisha raised her brows. "Okay, first, don't say 'girlfriend.' You sound like that chick in that old movie, *Clueless*. The one the blonde and Stacey Dash reformed into somethin' popular. Not. Good. Second, you can't run off right now 'cause I got to give you—"

"Kramisha!" Shaking her head, Stevie Rae backed away from the purple sheet of paper Kramisha had started to hand to her. "I am just one person! I cannot handle anythin' else right now other than the shit storm I'm already caught in—excuse my French. But you gotta keep your future-telling poems to yourself.

At least till Z gets here, gets settled, and helps me be sure Damien isn't gonna hurl himself off the top of the closest high building."

Kramisha gave her a narrowed-eye look. "Too bad you ain't just one person."

"What in the Sam Hill do you mean? 'Course I'm one person. Jeeze Louise, I wish there was more than one of me. Then I could keep an eye on Damien, be sure Dragon doesn't go totally postal, pick up Zoey from the dang airport on time *and* figure out what's goin' on with her, get some dang thing to eat, and start to deal with the fact that Neferet is up to something of massive cat-herding proportions tonight at Jack's funeral. Oh, and maybe one of the me's could take a long bubble bath and listen to my Kenny Chesney while I read the end of *A Night to Remember*."

"*A Night to Remember*? You mean that *Titanic* story I read last year in Lit class?"

"Yeah. We'd just started it when I died and un-died, so I never got to finish it. I kinda liked it."

"Here. I'll help ya out. THE SHIP SINKS. THEY DIE. The end. Now can we please move on to somethin' more important?" She lifted the piece of purple paper again.

"Yes, hateful, I do know what happens, but that doesn't mean it's not a good story." Stevie Rae tucked an annoying blond curl behind her ear. "You say I don't tell good lies? Okay, here's the truth. My mama would say I got too dang much on my plate right now to get even one more forkful of chicken-fried stress, so let's lay off the poem stuff for a while."

Totally surprising Stevie Rae, Kramisha took a big step into her personal space, and then grabbed her by the shoulders. Looking straight into her eyes, she said, "You ain't just one person. You a High Priestess. A *red* High Priestess. The only one they is. That means you gotta deal with stress. Lots of it. 'Specially right now when Neferet is creatin' all kinds of crazy messes."

"I know that, but—"

Kramisha squeezed her shoulders hard, and cut in saying, "Jack is dead. They's no tellin' who's next." Then the Poet Laureate blinked a couple of times, her smooth brown brow furrowing, leaned forward, and took a giant noisy sniff of the air right next to Stevie Rae's face.

Stevie Rae pulled out of her vise grip and stepped backward. "Are you sniffing me?"

"Yes. You smell weird. I noticed it before. When you was in the hospital."

"So?"

Kramisha studied her. "So, it reminds me of somethin'."

"Your mom?" Stevie Rae said with forced nonchalance.

"Don't even go there. And while I'm thinkin' a' it, where is you goin'?"

"I'm supposed to be helping Aphrodite get stuff to feed Damien's cat and Duchess. Then I have to pick up Z from the airport and let her know that Neferet has decided to step aside and let her light Jack's funeral pyre. Tonight."

"Yeah, we all heard 'bout that. It don't seem right to me."

"Zoey lighting Jack's fire?"

"No, Neferet lettin' her." Kramisha scratched her head and her yellow wig moved from side to side. "So, here's the thing: let Aphrodite take care of the Damien stuff right now. You need to go out there"—she paused and waved one long, gold-fingernailed hand vaguely at the trees that ringed the House of Night campus—"and do that communing-with-the-earth-green-glowy-thing you do. Again."

"Kramisha, I don't have time to do that."

"I ain't done yet. You need to recharge your business before all hell breaks loose. See, I'm not real sure Zoey is gonna be up for what might be happenin' tonight."

Instead of brushing Kramisha and her bossy self aside, Stevie Rae hesitated and thought about what she was saying. "You could be right," she said slowly.

"She don't want to come back. You know that, right?" Kramisha said.

Stevie Rae hitched her shoulders. "Well, would you? She's been through a lot."

"I don't think I would, that's why I'm sayin' this to you, 'cause I do understand. But Zoey ain't the only one of us who's been through a lot lately. Some of us is still goin' through a lot. We all have to learn to take care of our business and deal."

"Hey, she's comin' back—she *is* dealing," Stevie Rae said.

"I ain't just talkin' 'bout Zoey." Kramisha folded the purple piece of notebook paper in half and handed it to Stevie Rae, who took it reluctantly; when she sighed and started to unfold it, Kramisha shook her head. "You don't need to read it in front a' me." Stevie Rae looked up at the Poet Laureate with a question mark on her face. "Look, right now I'm gonna talk to you like a Poet Laureate to her High Priestess, so you need to listen up. Take this poem and go out to the trees. Read it there. Think about it real good. Whatever it is you have goin' on, you need to make a change. This is the third serious warnin' I've got 'bout you. Stop ignorin' the truth, Stevie Rae, 'cause what you do don't just affect yourself. Are you hearin' me?"

Stevie Rae drew in a deep breath. "I'm hearing you."

"Good. Go on now." Kramisha started to walk into the dorm.

"Hey, would you explain to Aphrodite that I had somethin' to do, so I'm not comin' in?"

Kramisha looked over her shoulder at Stevie Rae. "Yeah, but you'll owe me dinner at Red Lobster."

"Yeah, okay. I like the Loobster," Stevie Rae said.

"I'm gonna order anything I want."

"Of course you will," Stevie Rae muttered, sighed again, and headed for the trees.

CHAPTER SEVENTEEN

Stevie Rae

Stevie Rae wasn't entirely sure what the poem meant, but she was sure Kramisha was right—she needed to stop ignoring the truth and make a change. The hard part was, she wasn't sure she could find the truth anymore, let alone know how to change stuff. She looked down at the poem. Her night vision was so good she didn't even have to move out from under the shadows beneath the old pin oaks that framed the Utica Street side of the campus and the side road that led to the entrance of the school.

"Haiku is always so dang confusin'," she muttered as she re-read the three-line poem again:

You must tell your heart
The cloak of secrets smothers
Freedom: his to choose

It was about Rephaim. And her. Again. Stevie Rae plopped her butt down at the base of the big tree and let her back rest against its rough bark, taking comfort from the sense of strength the oak exuded. *I'm supposed to tell my heart, but what do I tell it? And I know keeping this secret is smothering me, but there's no one I can tell about Rephaim. Freedom is his to choose? Hell yeah, it is, but his daddy has such a hard grip on him that he can't see that.*

Stevie Rae thought how ironic it was that an ancient immortal and his half-bird, half-immortal son had what was basically an old-school version of the same abusive daddy/son relationship a zillion other kids she knew had with their jerk daddies. Kalona had been treating him like a slave and making him believe messed-up stuff about himself for so long that Rephaim didn't even realize how wrong it was.

Then of course it was equally messed up that she was where she was with Rephaim—Imprinted and bound to him because of a debt she promised the black bull of Light.

"Well, not really just 'cause of a debt," Stevie Rae whispered to herself. She'd been drawn to him way before that. "I l-like him." She stumbled over the words, even though the night was silent and only the listening trees were present. "I wish I knew if that's 'cause of our Imprint or 'cause there really is something, some-one inside him worth liking."

She sat there, staring up at the spiderweb of winter-bare boughs over her head. And then, because she was spilling her guts to the trees, she added, "The truth is I shouldn't ever see him again." Just imagining Dragon finding out that she'd saved and Im-printed with the creature who had killed Anastasia made her feel like she wanted to puke. "Maybe the freedom part of the poem means that if I stop seein' him, Rephaim will choose to leave. Maybe our Imprint will fade away if we stay apart." Just the thought of that made her want to puke, too. "I really wish someone would tell me what to do," she said morosely, resting her chin on her hands.

As if in answer to her, the night breeze brought her the sound of someone sobbing. Frowning, Stevie Rae stood up, cocked her head, and listened. Yep, someone was definitely bawling their eyes out. She didn't really want to follow the sound. The truth was, she'd had more than enough bawling lately to last for quite some time, but the cries were so heartbreaking, so deeply sad, that she couldn't just ignore it—that wouldn't be right. So Stevie Rae let the crying lead her up the little road that ended at the big, black iron gate that was the main entrance to the school.

At first she didn't understand what it was she was seeing. Yeah, she could tell the crying person was a woman, and she was outside the House of Night gate. As Stevie Rae got closer she could see that the woman was kneeling in front of the gate, just off to the right side of it. She'd leaned what looked like a big funeral wreath made of plastic pink carnations and green stuff against the stone pillar. In front of that she'd lit a green candle and, as she continued to cry, she was pulling a picture out of her purse. It was when the woman brought the picture to her lips to kiss it that Stevie Rae's eyes found her face.

"Mama!"

She'd barely whispered the word, but her mom's head came up and her eyes instantly found Stevie Rae.

"Stevie Rae? Baby?"

At the sound of her mama's voice, the knot that had been building inside Stevie Rae's stomach suddenly dissolved, and she ran to the gate. With no other thought except getting to her mama, Stevie Rae scaled the stone wall easily, landing on the other side.

"Stevie Rae?" she repeated, this time in a questioning whisper.

Finding it impossible to speak, Stevie Rae just nodded, making the tears that had started to pool in her eyes slosh over and spill down her face.

"Oh, baby, I'm so glad I got to see you one more time." Her mom dabbed at her face with the old-fashioned cloth handkerchief she was clutching in one hand, making an obvious effort to stop crying. "Sweetheart, are you happy wherever you are?" Not pausing for an answer, she kept talking, staring at Stevie Rae's face as if she was trying to memorize it. "I miss you so much. I wanted to come before and leave this wreath for you, and the candle and this real cute eighth-grade picture, but I couldn't get here because of the storm. Then when the roads was opened I couldn't make myself, 'cause visitin' here and leavin' all this for you would make it final. You'd really be *dead*." She mouthed the word, not able to speak it.

"Oh, Mama! I've missed you so much, too!" Stevie Rae hurled herself into her arms, buried her face in her mama's poofy blue coat, and breathing in the scent of home, sobbed her heart out.

"There, there, sweetheart. It's gonna be fine. You'll see. Everything'll be okay." She soothed and patted Stevie Rae's back and hugged her fiercely.

Finally, after what seemed like hours, Stevie Rae was able to look up at her mom. Virginia "Ginny" Johnson smiled through her tears and kissed her daughter, first on her forehead and then gently on her lips. Then she reached into the pocket of her coat and pulled out a second handkerchief, this one still neatly folded. "Good thing I brought more than one."

"Thanks, Mama. You always come prepared." Stevie Rae grinned and wiped her face and blew her nose. "You don't have any of your chocolate chip cookies with you, do ya?"

Her mama's brow furrowed. "Baby, how can you eat?"

"Well, with my mouth like I always have."

"Baby," she said, looking increasingly confused. "I do not care that you are *communing through the spirit world*." Mama Johnson said the last part with a woo-woo tone to her voice and an attempt at mystical hand gestures. "I'm just real glad that I get to see my girl again, but I am gonna admit it'll take a sec for me to get used to the idea of you bein' a ghost, and all, 'specially one that cries real tears and eats. It just don't make good sense."

"Mama, I'm not a ghost."

"Are you some kinda apparition? Again, baby, it don't matter to me. I'll still love you. I'll come here and visit you lots and lots if this is what you want to haunt. I'm just askin' so I can know."

"Mama, I'm not dead. Well, not anymore."

"Baby, have you had a paranormal experience?"

"Mama, you have no idea."

"And you ain't dead? At all?" Mama Johnson asked.

"No, and I really don't know why. It did seem that I died, but then I came back, and now I have this," Stevie Rae pointed to the red tattoo Markings of vines and leaves that framed her face. "Apparently, I'm the first ever Red Vampyre High Priestess."

Mama Johnson had stopped crying, but at Stevie Rae's explanation, tears filled her eyes and overflowed again. "Not dead . . . ," she whispered between sobs. "Not dead . . ."

Stevie Rae stepped into her mama's arms again and squeezed her tight. "I'm so sorry I didn't come and tell you. I wanted to. I really, really did. It's just that, well, I wasn't myself when I first was un-dead. And then all Hades broke loose at the school. I couldn't get away, and I couldn't just call you. I mean, how do you call your mama and say, 'Hi, don't hang up. It's really me and I'm not dead anymore.' I guess I just didn't know what to do. I'm so sorry," she repeated, closing her eyes and holding onto her mom with everything she had.

"No, no, it's fine. It's fine. All that matters is that you're here and you're okay." Her mama pried Stevie Rae off her so she could look her over while she wiped her eyes. "You are okay, aren't you, baby?"

"I'm fine, Mama."

Mama Johnson reached out and cupped Stevie Rae's chin, forcing her daughter to meet her gaze. She shook her head and in her firm, familiar, mom voice said, "It's not nice to lie to your mama."

Stevie Rae didn't know what to say. She stared at her mom as the dam of secrets and lies and longing began to break apart inside her.

Mama Johnson took her daughter's hands, one in each of hers, and looked into her eyes. "I'm here. I love you. Tell me, baby," she said softly.

"It's bad," Stevie Rae said. "Real bad."

Her mama's voice was filled with love and warmth. "Baby, there ain't nothin' as bad as you bein' dead."

That was what decided Stevie Rae—her mama's unconditional love. She took a deep breath, and when she let it out she blurted, "I've Imprinted with a monster, Mama. A creature who's half human and half bird. He's done bad things. Really bad things. He's even killed people."

Mama Johnson's expression didn't change, but her grip on Stevie Rae's hands tightened. "Is this creature here? In Tulsa?"

Stevie Rae nodded. "He's hidin', though. No one at the House of Night knows about him and me."

"Not even Zoey?"

"No, 'specially not Zoey. She'd really freak. Heck, Mama, anyone who knew would freak. I know I'm gonna get found out. It has to happen, and I don't know what to do. It's so awful. Everyone'll hate me. No one will understand."

"Not *everyone* will hate you, baby. I don't hate you."

Stevie Rae sighed and then smiled. "But you're my mama. It's your job to love me."

"It's a friend's job to love you, too, if they're real friends." Mama Johnson paused and then asked slowly, "Baby, does this creature have somethin' on you? I mean, I don't know much about vampyre ways, but everyone knows Imprinting with a vampyre is a serious thing. Did he somehow make you do it with him? If that's what happened we can go to the school. They'll have to understand and they must have some way to help you get rid of him."

"No, Mama. I Imprinted with Rephaim because he saved my life."

"He brought you back from the dead?"

Stevie Rae shook her head. "No, I'm not sure how I un-died, but it has somethin' to do with Neferet."

"Then I should thank her, baby. Maybe I'll—"

"No, Mama! You have to stay away from the school and away from Neferet. Whatever she did wasn't because she's good. She pretends to be, but she's the opposite."

"And this creature you call Rephaim?"

"He's been on the side of Darkness for a long time. His daddy is seriously bad news and has messed with his head."

"But he saved your life?" Mama Johnson asked.

"Twice, Mama, and he'd do it again. I know he would."

"Baby, think hard before you answer me two questions."

"Okay, Mama."

"First, do you see good in him?"

"Yes," Stevie Rae said without hesitation. "I really do."

"Second, would he hurt you? Are you safe with him?"

"Mama, he faced a monster more terrible than I can describe to save me, and when he did that, the monster turned on him and hurt him. Real bad. He did that so I wouldn't be hurt. I honestly think he'd die before he hurt me."

"Then, here's the truth from my heart to yours: I can't begin to understand how he could be a mixture of a man and a bird, but I'm settin' that craziness aside 'cause he saved you and you're bound to him. What that means, sweetheart, is when the time comes for him to choose between the bad things in his past and a different future with you, if he's strong enough he will choose you."

"But my friends won't accept him, and worse than that, the vampyres will try to kill him."

"Baby, if your Rephaim's done the bad things you say he has, and I do believe you, then he's got some consequences to pay. That's for him to do, not you. What you need to remember is this: the only person's actions you can control are you own. You do what's right, baby. You've always been good at that. Protect your own. Stand up for what you believe in. That's it—that's all you can do. And if this Rephaim stands beside you, you may be surprised at what happens."

Stevie Rae could feel her eyes filling up with tears again. "He said I had to go see you. He never knew his mama. She was raped by his daddy and she died when he was born. But he told me not too long ago that I had to find a way to see you."

"Baby, a monster wouldn't say that."

"He's not human, Mama." Stevie Rae was gripping her mama's hands so hard her fingers felt numb, but she couldn't let go. She didn't ever want to let go.

"Stevie Rae, you're not human either, not no more, and that don't make a dang bit of difference to me. This Rephaim boy saved your life. Twice. So I really don't care if he's part rhinoceros and has a horn growing outta his forehead. He saved my girl, and you tell him next time you see him that he's gettin' a big ol' hug from me for that."

A giggle escaped Stevie Rae's mouth at the mental image of her mama hugging Rephaim. "I'll tell him."

Mama Johnson's face hardened into her serious expression. "You know, the sooner you come clean with everybody 'bout him, the better. Right?"

"I know. I'll try. There's a lot goin' on right now and it's not a good time for me to dump this on everybody."

"It's always the right time for the truth," said Mama Johnson.

"Oh, Mama, I don't know how I got myself into this mess."

"Sure you do, baby. I wasn't even there and I can tell you that somethin' 'bout this creature got through to you, and that some-thin' might end up bein' his redemption."

"Only if he's strong enough," Stevie Rae said. "And I don't know if he is. Far as I know he's never stood up to his daddy be-fore."

"Would his daddy approve of you bein' with him?"

Stevie Rae scoffed, "No dang way."

"But he's saved your life twice and Imprinted with you. Baby, to me that says he's been standing up to his daddy for a while now."

"No, he did all that while his daddy was, well, let's just say out of the country. He's back now, and Rephaim is back to doin' whatever he wants him to do."

"Really? How do you know that?"

"He told me today when he—" Stevie Rae's words broke off and her eyes widened.

Her mama smiled and nodded. "See?"

"Ohmygood*ness*, you might be right!"

"'Course I'm right. I'm your mama."

"I love you, Mama," Stevie Rae said.

"And I love you right back, baby girl."

CHAPTER EIGHTEEN

Rephaim

"I cannot believe you are going to do this," Kalona said, pacing back and forth across the rooftop balcony of the Mayo.

"I am doing this because it is necessary, it is time, and it is the right thing to do!" Neferet's voice rose in tempo while she spoke as if she were exploding from the inside out.

"The *right* thing to do! As if you're a creature of Light?" Rephaim couldn't stop the words, nor could he school his voice to sound anything but incredulous.

Neferet rounded on him. She raised her hand. Rephaim could see threads of power quivering in the air around her, absorbing into her skin, crawling beneath it. The sight made his stomach tighten as he remembered the terrible touch of those Dark threads. Automatically, he moved a step back from her.

"Are you questioning me, bird creature?" Neferet looked like she was readying herself to hurl the Darkness at him.

"Rephaim does not question you, just as I do not question you." His father moved closer to Neferet, stepping between the Tsi Sgili and him as he continued to speak with the calm voice of authority. "We are both simply surprised."

"It is what Zoey and her allies would least expect me to do. So, even though it sickens me, I will abase myself—temporarily. By doing so I make Zoey impotent. If she so much as whispers against me, she will reveal herself to be the petulant child she really is."

"I would think you would rather destroy her than humiliate her," Rephaim said.

Neferet sneered at him and spoke to him as if he were an utter fool. "I have the ability to kill her tonight, but no matter how I orchestrated it, I would be implicated. Even those dotards on the High Council would be compelled to come here—to watch me, and to interfere with my plans. No, I am not ready for that, and until I am, I want Zoey Redbird gagged and put back in her place. She is a mere fledgling; she will be treated as such from here on out. And as I am taking care of Zoey I will also be revisiting her little group of friends—especially the one who calls herself the first red High Priestess." Neferet's laughter was mocking. "Stevie Rae? A High Priestess? I intend to reveal what she really is."

"And what is that?" Rephaim had to ask, though he kept his voice level, his expression as blank as he could make it.

"She is a vampyre who has known, and even embraced, Darkness."

"Ultimately she chose Light," Rephaim said, and realized that he'd spoken much too quickly when Neferet's eyes narrowed.

"But the fact that Darkness has touched her changes her forever," Kalona said.

Neferet smiled sweetly at Kalona. "You are so very right, my Consort."

"Couldn't knowing the touch of Darkness have a strengthening effect on the Red One?" Rephaim was unable to stop himself from asking.

"Of course it has. The Red One is a powerful vampyre, if young and inexperienced, which is exactly why she could be of excellent use to us," Kalona said.

"I believe there is even more to Stevie Rae than she has shown to her little friends. I saw her when she was in Darkness. She reveled in it," Neferet said. "I say we need to watch her and see what is beneath that *bright, innocent* exterior." Neferet enunciated the words sarcastically.

"As you wisssssh," Rephaim said, and was disgusted that the anger Neferet caused within him had him hissing like an animal.

Neferet stared at him. "I sense a change in you."

Rephaim forced himself to continue to meet her eyes steadily. "In my father's absence I was closer to death and Darkness than ever before during my long life. If you sense a change within me, perhaps that is it."

"Perhaps," Neferet said slowly. "And perhaps not. Why is it that I suspect you might not be entirely pleased your father and I have returned to Tulsa?"

Rephaim held himself very still so that the Tsi Sgili would not see the hate and anger that were flooding his body. "I am my father's favored son. As always, I stand beside him. The days he was absent from me were the darkest of my life."

"Really? How very terrible for you," Neferet said sarcastically. Then she dismissively turned from him to face Kalona. "Your *favored* son's words remind me—where are the rest of the creatures you call your children? Surely a handful of fledglings and nuns didn't manage to kill them all."

Kalona's jaw clenched and unclenched and his eyes blazed amber. Recognizing that his father was struggling to control his anger, Rephaim spoke up quickly. "I have surviving brothers. I saw them flee when you and my father were banished."

Neferet's eyes narrowed. "I am *banished* no more."

No more, Rephaim thought, meeting her gaze without so much as a blink, *but a handful of fledglings and nuns did manage it once.*

Again, Kalona drew her attention from him. "The others are not like Rephaim. They need help to hide in the city without being detected. They must have found safe places to nest farther from civilization." When he spoke, his anger only bubbled under the surface of his words and did not boil over, though Rephaim wondered at how blind Neferet had become. Did she really believe she was so powerful that she could continually bait an ancient immortal without paying the consequence of his wrath?

"Well, we're back. They should be here. They're aberrations of nature, but they do have their uses. During the daylight hours they can stay in there, far away from my bedchamber." She waved toward the lush penthouse suite. "At night they can lurk out here and await my orders."

"You mean *my* orders." Kalona hadn't raised his voice, but the power that rumbled through it drew prickles of gooseflesh up and down Rephaim's arms. "My sons only obey me. They are bound to me through blood and magick and time. I alone control them."

"Then I assume you can control getting them here?"

"Yes."

"Well, summon them or have Rephaim herd them here, or whatever it is you do. I can't be expected to take care of everything."

"As you wish," Kalona said, echoing Rephaim's earlier statement.

"Now I'm going to go abase myself before a school full of lesser beings because you did not keep Zoey Redbird from returning to this realm." Her eyes looked like green ice. "And that is why *you* now obey only *me*. Be here when I return." Neferet left the balcony. Her long cloak should have caught in the door she slammed behind her, but at the last moment it rippled and skittered closer to the Tsi Sgili's body, lapping around her ankles like a sticky pool of tar.

Rephaim faced his father, the ancient immortal he'd been serving faithfully for centuries. "How can you allow her to speak to you like that? To use you like that? She called my brothers aberrations of nature, but it is she who is the true monster!" Rephaim knew he shouldn't have spoken to his father like that, but he couldn't help himself. Seeing the proud and powerful Kalona being ordered around like a servant was unbearable.

As Kalona approached Rephaim braced himself for what was surely to come. He'd seen his father's wrath unleashed before—he knew what to expect. Kalona unfurled his great wings and loomed over his son, but the blow Rephaim expected did not come. Instead when he met his father's gaze he saw despair and not anger.

Looking like a fallen god, Kalona said, "Not you, too. I expected her disrespect and disloyalty; she betrayed a goddess to free me. You, though, you I never believed would turn on me."

"Father! I have not!" Rephaim said, putting from his mind all thoughts of Stevie Rae. "I simply cannot bear the way she treats you."

"That is why I must discover a way to break that accursed oath." Kalona made a wordless sound of frustration and paced over to the balustraded stone railing, staring out into the night. "If only Nyx had stayed out of the battle with Stark. Then he would have remained dead and I know in my soul Zoey would never have found the strength to return to this realm and her body, not with two of her lovers dead."

Rephaim followed his father to the railing. "Dead? You killed Stark in the Otherworld?"

Kalona snorted, "Of course I killed that boy. He and I battled. He could not possibly have defeated me, even if he did manage to become a Guardian and wield the great Guardian claymore."

"Nyx resurrected Stark?" Rephaim said, incredulous. "But the

Goddess doesn't interfere with human choice. It was Stark's *choice* to defend Zoey against you."

"Nyx did not resurrect Stark. I did."

Rephaim blinked in shock. "You?"

Kalona nodded and continued to stare out at the night sky, not meeting his son's gaze as he spoke in a strained voice as if he had to force each word from his throat. "I killed Stark. I believed Zoey would retreat then and remain in the Otherworld with the souls of her Warrior and mate. Or perhaps her spirit would shatter forever and she would be a wandering Caoinic Shi'." Kalona paused and then added, "Though I did not wish the latter on her. I do not hate her as does Neferet."

To Rephaim it seemed his father was talking aloud to himself more than speaking to him, so when Kalona went silent he was silent and patient, not wanting to interrupt him, waiting for him to continue.

"Zoey is stronger than I anticipated." Kalona continued speaking to the night. "Instead of retreating or shattering, she attacked." The winged immortal chuckled at the memory. "She skewered me with my own spear and then ordered me to return Stark's life to repay the life debt I owed for killing that boy of hers. I refused, of course."

Unable to stay silent, Rephaim blurted, "But life debts are powerful things, Father."

"True, but I am a powerful immortal. Consequences that govern mortals do not apply to me."

Rephaim's thoughts, like a cold wind, whispered through his mind: *Perhaps he is wrong. Perhaps what is happening to Father is part of the consequences he has considered himself too powerful to pay.* But Rephaim knew better than to correct Kalona, so he simply continued, "You refused Zoey, and then what happened?"

"Nyx happened," Kalona said bitterly. "I could refuse a child-like High Priestess. I could not refuse the Goddess. I could never refuse the Goddess. I breathed a sliver of my immortality into Stark. He lived. Zoey returned to her body and managed to rescue her Warrior from the Otherworld, too. And I am under the control of a Tsi Sgili who I believe to be utterly mad." Kalona looked at Rephaim. "If I do not break this bondage she may take me into madness with her. She has a connection with Darkness that I have not so much as sensed in centuries. It is as powerful as it is seductive and dangerous."

"You should kill Zoey." Rephaim spoke the words slowly, haltingly, hating himself for every syllable because he knew the pain Zoey's death would cause Stevie Rae.

"I have, of course, already considered that." Rephaim held his breath when Kalona paused. "And I have come to believe that if I kill Zoey Redbird it would be an open affront to Nyx. I have not served the Goddess in many ages. I have done things she would view as"—Kalona paused again, this time struggling with his words—"unforgivable. But I have never taken the life of any priestess in her service."

"Do you fear Nyx?" Rephaim asked.

"Only a fool does not fear a goddess. Even Neferet avoids Nyx's wrath by not killing Zoey, though the Tsi Sgili does not admit so to herself."

"Neferet is so swollen with Darkness that she no longer thinks rationally," Rephaim said.

"True, but just because she is irrational that does not mean she isn't clever. For instance, I believe she may be correct about the Red One—she could be used or perhaps even turned from the path she has chosen." Kalona shrugged. "Or she can continue to stand with Zoey and be destroyed when Neferet comes against her."

"Father, I do not believe it is simply that Stevie Rae stands with Zoey. I believe she stands with Nyx, too. Is it logical to assume Nyx's first red High Priestess would be special to the Goddess, and therefore should she remain untouched like Zoey?"

"I see validity in your words, my son." Kalona nodded his head in solemn agreement. "If she does not turn from the path of the Goddess, I will not harm the Red One. Instead of me, Neferet will be incurring Nyx's wrath if she destroys Stevie Rae."

Rephaim maintained a tight control on his voice and expression. "That is a wise decision, Father."

"Of course there are other ways of hindering a High Priestess without killing her."

"What do you plan to do to hinder the Red One?" Rephaim asked.

"I do not plan to do anything to the Red One until Neferet manages to coerce her from her path, and then I will either direct her powers or step aside while Neferet destroys her." Kalona waved away the question. "I was thinking of Zoey. If Zoey can be persuaded to come against Neferet publically, the Tsi Sgili will be completely distracted. You and I can focus on breaking my bond to her."

"But, as Neferet said, after tonight if Zoey speaks against her she will be admonished and discredited. Zoey is wise enough to know that. She won't publically clash with Neferet."

Kalona smiled. "Ah, but what if her Warrior, her Guardian, the one person on this earth she trusts above all others, begins to whisper to her that she shouldn't allow Neferet to get away with her evil deeds? That she must fulfill her role as High Priestess, no matter the supposed consequences, and stand up to Neferet."

"Stark would not do that."

Kalona's smile widened. "My spirit can enter Stark's body."

Rephaim gasped. "How?"

Still grinning, Kalona shrugged his broad shoulders. "I do not know. I have not experienced this ever before."

"So this is more than entering the realm of dreams and finding a sleeping spirit?"

"Much more. Stark was completely awake and I followed a connection I believed would lead me to A-ya in the realm of dreams, if Zoey had been sleeping. The connection took me to Stark—*into* Stark. I believe he sensed something, but I do not believe he knew it was me." Kalona cocked his head, considering. "Perhaps my ability to mingle my spirit with his is a result of the sliver of my immortality I breathed within him."

. . . Immortality I breathed within him. His father's words swirled around and around in Rephaim's mind. Something was there—something they were both missing. "Have you never shared your immortality with another being?"

Kalona's smile faded. "Of course not. My immortality is not a power I would willingly share with another."

And suddenly what had been niggling at the edge of Rephaim's thoughts burst into understanding. No wonder Kalona had appeared different since he'd returned from the Otherworld. It all made sense now. "Father! What was the exact wording of the oath you swore to Neferet?"

Kalona frowned at his son, but he recited the oath: "If I failed in my sworn quest to destroy Zoey Redbird, fledging High Priestess of Nyx, Neferet shall hold dominion over my spirit for as long as I am an immortal."

Excitement coursed through Rephaim's body. "And how do you know Neferet actually has dominion over your spirit?"

"I did not destroy Zoey; she must have dominion over me."

"No, Father. If you shared your immortality with Stark, you are no longer completely an immortal, just as Stark is no longer completely a mortal. The conditions of the oath do not exist, nor did they ever. You are not truly bound to Neferet."

"I am not truly bound to Neferet?" Kalona's expression shifted from disbelief to shock, and finally to joy.

"I do not believe you are," Rephaim said.

"There is only one way to be certain," Kalona said.

Rephaim nodded. "You must openly disobey her."

"That, my son, will be a pleasure."

As he watched his father throw his arms back and shout joyously to the sky, Rephaim knew that tonight would change everything, and no matter what he had to figure out a way to be sure Stevie Rae was safe.

CHAPTER NINETEEN

Zoey

"You look really tired." I touched Stark's face as if I could smooth away the dark circles under his eyes. "I thought you slept most of the whole flight."

Stark kissed my palm and made what looked to be an attempt at his cocky smile, which failed miserably. "I'm cool. It's just jet lag."

"How can you be jet-lagged before they've even opened the door of the jet?" I pointed my chin in the direction of the vampyre flight attendant who was busy doing whatever it was they did to get a plane open after landing. There was a whooshing sound and the seat belt light made an annoyingly loud *ding! ding!* sound.

"There, the door's open. I can be jet lagged now," Stark said as he unbuckled his seat belt.

Knowing he was completely full of bullpoopie, I grabbed his wrist and made him stay in his seat. "You know I can tell something's wrong."

Stark sighed. "I'm just having bad dreams again, that's all. And when I wake up I can't ever really remember them. Somehow that seems like the worst part. It's probably a weird side effect from being in the Otherworld."

"Great. You have PTSD. I knew it. Hey, I think I remember

reading in one of the House of Night newsletters that Dragon is one of the school counselors. Maybe you could see him and—"

"No!" Stark interrupted, and then kissed my nose when I frowned at him. "Stop worrying. I'm fine. I don't need to talk to Dragon about my bad dreams. Plus, I don't know what the hell PTSD is, but it sounds enough like an STD to be dodgy."

I couldn't help it, I giggled. "Dodgy? You sound like Seoras."

"Aye, wumman, then it's mindin' me you should be! Get yur arse outta yur chair."

I scowled and shook my head. "Do. Not. Call. Me. Woman. Plus, it's freakish how well you can do that accent." He did have a point about getting out of the stupid plane, though, so I stood up and waited for him to grab my carry-on bag. While we were walking up the ramp from the plane I added, "And PTSD stands for Post-Traumatic Stress Disorder."

"How do you know that?"

"I Googled your symptoms and it came up."

"You did what?" he said so loud a woman wearing an appli- quéd sweatshirt gave us the stank eye.

"Sssh." I wrapped my arm through his so that we could talk without everyone gawking. "Look, you've been acting weird: tired, distracted, grumpy, and you're forgetting things. I Googled. PTSD came up. You probably need counseling."

He gave me his you-are-an-insane-woman look. "Z, I love you. I'll guard you and stand beside you for the rest of my life. But you gotta quit Googling health-related stuff. Especially health-related stuff about me."

"I just like to be well informed."

"You like to scare the crap out of yourself Googling bizarre health stuff."

"So?"

He grinned at me, and this time he did look cocky and cute. "So you admit it."

"Not necessarily," I said, elbowing him. I didn't get to say anything else because just then I was enveloped in what felt like a mini Oklahoma tornado.

"Zoey! Ohmygood*ness,* it's so good to see you! I missed you like crazy! Are you okay? It's awful 'bout Jack, ain't it?" Stevie Rae was hugging me and crying and talking all at the same time.

"Oh, Stevie Rae, I've missed you, too!" And then I was bawling along with her and we just stood there holding tight to each other like touch could somehow make everything that was crazy and wrong in our world better.

Over Stevie Rae's shoulder I saw Stark standing there, smiling at us. He was pulling out the little travel pack of Kleenex that he kept in his jeans' pocket ever since he'd gotten back from the Otherworld, and I thought that maybe, just maybe, touch added to love might make *almost* everything better in our world.

"Come on," I said to Stevie Rae as we took the tissues from Stark and the three of us walked arm-in-arm through the giant revolving door that spewed us out into a cold Tulsa night. "Let's go home, and on the way there you can tell me all about the giant, stinking pile of bullpoopie that's waiting for me."

"Language, *u-we-tsi-a-ge-ya.*"

"Grandma!" I unhooked myself from Stevie Rae and Stark and ran into her arms. I hugged her tightly, letting love and the soothing scent of lavender surround me. "Oh, Grandma, I'm so glad you're here!"

"*U-we-tsi-a-ge-ya,* daughter, let me look at your face." Grandma held me at arm's length, her hands on my shoulders, while she studied my face. "It is true; you are whole and well again." She closed her eyes and squeezed my shoulders, murmuring, "Thank the Great Mother for that." Then we were hugging and laughing at the same time.

"How did you know I'd be here?" I asked when I was finally able to stop hugging her.

"Did your super cool Spidey Senses tell you?" Stevie Rae asked as she stepped up and hugged Grandma hello.

"No," she said, turning her attention from Stevie Rae to Stark, who was gazing down at her. "Something much more mundane." She smiled seraphically. "Or I suppose I should say some-*one* much more mundane, although I am not at all sure *mundane* is a good word to use when referring to this valiant Warrior."

"Stark? You called my grandma?"

He shot me his cocky grin and said, "Yeah, I like having an excuse to call another beautiful woman named Redbird."

"Come here, you charmer," Grandma said.

I shook my head as Stark hugged Grandma carefully, like he wasn't sure if she'd break or not. *He'd called my grandma and told her when our plane was landing.* Stark's eyes met mine over Grandma's shoulder. *Thank you,* I mouthed silently to him. His grin got bigger.

Then Grandma was there at my side again, taking my hand.

"Hey, why don't Stevie Rae and I go get the car while you and your grandma talk?"

I barely had time to nod yes, and the two of them were gone, leaving Grandma and me to find a bench positioned conveniently close by. We sat for a second without saying anything. We just held hands and looked at each other. I didn't realize I was crying until Grandma delicately wiped the tears from my face.

"I knew you'd return to us," she said.

"I'm sorry I worried you. I'm sorry that I didn't—"

"Ssh," Grandma shushed me. "There is no need for apologies.

You did your best, and your best has always been good enough for me."

"I was weak, Grandma. I'm still weak," I said honestly.

"No, *u-we-tsi-a-ge-ya,* you are young, that is all." She touched my face gently. "I am sorry about your Heath. I will miss that young man."

"I will, too," I said, blinking hard so I wouldn't start crying again.

"But I feel you two will know one another again. Perhaps in this lifetime, perhaps in the next."

I nodded. "That's what Heath said, too, before he moved on to the next realm of the Otherworld."

Grandma's smile was serene. "The Otherworld—I know that it was under heartbreaking circumstances, but you were given a great gift when you were allowed to travel there and back."

Her words made me think—really think. Since I'd returned to the real world I'd been tired and sad and confused and then, finally, with Stark I'd been content and in love. "But I haven't been thankful," I said the words aloud as I realized them. "I haven't understood the gift I'd been given." I wanted to smack myself in the head. "I'm a crappy High Priestess, Grandma."

Grandma laughed. "Oh, Zoeybird, if that were true you would not question yourself or call yourself to task for your mistakes."

I snorted. "I don't think High Priestesses are supposed to make mistakes."

"Of course they are. How else would they learn and grow?"

I started to say that I'd made enough mistakes that I should have grown to be, like, a zillion feet tall, but I knew that wasn't what Grandma meant. I sighed and said, "I have a bunch of faults."

"It is a wise woman who recognizes that." Sadness made her smile fade. "It is one of the key differences between you and your mother."

"My mother." I sighed again. "I've been thinking about her lately."

"As have I. Linda has been close to my mind during the past several days."

I raised my brows at Grandma. Usually when someone was "close to her mind" it meant something was going on with that person. "Have you heard from her?"

"No, but I believe I soon will. Hold good thoughts for her, *u-we-tsi-a-ge-ya*."

"I will," I said.

My Bug puttered up then, looking familiar and cute with its shiny aqua blue paint and sparkly chrome.

"Best be getting back to your school, Zoeybird. You'll be needed there tonight," she said in her no-nonsense-Grandma-voice.

We stood and hugged again. I had to make myself let go of her. "Are you staying in Tulsa tonight, Grandma?"

"Oh, no, honey. I have too much to do. There's a big powwow in Tahlequah tomorrow and I've made lovely new lavender sachets." She smiled at me. "I beaded redbirds into them."

I grinned and hugged her one last time. "Save one for me, okay?"

"Always," she said. "I love you, *u-we-tsi-a-ge-ya*."

"I love you, too," I said.

And then I watched as Stark jumped out of the Bug and took Grandma's arm, helping her cross the busy street between the airport arrivals terminal and short-term parking. He jogged back to me, dodging cars. When he opened the door of the car for me I paused, pressed my hand to his chest, and tugged at his shirt until he bent down so I could kiss him. "You're the best Warrior in the world," I whispered against his lips.

"Aye," he said, eyes sparkling.

Scrunching myself into the back of my Bug I met Stevie Rae's eyes in the rearview mirror. "Thanks for giving me some alone time with my grandma."

"Not a problem, Z. I heart me your grandma."

"Yeah, me too," I said softly. Then I straightened my shoulders and, feeling totally empowered, continued, "Okay. So. Tell me about the bullpoopie I'm getting ready to step into back at school."

"Hold on to your horses 'cause it really is one red-hot mess," Stevie Rae said as she signaled and pulled away from the curb.

"You don't even like horses," I said.

"Exactly," she said, which made absolutely no sense, but also made me laugh. Yep, hot mess of bullpoopie or not, I was seriously glad to be home.

"I still can't believe the High Council could be that naïve," I said for what felt like the gazillionth time as Stevie Rae helped me decide on what outfit I was gonna wear to *light Jack's funeral pyre*. I shuddered.

Without knocking, Aphrodite breezed into the room. She took one look at the black, long-sleeved, high-necked sweater and black jeans I was holding up and said, "Oh, for shit's sake. You can't wear that. You're lighting the funeral pyre of a *gay*. Do you know how mortified Jack would be if he saw you in that, not to mention Damien? It looks like an early 1990s Anita Blake reject outfit."

"Who's Anita Blake?" Stevie Rae asked.

"Vampire killer chick written by a human chick who has a Totally Tragic fashion sense." Aphrodite was wearing a skintight sapphire-colored dress that was a little shimmery, but not so much so that it looked like one of those prom rejects from David's Bridal. Actually, she looked gorgeous and classy like she usually does. Probably because Victoria, her personal shopper at super posh Miss Jackson's at Utica Square, had pulled the dang thing for her as soon as it came in *and* charged her mommy's platinum credit card. *Sigh*. It kinda made my head hurt.

Anyway, she marched over to my closet, opened it, and after one disdainful look at my wardrobe took out the dress she'd given me the night I'd gone to my first Dark Daughters' Ritual. It was black, long-sleeved, and (unlike the sweater and jeans) flattering. It was also trimmed around the low, round neckline, the flowy sleeves, and the hem with little red glass beads that sparkled whenever I moved and matched perfectly the Leader of the Dark Daughters triple moon that rested around my neck. I met her eyes. "This dress doesn't have such nice memories attached to it," I said.

"Yeah, well, it looks good on you. It's appropriate. And, most important, Jack would totally love it. Plus, according to my mother, memories change like people do, especially if there's enough alcohol involved."

"Look, Aphrodite, do not tell me you are gonna be drinkin' tonight. That's just not appropriate," Stevie Rae said.

"No, bumpkin. Or at least not until afterward." She tossed the dress at me. "Now put this on and hurry up. The Twins and Darius are bringing Damien up here so we can all walk out to the pyre together—a show of nerd herd solidarity and all, which I believe is a good decision," she added quickly when Stevie Rae sucked in air and opened her mouth to interrupt. "Oh, and hi. It's good to see you and your hypochondriac boyfriend back in the real world."

"Fine. I'll wear this." I ducked into our bathroom, then popped my head out and met Aphrodite cool blue eyes. "Oh, and Stark is my Guardian and Warrior first, my boyfriend second. *And* he is darn sure not a hypochondriac. You know that. You saw what happened to him."

"Huh," Aphrodite scoffed under her breath.

I ignored the rude sound but kept the door open so I could still talk to them while I got dressed. When I saw the seer stone I paused, and decided to let it hang down beneath the top of the dress—no way did I feel like answering questions about Skye and Sgiach tonight. I combed my hair quickly and said, "Hey, do you guys think Neferet's letting me light the pyre because she expects me to mess it up?" Hell, *I* expected to mess it up, why wouldn't she?

"Well, I think her plan's much more nefarious than you fumbling around with some words 'cause you're bawling, 'cause you actually cared 'bout Jack," Stevie Rae said.

"Nef what?" said Shaunee as she, too, walked right into my room without so much as a howdy do.

"Arious who?" chimed in Erin. "What's she doing, Twin? Tryin' to pick up the Damien vocab slack?"

"Totally sounds like it, Twin," Shaunee replied.

"I like words, and you two can go suck a lemon," Stevie Rae said.

Aphrodite started to laugh and then covered it with a cough when I left the bathroom and glared at all of them. "We're getting ready to go to a funeral. I think we should show a little more respect for Jack, being as he was our friend and all."

The Twins instantly looked contrite. They came over to me and each gave me a hug, mumbling *hi*s and *glad you're back*s.

"Z has a point about bein' more serious, and not just 'cause it's Jack's funeral and that's real terrible. We all know there's no way Neferet has suddenly decided to do the right thing and respect Zoey and her powers," Stevie Rae said.

"We need to be on our guard," I agreed. "Stay close to me. Be ready. If I have to cast a protective circle, I don't imagine I'll have much time to do it."

"Why don't you cast one to begin with?" Aphrodite said.

"I was gonna, but I looked up stuff about a vampyre funeral, and the High Priestess usually doesn't cast one. It's her job, well, uh, I mean *my* job tonight, to stand as respectful witness to the loss of a fellow vampyre, and to help send the vampyre's spirit to Nyx's Otherworld. There's no circle casting involved in that, just prayers to Nyx and such."

"You should be good at that, Z, since you just got back from the Otherworld," Stevie Rae said.

"I just hope I do Jack proud." I felt the tears start to sting my eyes and I blinked hard, forcing them back. The last thing any of my friends needed was for me to be a bawling, snotting mess tonight.

"So none of you have any idea what Neferet's up to?" I asked them.

There was a bunch of head shaking, and Aphrodite said, "All I can think is that she's going to somehow try to humiliate you, but I don't see how that can happen if you stay calm and strong and focus on why we're all here tonight."

"For Jack," Shaunee said.

"To say bye to him," Erin said, her voice shaking a little.

"Well, that's nice and all," Stevie Rae said, and we looked at her. "But I think funerals, no matter what they're like, are mostly for the people left behind, like Damien."

"That's a really good point, Stevie Rae." I smiled at her in gratitude. "I'll remember that."

Stevie Rae cleared her voice. "I know because I saw my mama today, and she was kinda holdin' a mini funeral for me. It was her way of tryin' to find closure."

I had a moment of intense shock while the Twins exploded with "Ohmygoddess, how awful!"

"She came here?" Aphrodite asked. I was surprised at how kind her voice sounded.

Stevie Rae nodded. "She was out by the front gate leavin' me a funeral wreath, but really what she was doin' was what Damien is gonna try to do tonight: saying goodbye."

"You talked to her, didn't you?" I said. "I mean, she knows you're not dead anymore, right?"

Stevie Rae smiled, even though her eyes still looked super sad. "Yeah, but it made me feel awful that I hadn't gone to her first. It was terrible to see her cry so much."

I went to my BFF and hugged her. "Well, at least she knows now."

"And at least you have a mom who cares enough to cry about you," Aphrodite said.

I met Aphrodite's gaze with complete understanding. "Yeah, that's true."

"Y'all please, your mamas would be crying if something happened to you," Stevie Rae said.

"Mine would in public because it's expected of her, and because she'd be so prescription-med-ed up that she could work up a tear over just about anything," Aphrodite said blandly.

"Well, I guess mine would cry, too, but it'd be all about *how could she have done this to me* and *now she's going straight to hell and it's all her fault.*" I paused and then added, "My grandma would say it's too bad that my mom doesn't understand that there's more than just one right answer about forever." I smiled at my friends. "I know 'cause I've been there and it's wonderful. Really, really wonderful."

"Jack's there, isn't he? Safe, in the Otherworld, with the Goddess?"

We all looked up to see Damien standing in the doorway that

the Twins had left open. Darius was on one side of him and Stark was on the other. Damien looked absolutely horrible, even though he was dressed immaculately in Armani. He was so pale it seemed I could see through his skin, and the shadows under his eyes looked like bruises. I walked over to him and took him into my arms. He felt thin and frail and totally un-Damien-like.

"Yes. He is with Nyx. I give you my word on that as one of her High Priestesses." I hugged him and whispered, "I am so sorry, Damien."

Damien returned my hug and then, with an effort, stepped back. He wasn't crying. Instead he looked drained—empty—hopeless.

"I'm ready to go, and I'm really glad you're here."

"So am I. I wish I'd been here before." I felt tears start to threaten again. "Maybe I could have—"

"No, you couldn't have," Aphrodite said, stepping up to stand beside me. Again, her voice was softened with understanding and she sounded way older than nineteen. "You couldn't stop Heath's death. You wouldn't have been able to stop Jack's." My eyes briefly met Stark's and I saw in his gaze a reflection of what I was thinking—that I'd stopped his death. Even if it meant he had nightmares and still wasn't one hundred percent, at least he was *alive.*

"Seriously, stop it, Z," Aphrodite said. "All of you—don't start the self-blame game. The only one responsible for Jack being dead is Neferet. We know that, even if no one else does."

"I can't deal with that right now," Damien said, and for a second I thought he might actually faint. "Do we have to face down Neferet tonight?"

"No," I said quickly. "I'm not planning anything like that."

"But we can't control what she'll do," Aphrodite said.

"Stark and I will stay close. The rest of you be sure you're near

Zoey and Damien. We won't begin anything, but if Neferet attempts to harm any of us, we will be ready."

"I've seen her in front of the Council. I don't think she's gonna do anything as obvious as attackin' Z," Stevie Rae said.

"Whatever she does, we'll be ready," Stark echoed Darius's words.

"I won't be ready," Damien said. "I don't think I'll ever be able to fight anything again."

I took Damien's hand in mine. "Well, tonight you won't have to. If there's a battle to be fought, your friends will do it. Now let's go see to Jack."

Damien drew in a long, shaky breath, nodded, and we left my room. Still holding Damien's hand, I led the group down the stairs and out into the common room, which was completely empty. I mentally sent a small prayer up to the Goddess: *Please let everyone already be out there—please let Damien know how much Jack was loved.*

We walked down the sidewalk that led around the front part of the school. I knew where we were going. I remembered all too well that Anastasia's pyre had been placed in the center of the school grounds, directly in front of Nyx's Temple.

As we moved along the sidewalk in silence a small sound caught me and I glanced at a bench that rested under a redbud tree near the front of the school. Erik was sitting there, alone. His face was in his hands and the sound I'd heard was his crying.

CHAPTER TWENTY

Zoey

I almost kept walking by, and then I remembered that before he'd gone through the Change, Erik had been Jack's roommate. And because of that I also remembered that it didn't matter just then what had happened between him and me. I was serving the role of High Priestess tonight for Jack, and I knew beyond any doubt Jack wouldn't want me to let Erik sit out there all by himself, crying.

Plus I had a sudden flash though my mind of the time when Erik had found me crying after my first, disastrous, Dark Daughters' Ritual. Back then he'd been sweet and thoughtful and had made me feel like maybe I could really handle the craziness that happened at this school.

I owed him a favor in return.

I squeezed Damien's hand and brought him and my whole group to a halt. "Honey," I said to Damien, "I want you to go with Stark and everyone else to the pyre. There's something I have to do real quick. Plus, from everything I can find to read on vamp funerals and such, you—'cause Jack really was your Consort—need to spend time meditating before the pyre is lit." At least I hoped that was what Damien needed to do.

As if she'd materialized in response to my words, a vampyre stepped out of the shadows, coming from the direction of the funeral pyre. "You are absolutely correct, Zoey Redbird," she said.

I, along with all of my friends, gave her big question-mark looks.

"Oh, I should introduce myself." She offered me her forearm in the traditional vampyre greeting. "I am Beverly—" She paused, cleared her throat, and started again. "I am Professor Missal. The new Spells and Rituals instructor."

"Oh, uh, nice to meet you." I returned her greeting by grasping her forearm. Yeah, she had a full vamp tattoo—a pretty pattern that reminded me of musical notes—but I swear she looked younger than Stevie Rae. "Um, Professor Missal, would you lead Damien and the rest of the kids to the pyre? There's something I need to do here."

"Of course. Everything will be ready for you." She turned to Damien and said gently, "Please follow me."

Damien said a faint okay, but he looked super glassy eyed. Still, he began following the new professor. Stark hung back. His eyes shifted to the shadows and the bench on which Erik sat. Then they returned to me.

"Please," I said. "I need to talk to him. Trust me, 'kay?"

His face relaxed. "No problem, *mo bann ri.*" Before he started after Damien, he added softly in his excellent Scottish accent, "It's waitin' for you I'll be when yur finished."

"Thank you." I tried to tell him with my eyes how much I loved and appreciated his loyalty and his trust.

He smiled and moved off with the rest of the group. Well, except for Aphrodite. And Darius, who hovered about like her shadow.

"What?" I said.

"Like we can leave you alone?" Aphrodite rolled her eyes. "Seriously. How clueless are you? Neferet managed to cut off Jack's head without actually being there. Darius and I aren't leaving you alone to comfort Erik the Douche."

I looked at Darius, but he shook his head and said, "Sorry, Zoey, Aphrodite has a point."

"Could you at least stay back here out of earshot?" I asked in exasperation.

"Like we want to hear Erik's crybaby crap? No problem. Just hurry up. No one needs to be kept waiting for a douche bag," Aphrodite said.

I didn't even bother to sigh as I walked away from them, making a path to Erik. Okay, seriously. The guy didn't even know I was there. I was standing in front of him. His face was in his hands and he was crying. Really crying. Knowing what an excellent actor he was, I cleared my throat and got ready to be semi-sarcastic, or at the very least passive-aggressive.

When he looked up at me everything changed. His eyes were puffy and red. Tears soaked his cheeks. Snot even ran out of his nose. He blinked a couple of times, like he was having a hard time focusing on me. "Oh, uh, Zoey," he said, and made an effort at pulling himself together. He sat up straighter, and wiped his snotty nose on the back of his sleeve. "Um, hey. You're back."

"Yeah, I landed a little while ago. I'm going to light Jack's pyre. Wanna come with me?"

A sob erupted from deep within him. Erik bowed his head and began to weep.

It was totally awful.

I so didn't know what to do.

And I swear I heard Aphrodite snorting off in the distance.

"Hey." I sat next to him and awkwardly patted his shoulder. "I know it's terrible. You guys were really good friends."

Erik nodded his head. I could see he was making an effort to get himself under control, so I sat there and babbled while he sniffed and wiped his face on his sleeve (eesh).

"It really sucks. Jack was too darn nice and sweet and young and *everything* to have something like this happen to him. We're all gonna miss him so much."

"Neferet did this." He spoke quietly, and I saw him glancing around like he was scared of being overheard. "I don't know how. I don't fucking even know why, but she did it."

"Yeah," I said.

Our eyes met.

"Are you going to do something about it?" he said.

My gaze didn't falter one little bit. "Absolutely everything in my power."

He almost smiled. "Well, that's good enough for me." He wiped his face again and ran a hand through his hair. "I was leaving."

"Huh?" I said brilliantly.

"Yeah, going. Leaving the Tulsa House of Night for L.A. They want me there—in Hollywood. I was supposed to be the next Brad Pitt."

"*Was*?" I asked, totally confused. "What's stopping you?"

Slowly, Erik raised his right hand and held it, palm out, toward me. I blinked several times, not really understanding what I was seeing.

"Yeah, it's what you think," he said.

"It's Nyx's Labyrinth." Of course I recognized the raised sapphire-colored tattoo that filled his palm, but it was like my mind was having a hard time catching up with my eyes, and I wasn't getting it until Aphrodite's voice came from behind me. "Oh, for shit's sake! Erik's a Tracker."

Erik's eyes shifted from me to Aphrodite. "Happy now? Go ahead and laugh. You know this means I can't leave the Tulsa House of Night for four years—that I have to stay here and follow a damn *essence* and be the asshole who is there when every kid for the next *four years* is Marked and finds out he might or might not die, but for sure has to change his life forever."

There was a moment of silence and then Aphrodite said, "Is that what's bothering you? That you're the new Tracker and it's a tough job, or is what's really bothering you that you have to put off Hollywood for four years and in that time there's sure to be 'the next Brad Pitt'?"

I whirled around and faced her. "He was Jack's roommate! Do you remember what it's like to lose a roommate?" I saw her expression shift and soften, but I just shook my head. "No. You and Darius go on. I'll follow you." When Aphrodite still hesitated I spoke directly to her Warrior. "As your High Priestess I'm commanding you. I want to be alone with Erik. Take Aphrodite and meet me at Jack's pyre."

Darius didn't hesitate for another second. He bowed solemnly to me, then he took Aphrodite by the elbow and literally pulled her away. I sighed deeply and sat down next to Erik on the bench.

"Sorry about that. Aphrodite means well, but like Stevie Rae would say, she's not very nice sometimes."

Erik snorted. "You don't need to tell me that. She and I dated, remember?"

"I remember," I said quietly. Then added, "You and I dated, too."

"Yeah," he said. "I thought I loved you."

"I thought I loved you, too."

He looked at me. "Were we wrong?"

I looked back at him. Really looked back at him. Goddess, he was hot in a seriously Superman/Clark Kent kind of way. Tall and dark and blue eyed and muscly. But there was more to him than that. Yeah, he was controlling and arrogant, but somewhere inside him I knew there was a really, really good guy. I just wasn't the right girl for that guy.

"Yeah, we were wrong, but that's okay. Recently I've been reminded that it's okay not to be perfect, especially if you learn from your mess-ups. So how about we learn from ours? I think we could make better friends anyway."

His gorgeous lips turned up. "I think you might be right."

"Plus," I added, bumping him with my shoulder, "I don't have enough pretty straight guys as my friends."

"I'm a pretty straight guy. I mean, a *really* straight guy who is also, as you say, pretty."

"Yep, you are," I said. Then I held out my hand. "Friends?"

"Friends." Erik took my hand in his and then, with a rakish smile, he dropped gracefully from the bench to one knee. "My lady, let's always be friends."

"Okie dokie," I said, kinda breathlessly, 'cause, well, no matter how much I loved Stark, Erik was seriously hot and a super good actor.

He bowed and kissed my hand. Not in a creepy I'm-trying-to-get-into-your-pants way, but in a real old-school-gentleman way. Still on his knee, he looked up at me and said, "You have to say something tonight that gives us hope and helps Damien, because right now lots of us are just floating out there wondering what the fuck—and Damien is seriously not doing well."

My heart clenched. "I know."

"Good. No matter what else, I believe in you, Zoey."

I sighed. Again.

He smiled and stood up, pulling me up with him. "So please let me escort you to this funeral."

I took Erik's arm and stepped into a future I couldn't have begun to imagine.

It was an awesome, sad, incredible sight. Unlike the last time a funeral pyre had burned for a vampyre at the House of Night, the entire school was there. Fledglings and vampyres made a huge circle around a benchlike structure that had been built in the very center of the school grounds. I could still see the charred grass that bore witness to the fact that not long ago Anastasia Lankford's body had been consumed by the Goddess's fire in that very same place. Only the school hadn't come out to witness and show respect for her then. Too many of them had been under the control of Kalona—or just downright scared. Tonight was different. Kalona's control had been broken and Jack was getting a Warrior's sendoff.

My eyes found Dragon Lankford even before I looked at the funeral pyre. He was standing behind Jack in the shadow of the closest oak tree. But the shadows didn't cloak his pain. I could see tears falling silently down his chiseled face. *Goddess help Dragon,* was my first prayer of the night. *He's such a good man. Help him find peace.*

Then I looked at Jack.

What I saw made me gasp and smile through my tears. As was traditional for vampyre funerals, he'd been wrapped, head to toe, in the traditional vampyre shroud, but Jack's covering was purple. Super shiny. Super brilliant. Super purple.

"She actually did it." Erik's choked voice came from beside me. "I knew purple was his favorite color, so I went to The Dolphin at Utica Square and bought purple sheets. Lots of them. Then I told Sapphire over in the infirmary to wrap Jack in them, even though I didn't think she really would."

I turned to Erik, went up on my tiptoes, and kissed his cheek. "Thank you. Jack would absolutely love that you did that. You were a good friend to him, Erik."

He nodded and smiled but didn't say anything, and I saw that he was crying again. Before I could join him and bawl so hard I couldn't possibly be mistaken for anyone's High Priestess, I looked away from him and my eyes found Damien. He was on his knees at the head of Jack's pyre. Duchess was sitting beside him and his chubby cat, Cammy, was curled up mournfully between his knees. Stark was standing next to Duchess and I could see that he was petting her and murmuring to the dog and Damien at the same time. Stevie Rae was next to Stark, looking super miserable and bawling steadily. Aphrodite stood at Damien's other side, with Darius right behind her. The Twins were to her left. And from each side of my group of best friends, the entire school stretched in a quiet, respectful circle around the pyre. Many of the fledglings and vampyres, including Lenobia and most of the other professors, were holding purple candles. It didn't seem like anyone except Stark was talking, but I could hear lots of sobbing.

Neferet was nowhere to be seen.

"You can do it," Erik whispered.

"How?" I barely spoke the word.

"Like you always do—with Nyx's help," he said.

"Please, Nyx, help me. I can't do this on my own," I whispered aloud. And then Professor Missal was there, ushering me forward. So, moving with what I hoped were the confident strides of a grown-up *real* High Priestess, I walked directly to Damien.

Stark saw me first. When his eyes met mine I didn't see any hint of jealousy or anger, even though I knew Erik was walking right behind me. My Warrior, my Guardian, my lover, stepped aside and bowed formally to me.

"Merry meet, High Priestess." His voice rang over the school grounds. Everyone turned to me and it seemed, as one, the House of Night bowed, acknowledging me as their High Priestess.

It gave me a feeling like I'd never had before. Professors, vampyres hundreds of years old, and the youngest of fledglings were all looking to me—believing in me, trusting in me. It was as terrifying as it was awesome.

Do not ever forget this feeling, the Goddess's voice sang through my mind. *A true High Priestess is humble as well as proud, and never forgets the responsibility that being a leader entails.*

I stopped before Damien and bowed to him, fist closed over my heart. "Merry meet, Damien." Then, not caring that I was deviating from the vampyre funeral etiquette text that I'd read on the plane, I took Damien's hands and tugged, so that he stood up. I wrapped my arms around him and repeated, "Merry meet, Damien."

He sobbed once. His body felt stiff and he moved slowly, like he was afraid he might break into a zillion pieces, but he hugged me back really hard. Before I stepped away from him I closed my eyes, centered myself, and whispered, "Air, come to your Damien. Fill him with lightness and hope, and help him get through this night." Air responded instantly. It lifted my hair and wrapped around Damien and me. I heard him suck in a breath, and when he exhaled, some of the terrible tightness went out of his body. I stepped back and met his sad eyes. "I love you, Damien."

"I love you, too, Zoey. Go ahead." He nodded toward Jack's purple-shrouded body. "Do what you have to do. I know Jack's not really there anyway." He paused and choked back a sob and then added, "He'd be glad it's you, though."

Instead of bursting into tears and falling to the ground in a soggy puddle like I wanted to, I turned to face the pyre and the House of Night. I drew two deep breaths, let them out, and with the third I whispered, "Spirit, come to me. Make my voice loud enough for everyone to hear." The element with which I have the closest affinity filled me and strengthened me. When I began speaking my voice was like a beacon from the Goddess, and it echoed with sound and spirit over the school grounds.

"Jack isn't here. In our minds we all understand that. Damien just said it to me, but tonight I want you all to *know* it." I could feel everyone's eyes on me, and I spoke slowly and distinctly the words that were Goddess-touched as they came to my mind. "I've been to the Otherworld and I can promise you that it is as beautiful and amazing and *real* as your hearts want to believe. Jack is there. He doesn't feel any pain. He's not sad or worried or scared. He's with Nyx in her meadows and groves." I paused and smiled through the brightness of tears. "He's probably frolicking gaily in those meadows and groves." I heard Damien's surprised giggle echoed by a few of the fledglings. "He's meeting familiar friends, like my Heath, and probably decorating like crazy." Aphrodite snorted a laugh and Erik chuckled. "We can't be with him right now." I looked at Damien. "It's hard. I know it's hard. But we can be sure that we'll see him again—in this life or the next. And when we do, no matter who we are or where we are, I promise you that one thing about our spirit, our essence, will stay the same: love. Our love lives on and will last forever. And that's a promise that I know comes straight from the Goddess."

Stark handed me a long wooden staff that had something sticky wrapped around the other end of it. I took it, but before I walked to the pyre my eyes found Shaunee.

"Will you help me?" I asked her.

She wiped away her tears, faced south, lifted her arms, and in a voice magnified by love and loss, she called, "Fire! Come to me!" The hands she held up over her head glowed as, with me, Shaunee walked to the head of the giant pile of timber on which Jack's body lay.

"Jack Swift, you were a sweet, special boy. I'll always love you like a brother and a friend. Until next time I see you, merry meet, merry part, and merry meet again." When I touched the end of my torch to the pyre, Shaunee flung her element into it, instantly setting it to light with an otherworldly glow that shimmered yellow and purple.

I'd turned to Shaunee and was opening my mouth to thank her and her element when Neferet's voice pierced the night.

"Zoey Redbird! Fledgling High Priestess! I ask that you stand witness!"

CHAPTER TWENTY-ONE

Zoey

I didn't have to look hard to find her. Neferet was standing on the steps of Nyx's Temple, off to my left. As everyone turned to whisper and stare at her, I felt Stark move to my side, so that it would only take one quick motion for him to come between Neferet and me. I was also aware of Stevie Rae. Suddenly she was there on my other side, and from the corners of my vision I could see the Twins and even Damien. My circle of friends surrounded me, letting me know wordlessly that they had my back.

When Neferet began to walk toward me I automatically began centering myself. I thought, *She must have gone totally, utterly insane to ask me to perform the funeral and then attack me in front of the entire school.* But sane or insane, it really didn't matter. She was evil and dangerous and coming against me, and I Was Not Going To Run.

So her next words shocked me almost as much as what she began to do.

"Hear me, Zoey Redbird, Fledgling High Priestess, and bear witness. I have wronged Nyx and you and this House of Night."

Her voice was strong and clear and beautiful, and it seemed to make music in the air around her. In the tempo she was creating, Neferet began to take her clothes off.

It should have been embarrassing or uncomfortable or erotic, but it wasn't any of those things. It was simply beautiful.

"I have lied to you and to my Goddess." Her shirt came off, fluttering behind her like a petal falling from a rose. "I have deceived you and my Goddess about my intentions." She unwrapped the black silk skirt she was wearing and stepped out of it as if it were a pool of dark water. Completely naked, she walked directly up to me. The purple and yellow flames of Jack's pyre flickered against her flesh, making her look like she, too, burned, only without being consumed. When she reached me she dropped to her knees, threw back her head, and opened her arms, saying, "Worst of all, I allowed a man to seduce me away from the love of my Goddess and her Path. Now here, bared to you, our House of Night, and to Nyx, I ask to be forgiven for my wrongdoings, for I find that I cannot live this terrible lie another moment." As she finished speaking she lowered her head and her arms and then formally, respectfully, deeply, Neferet bowed to me.

In the complete silence that followed her pronouncement my mind whirred in a cacophony of conflicting thoughts: *She's pretending—I wish she wasn't—it's because of her that Heath and Jack are dead—She's a master manipulator.* Trying to figure out what I should say—what I should do—I looked around, helplessly, for some clue. The Twins and Damien were staring openmouthed at Neferet, totally shocked. I glanced at Aphrodite. She was staring at Neferet, too, but the look on her face was open disgust. Stevie Rae and Stark were both looking at me. Ever so slightly, without saying a word, Stark shook his head once, *no.* I looked from him to Stevie Rae, who mouthed two words to me: *she lies.*

Hardly breathing, I glanced around the circle made by the House of Night. Some were looking at me questioningly, expectantly, but most of them were gawking at Neferet in awe, openly sobbing with what was obviously a mixture of happiness and relief.

At that moment, one thought crystallized and sliced dagger-like through all of the others in my mind: *If I don't accept her apology the school will turn against me. I'll look like a vindictive brat, and that is exactly what Neferet wants.*

I had no choice. All I could do was react and hope my friends trusted me enough to know that I could tell the difference between truth and manipulation.

"Stark, give me your shirt," I said quickly.

He didn't hesitate. He unbuttoned it and handed it to me.

Being sure my voice still carried the power of spirit with it I said to her, "Neferet, for myself I forgive you. I never wanted to be your enemy." She looked up at me; her green eyes were absolutely guileless.

"Zoey, I—," she began.

I spoke over her, cutting off the sweet sound of her voice. "But I can only speak for myself. You'll have to seek the Goddess for her forgiveness. Nyx knows your heart and your soul, so it's there that you'll find her answer."

"Then I already have it, and it fills my heart and soul with joy. Thank you, Zoey Redbird, and thank you, House of Night!"

There were murmurs all around the circle of "Thank the Goddess!" and "Blessed be!" I made myself smile as I bent and wrapped Stark's shirt around her shoulders. "Please, get up. You shouldn't be on your knees in front of me."

Neferet stood gracefully, and put on Stark's shirt, buttoning it carefully. Then she turned to Damien. "Merry meet, Damien. May I have your permission to send my personal prayer for Jack's spirit up to the Goddess?"

Damien didn't speak. He just nodded, and I couldn't tell through the sadness and grief on his face whether he believed Neferet's show or not. She continued to act her part perfectly.

"Thank you." Neferet stepped closer to Jack's fiery pyre, put

her head back, and lifted her arms. Unlike me, she didn't am-
plify her voice. Instead she spoke so softly that none of us could
hear her. Her face was tilted just right so that I had a perfect view
of it. Her expression was serene and sincere, and I wondered
how it was possible that something I was sure was so rotten inside could have such a gorgeous outside.

I think it was because I was staring at her so hard, trying to
find the chink in her armor, that I saw all of what happened next.

Neferet's expression changed. Her face was still tilted up, but it
was obvious, at least to me, that she'd seen something above us.

Then I heard it. It was a kinda familiar sound. I didn't recognize it right away, even though it made the hairs on my arms
rise. I didn't look up, though. I kept watching Neferet. Whatever
she was looking at was annoying and worrying her. She didn't
change her posture or stop speaking her "prayer," but her eyes
did dart around as if she was checking to see if anyone else had
noticed what she'd seen. I snapped my eyelids shut and hoped
that I looked like I was praying, meditating, concentrating—
anything but watching her. I gave it a couple of seconds, then
slowly opened my eyes.

Neferet definitely wasn't looking at me. She was staring at
Stevie Rae, but my BFF wasn't aware of it. Stevie Rae was too
busy gawking straight up, too. Only her expression wasn't annoyed or worried—it was radiant, as if she was looking at something that filled her with utter happiness, utter love.

Confused, I looked back at Neferet. She was still watching
Stevie Rae, and her expression had shifted again. I saw her eyes
widen, as if in realization, and then her face was suffused with
pleasure, like what she'd just figured out had made her super
happy.

I couldn't seem to take my eyes off Neferet, but I was reaching
for Stark's hand automatically, as if I knew my world was getting

ready to explode when Dragon Lankford's voice was a clarion call that changed everything.

"Raven Mocker above! Professors, get the fledglings under cover! Warriors, to me!"

Time started to move in fast-forward then. Stark pushed me behind him while he stared upward. I heard him curse, and I knew it had to be because he didn't have his bow with him.

"I want you to get into Nyx's Temple!" Stark shouted above the sound exploding around us, already moving me in that direction.

Over his shoulder I could see the pandemonium that had broken out. Some of the kids were screaming; professors were calling to their students and trying to reassure them; Sons of Erebus Warriors had weapons drawn, ready for the coming battle. Everyone was moving except Neferet and Stevie Rae.

Neferet was still standing beside Jack's burning pyre—still staring at Stevie Rae and smiling. Stevie Rae looked like she'd been rooted to her spot. She was gazing upward, shaking her head back and forth, back and forth, and she was sobbing.

"No, wait," I told Stark, moving around him so he quit pushing me toward the temple. "I can't go. Stevie Rae is—"

"FALL FROM THE SKY, FOUL BEAST!"

Neferet's shout cut me off. She'd flung her arms up, fingers outstretched like she was trying to grab something out of the air.

"Can you see that?" Stark asked me urgently, staring up at the sky.

"What? See what?"

"Black, sticky, threads of Darkness." He grimaced in horror. "She's using them. And that means she was lying her ass off about asking for forgiveness," he said grimly. "She's definitely still allied with Darkness."

Then there wasn't time to say any more because, with a terrible scream, an enormous Raven Mocker fell from the sky, landing in a heap in the middle of the school grounds.

I recognized him right away. It was Rephaim, Kalona's favored son.

"Kill it!" Neferet commanded.

Dragon Lankford didn't need the order. He was already moving. Blade flashing in the firelight, he descended on the Raven Mocker like an avenging god.

"No! Don't hurt him!" Stevie Rae screamed and hurled herself between Dragon and the fallen creature. Her arms were raised, palms outward, and she was glowing green, like her body had suddenly grown iridescent moss. Dragon hit the glowy green barrier and bounced off it like he'd smacked into a giant rubber ball. It was creepy and cool at the same time.

"Ah, hell," I murmured, already moving toward Stevie Rae. I had a bad feeling about what was going on. A really, really bad feeling.

Stark didn't try to stop me. He just said, "Stay close to me and out of that damn bird's reach."

"Why are you protecting this creature, Stevie Rae? Are you in league with it?" Neferet was standing beside Dragon, who had gotten back on his feet and was literally trembling with the effort it took not to rush against Stevie Rae again. Neferet sounded baffled, but her eyes flashed fiercely, like she was a cat and Stevie Rae was her trapped mouse.

Stevie Rae ignored Neferet. She looked at Dragon and said, "He's not here to hurt anyone. I promise."

"Free me, Red One." The Raven Mocker spoke as I finally reached Dragon and Neferet. He, too, had gotten to his feet, which surprised me because it seemed that the fall should have killed him. Actually, the only evidence I could see of him being hurt at all was a gash in his disturbingly human-looking bicep that was just beginning to weep blood. He was backing slowly away from Stevie Rae, but a weird green bubble had formed around them, and it wouldn't let him get very far from her.

"It's no good, Rephaim. I'm not gonna lie and pretend anymore." Stevie Rae glanced at Neferet and at the crowd of fledglings and professors who had stopped running away and instead were watching her, shock and horror clear on their faces. Then, setting her jaw and lifting her chin, Stevie Rae looked back at the Raven Mocker. "I'm not *that* good of an actress. I don't ever want to be *that* good of an actress."

"Do not do this."

The Raven Mocker's voice shocked me. It wasn't because he sounded human. I'd heard him speak before and knew that, if he wasn't hissing in anger, he could talk like a guy. What shocked me was the tone of his voice. He sounded scared and very, very sad.

"It's already done," Stevie Rae told him.

And that's when I finally found my voice. "What in the hell is going on, Stevie Rae?"

"I'm sorry, Z. I wanted to tell you. I really, really wanted to. I just didn't know how." Stevie Rae's eyes pleaded with me to understand.

"Didn't know how to tell me what?"

Then it hit me—the smell of the Raven Mocker's blood. With a rush of horror, I knew the scent of it. It had been on Stevie Rae before, and I realized what she was talking about, what she'd been trying to tell me.

"You've Imprinted with that creature." I was thinking the words, but Neferet was the one who said them out loud.

"Oh, Goddess, no, Stevie Rae," I said, my lips feeling cold and numb. Disbelieving, I kept shaking my head back and forth like denial could make this whole nightmare go away.

"*How?*" The words sounded ripped from Dragon.

"It was not her fault," the Raven Mocker said. "I am responsible."

"Do not speak to me, monster." Dragon sounded deadly.

The Raven Mocker's red-tinged gaze moved from the Sword Master to me. "Do not blame her, Zoey Redbird."

"Why are you talking to me?" I yelled at it. Still shaking my head I looked at Stevie Rae. "How could you have let this happen?" I asked, and then clamped my mouth shut as I realized how much I suddenly sounded like my mother.

"Holy shit. I knew something freaky was going on with you, Stevie Rae, but I had no clue about a weirdness of this degree," Aphrodite said, coming up beside me.

"I shoulda said somethin'," Kramisha said from several feet away where she was standing beside the Twins and Damien, who were all staring disbelievingly back and forth from Stevie Rae to the Raven Mocker. "I knew them poems 'bout a beast and you and such was bad. I just didn't know they was literal."

"Because of the alliance between these two, Darkness has already tainted the school," Neferet said solemnly. "This creature must be responsible for Jack's death."

"That's a bunch of hogwash!" Stevie Rae said. "You killed Jack as a sacrifice to Darkness 'cause it gave you control of Kalona's soul. You know it. I know it. And Rephaim knows it. That's why he was up there watching you from a distance. He wanted to be sure you didn't do anything too terrible tonight."

I watched Stevie Rae stand up to Neferet and recognized the strength and the hopelessness I saw in my BFF, because I'd felt both things the times I'd stood up to Neferet, too—especially back when it was just me against her and an entire school full of vamps and fledglings had no clue that she was anything less than perfect.

"He has utterly twisted her," Neferet said, speaking to the re-gathering crowd. "They should both be destroyed at once."

My gut lurched and, with a certainty I felt only when I was being Goddess-led, I *knew* I had to do something.

"Okay, that's enough." With Stark moving restlessly at my side and keeping his gaze trained on the birdguy, I moved closer to Stevie Rae. "You gotta know how bad this looks."

"Yeah, I do."

"And you really are Imprinted with him?"

"Yeah, I am," she said firmly.

"Did he attack you or something?" I asked, trying to make some sense of it.

"No, Z, the opposite. He saved my life. Twice."

"Of course he did. You're in league with the creature and al-lied with Darkness!" Neferet turned to face the watching fledg-lings and vampyres.

The green glow surrounding Stevie Rae intensified as did her voice. "Rephaim saved me from Darkness. He was why I sur-vived accidentally invoking the white bull. And just because most of these folks can't see what you're doing, don't ever forget that I can. I see the threads of Darkness that follow your com-mand."

"You sound very familiar with that subject," Neferet said.

"'Course I am," Stevie Rae said angrily. "Before Aphrodite's sacrifice I was filled with Darkness. I'll always recognize it; just like I'll always choose Light over it."

"Really?" Neferet's smile was smug. "And that's what you're do-ing when you choose this creature? Choosing *Light*? Raven Mock-ers were created in anger and violence and hatred. They live for death and destruction. This one killed Anastasia Lankford. How can that be mistaken for Light and the Path of the Goddess?"

"It was wrong." Rephaim wasn't speaking to Neferet. He was looking directly at Stevie Rae. "What I was before I knew you was wrong. Then you found me and pulled me from a dark place." I held my breath as the Raven Mocker slowly, gently, touched Stevie Rae's cheek, wiping a tear away. "You showed me kindness and for a little while I glimpsed happiness. That is enough for me. Release me, Stevie Rae, my Red One. Let them exact their vengeance upon me. Perhaps Nyx will take pity on my spirit and allow me to enter her realm where someday I will see you again."

Stevie Rae shook her head. "No. I can't. I won't. If I'm yours then you're mine, too. I'm not gonna let you go without a fight."

"Does that mean you'll fight your friends for him?" I shouted at her, feeling like everything was spinning out of control.

Calmly, Stevie Rae looked at me. I saw the answer in her eyes before she spoke in a sad but firm voice. "If I have to, I will." And then she said the one thing—the only thing—that finally made sense of the whole crazy mess, and it changed everything for me. "Zoey, you would have fought anyone to protect me when I was filled with Darkness, even when you didn't know for sure if I'd ever be myself again. He's already Changed, Z. He's turned from Darkness. How can I do any less for him?"

"That thing killed my mate!" Dragon bellowed.

"For that, as well as for a multitude of other offenses, he must die," Neferet said. "Stevie Rae, if you choose to stand with the creature, then you choose to stand against the House of Night, and you will deserve to perish with him."

"Okay, no. Hang on," I said. "Sometimes things aren't just black and white, and there's more than one right answer. Dragon, I know this is terrible for you, but let's all just take a breath and step back for a second. You can't really be talking about killing Stevie Rae."

"If she stands with Darkness she deserves the same fate as the creature," Neferet said.

"Oh, please. You just admitted that *you* stood with Darkness, and Zoey forgave you for it," Aphrodite said. "I'm not saying that I'm cool with this whole birdboy/Stevie Rae weirdness, but how can it be okay for you to get forgiveness, but not okay for those two?"

"Because I no longer am under the influence of Darkness, which was personified by this creature's father," Neferet said smoothly. "I am not allied with him anymore. Let's ask the creature if he can say the same." She looked at the Raven Mocker. "Rephaim, will you swear that you are no longer your father's son? That you no longer are allied with him?"

This time Rephaim did answer Neferet directly. "Only my father can free me from his service."

I could see the smugness in Neferet's face. "And have you asked Kalona to free you from him?"

"I have not." Rephaim looked from Neferet to Stevie Rae. "Please understand."

"I do. I promise you I do," she told him. Then she shouted at Neferet. "He hasn't asked Kalona to free him because he doesn't want to betray his daddy!"

"His reasons for choosing Darkness are not important," Neferet said.

"Actually, I think they are," I said. "And another thing, we're talking about Kalona like he's here. Isn't he supposed to have been banished from your side?"

Neferet turned her cold green eyes on me. "The immortal is no longer at my side."

"But it's sounding like he's here in Tulsa. If he's banished, what is he doing here? Uh, Rephaim," I tripped over his name. It was super weird to be talking to the scary creature like he was an ordinary guy. "Is your dad in Tulsa?"

"I-I cannot speak of my father," the Raven Mocker said haltingly.

"I'm not asking you to say anything bad or even tell us where exactly he is," I said.

I was surprised to be able to see the anguish in his red-tinged eyes. "I am sorry. I cannot."

"See! He will not speak against Kalona; he will not stand against Kalona," Neferet's voice shot out. "And because the Raven Mocker is here, we know that Kalona is either in Tulsa already, or on his way. So when he attacks this school, as he surely will, you will, again, be by his side *fighting against us.*"

Rephaim turned his scarlet gaze to Stevie Rae. In a voice filled with despair he said, "I will not harm you, but he is my father and I—"

Neferet cut in, "Dragon Lankford, as High Priestess of this House of Night I command you to protect it. Kill this vile Raven Mocker and *anyone* who would stand with him."

I saw Neferet raise her hand and flick her wrist toward Stevie Rae. The green glowy bubble that had been surrounding her and the Raven Mocker shivered, and Stevie Rae groaned. Her face went real white, and she put her hand to her stomach like she was going to be sick.

"Stevie Rae?" I started to go to her, but Stark grabbed my hand, holding me back.

"Neferet's using Darkness," he said. "You can't get between her and Stevie Rae—it'll cut you down."

"Darkness?" Neferet's voice sounded swollen with power. "I'm not using Darkness. I'm using the righteous vengeance of a goddess. Only that could let me break this barrier. Now, Dragon! Show this creature the consequence for standing against my House of Night!"

Stevie Rae groaned again, and dropped to her knees. The green glow vanished. Rephaim was bending over Stevie Rae, so his back was completely exposed and vulnerable to Dragon's sword.

I raised the hand Stark wasn't clutching, but what was I going to do? Attack Dragon? To save the Raven Mocker who had killed his mate? I was frozen. I wouldn't let Dragon hurt Stevie Rae, but he wasn't attacking her—he was attacking our enemy, *an enemy my BFF had Imprinted with*. It was like watching one of those slasher movies and waiting for the throat-cutting, dismembering, totally gross carnage to start, only this was for real.

There was a great whooshing sound, like a controlled gale, and Kalona dropped from the sky, landing between his son and Dragon. He had that terrible black spear in his hand, the one he'd materialized in the Otherworld, and with it he deflected the Sword Master's blow with such force that he knocked Dragon to his knees.

The Sons of Erebus leaped into action. More than a dozen of them rushed to defend their Sword Master. Kalona was a deadly blur, but even he was struggling to handle so many Warriors at once.

"Rephaim! Son!" Kalona called to him. "To me! Defend me!"

CHAPTER TWENTY-TWO

Stevie Rae

"You can't kill anyone!" Stevie Rae cried as Rephaim picked up a fallen Son of Erebus's sword.

He looked at her and whispered, "Force Kalona to go against Neferet's wishes. It is the only way to end this." Then he ran to do his father's bidding.

Force Kalona to go against Neferet? What is Rephaim talking about? Isn't Kalona under her control? Stevie Rae struggled to stand up, but those terrible black threads had not just sliced through her earth shield, they had also drained her. She felt weak and light-headed and wanted to puke her guts out.

Then Zoey was there, crouching beside her, and Stark was standing guard in front of the two of them, positioning himself between them and the bloody battle between the Sons of Erebus and Kalona and Rephaim. Stevie Rae looked up just in time to see a giant sword materialize in his hand. She grabbed Zoey's wrist.

"Don't let Stark hurt Rephaim!" Stevie Rae begged her BFF. Zoey met her eyes. "Please," she told her. "Please trust me."

Zoey nodded once, then called to her Warrior. "Don't hurt Rephaim."

Stark turned his head, though he didn't take his eyes from the battle. "I'll damn sure hurt him if he attacks you," he retorted.

"He won't," Stevie Rae said.

"I wouldn't bet on it," Aphrodite said, running up to the two of them while Darius, his own sword drawn, joined Stark, joining the barrier between danger and their priestesses. "Bumpkin, you have royally fucked up this time."

"Hate to agree with Aphrodikey," Erin said.

"*Really* hate to, but she's right," Shaunee said.

Damien, looking haggard, knelt on the other side of Stevie Rae. "We can yell at Stevie Rae later. Right now let's just figure out how to get her out of this mess," he said.

"You don't understand," Stevie Rae told him, her eyes filling up with tears. "I don't want out of it, and the only thing that's a mess is that y'all found out like this instead of me tellin' you 'bout Rephaim."

Damien stared at her for what seemed like a long time before he replied, "Oh, I see. I do understand because before I lost it, I learned a lot about love."

Before Stevie Rae could say anything else, a painful cry from one of the Sons of Erebus Warriors drew all of their eyes. Kalona had just stabbed him in the meaty part of his thigh, and the young Warrior had gone down, but as quickly as he'd fallen, another Warrior dragged him out of the way and yet another took his place, closing the break in the deadly circle around the winged beings.

They were fighting back to back. Stevie Rae wanted to curl up and die as she watched the House of Night Warriors press the attack over and over. Perfectly matched, perfectly in tune, Kalona and Rephaim complemented each other's movements. In one part of her brain, Stevie Rae could acknowledge the beauty of the lethal dance that was going on between the Warriors and the winged beings—there was a grace and a symmetry to the fight that was awe-inspiring. But in most of her brain she just wanted to scream at Rephaim, *Run! Fly away! Get outta here! Save yourself!*

A Warrior lunged at Rephaim and at the very last moment he parried the blow. Sick and scared and almost completely defeated by the terrible unknown of what was going to happen to both of them, it took Stevie Rae longer than it should have for her to really see what Rephaim was doing—or rather, *not* doing. And when she did see it, Stevie Rae felt the sweet stirring of hope.

"Zoey," she clutched her friend's hand, unwilling to look away from the battle. "Watch Rephaim. He's not attacking. He's not hurting anyone. He's only defending himself."

Zoey paused, observing, and then said, "You're right. Stevie Rae, you're right! He's not attacking."

Pride for Rephaim made Stevie Rae's chest hurt, like her heart was thudding too hard to be held inside her rib cage. The Warriors kept attacking, brutal and deadly in their intent. Kalona kept wounding, maiming, and even killing. Rephaim continued to only defend himself—he blocked blows, he feinted and lunged, but he harmed none of the Warriors who were so obviously trying to kill him.

"She's correct," Darius said. "The Raven Mocker is entirely on the defensive."

"Press them! Kill them!" Neferet shouted. Stevie Rae took her gaze from Rephaim long enough to glance at her. Neferet looked bloated with power, reveling in the violence and destruction that was happening before her. Why didn't anyone else see the horrible Darkness that pulsed and slithered in excitement around her, wrapping around her legs, caressing her body, feeding from her power as, in turn, Neferet fed from the death and destruction around her?

With an avenging Dragon Lankford leading them, the Sons of Erebus Warriors redoubled their attack.

"I have to stop it," Stevie Rae spoke more to herself than aloud. "Before it's gone too far and he can't help but kill somebody, I have to stop it."

"There's no stopping it," Zoey said quietly. "I think Neferet planned something like this all along. Kalona's probably here because she told him to be."

"Kalona may be, but Rephaim isn't," Stevie Rae said firmly. "He came here to be sure I'm okay, and I'm not gonna let him go down because of that."

Still watching the bloody battle, Stevie Rae imagined she was a tree—a giant, strong oak, and her legs were roots going way, way down deep into the earth. So deep that Neferet's sticky threads of Darkness couldn't reach her. And then she imagined pulling power from the spirit of the earth—rich and fertile and mighty. The pure essence of the earth surged up into her body. Stevie Rae stood. She waved away Z's hand, and when she did Stevie Rae caught sight of her own hand. It was glowing with a soft, familiar green. She started walking forward, toward Rephaim.

"Whoa, where do you think you're going?" Stark asked. Beside him, Darius looked solid and very much in her way.

"To dance with beasts, so I'm gonna penetrate their disguise." The quote from Kramisha's poem drifted through her mind, dream-like.

"Okay, crazy much?" Aphrodite said. "You need to stay your butt here and out of that mess over there."

Stevie Rae ignored Aphrodite and faced down the two Warriors. "I'm Imprinted with him. My decision's made. If you gotta fight me—fight me, but I'm goin' over there to Rephaim."

"No one's fighting you, Stevie Rae," Zoey said. "Let her go," she told Stark and Darius.

"I need your help," Stevie Rae told Zoey. "If you'll trust me, come with me and give me a boost with spirit."

"No! You can't get mixed up in that," Stark told Zoey.

Zoey smiled at him. "But we've already mixed it up with Kalona and we won, remember?"

Stark snorted. "Yeah, after I died."

"Don't worry, Guardian. I'll save you again if I need to." Zoey turned back to Stevie Rae. "You said Rephaim saved your life?"

"Twice, and he had to stand up to Darkness to do it. Rephaim has good inside him. You got my promise on that, Z. Please, *please* trust me."

"I trust you. I'll always trust you," Zoey said. "I'm going with Stevie Rae," she told Stark, who didn't look happy at all about that news.

"I'm going too," Damien said, dry-eyed. "If you need air, it'll be there for you. I still believe in love."

"I don't like the birdthing, but air's not going without fire," Shaunee said.

"Ditto, Twin," Erin said.

Stevie Rae met each of their gazes. "Thank y'all. This means more than I can ever tell ya."

"Oh, for shit's sake. Let's go save the unattractive birdboy so the bumpkin can live unhappily ever after," Aphrodite said.

"Yeah, let's do that, only take both *un*s outta that sentence," Stevie Rae said, and with the circle forming around her, flanked by Stark and Darius, Stevie Rae led them forward. Still channeling the earth, she didn't hesitate, but strode over to the scene of blood and destruction, getting as close to Rephaim as she could.

"No!" he yelled, catching a glimpse of her. "Stay back!"

"Like heck I will!" Stevie Rae looked at Damien. "Time to cowboy up. Call air."

Damien faced east. "Air, I need you. Come to me!" Wind whirled around him, lifting his and everyone else's hair.

Stevie Rae raised her brows at Shaunee, who rolled her eyes, but faced south and called, "Fire, come burn for me, baby!" While heat joined air, and without any prompting, Erin faced west and said, "Water, come on and join the circle!" The scent of spring showers touched their faces.

As quickly as water joined them, Stevie Rae looked northward and said, "Earth, you're already with me. Please join the circle, too." The root-like connection to the ground that she already had intensified, and Stevie Rae knew she was like a lighthouse shining bright mossy green.

From beside her, Z said, "Spirit, please complete our circle."

There was a wonderful sense of well-being that Stevie Rae held onto as she stepped out from her group, as if she was their spearhead. Fully empowered by her element, she raised her arms, channeled the timeless, wise strength of trees, said, "Earth, make a barrier to end this fightin'. Please." She pointed at the men.

"Help her, air," Damien said.

"Fire her up, fire," Shaunee added.

"Support her, water," Erin said.

"Fill her, spirit," Zoey said.

Stevie Rae felt a shot of adrenaline rush from the circle of earth around her, up through her feet, and into her hand. Vinelike, green tendrils shot from the ground, making a caged barrier all around Rephaim and Kalona, completely halting the fighting.

They all turned to look at her.

"There, that's better. Now we can figure this out," Stevie Rae said.

"So, Zoey and your circle—you've decided to ally with Darkness, too," Neferet said.

Before Z could respond Stevie Rae said, "Neferet, that's as nutty as squirrel turds. Z just got back from hangin' out with Nyx in the Otherworld. She managed to kick Kalona's ass there, and bring her Warrior back safe and sound with her—somethin' no other High Priestess has ever been able to do. She's not exactly Darkness material." Neferet opened her mouth to speak and Stevie Rae cut her off. "No! I only have one more thing to say to you—no matter who you fool, I want you to know I'll never believe you've changed. You're a liar, and you're really, really not nice. I have seen the white bull, and I know the Darkness you're playin' with; I know just how wacked you are. Heck, Neferet, I can see that stuff slithering 'round you right now. So. Back. The. Hell. Off."

She turned her back to Neferet and focused on Kalona. She opened her mouth and suddenly her words dried up. The winged immortal looked like an avenging god. His bare chest was spattered with blood and his black spear dripped gore. His eyes shined amber as they stared at her with an expression that was amusement mixed with disdain.

How did I ever think I could stand up to him? Stevie Rae's mind shouted inside her head. *He's too powerful, and I'm nothing—just nothing . . .*

"Strengthen her, spirit," Zoey's voice whispered to her, carried on the wind Damien had conjured.

Stevie Rae pulled her gaze from Kalona's, meeting Zoey's eyes. Her BFF smiled. "Go on. Finish what you started. You can do it."

Stevie Rae felt a rush of gratitude. As her gaze returned to Kalona, she pulled deeply from the roots she imagined connecting her to her element and with that lifeline of power, and the support of her friends, she finished what she'd started.

"Okay, everybody knows that you used to be Nyx's Warrior, but that you're here 'cause somethin' messed up with that," she said matter-of-factly, "which means *you* messed up. It also means that even though you've gone all evil and stuff, you used to know about honor and loyalty and maybe even love. So I have somethin' to tell you about your son, and I want you to listen to me. I don't know how or why it happened, but I love him, and I think he loves me." Here she paused and met Rephaim's gaze.

"I do," he said clearly and distinctly so that his voice carried to everyone watching. "I love you, Stevie Rae."

She took one moment to smile at him, full on, filled with pride, and happiness, and above all, love. Then she refocused on Kalona. "Yes, it's weird. No, it's never gonna be a normal relationship, and Goddess knows we're gonna have to deal with lots of issues with my friends, but here's what's most important: I can give Rephaim kindness and a life where he'll know peace and happiness. But I can't do that unless you do somethin' first. You have to free him, Kalona. You have to let him make his own choice between staying with you or changing his path. I'm gonna go out on a limb here and believe with everything inside me, that somewhere deep inside *you* is still a tiny sliver of Nyx's Warrior, and *that* Kalona, the one who protected our Goddess, would do the right thing. Please be that Kalona again, if only just for one second."

Into the long silence where Kalona stared unblinkingly at Stevie Rae, Neferet's voice intruded—disdainful and arrogant. "Enough of this silly charade. I'll take care of the grass barrier. Dragon, exact your revenge on the Raven Mocker. And you, Kalona, you I order to be banished from my side as you were before. Nothing has changed between us." As she spoke, Stevie Rae watched her pull from the shadows all around them, and from her own body, the slithering black tentacles that seemed to always be near her now.

Stevie Rae readied herself. It was going to be awful, but she was dang sure not backing down, and that meant she was gonna have to stand up to Darkness again.

But just as she felt the first tug of pain and chill, and the drain Darkness caused within the earth, the winged immortal raised one hand slightly, and said, "Halt! I've long allied with Darkness. Obey my command. This is not your battle. *Begone!*"

"No!" Neferet shrieked as the sticky threads, invisible to almost everyone present, began to slither away to be reabsorbed into the shadows from whence they came. Neferet turned on Kalona. "Foolish creature! What are you doing? I ordered you to leave. You *must* obey my command! I am High Priestess here!"

"I am not under your control! Nor have I ever been." Kalona's smile was victorious and he looked so magnificent for a moment Stevie Rae's breath caught at the sight of him.

"I don't know what you're talking about," Neferet recovered quickly. "It is I who was under your control."

Kalona glanced around the school grounds, taking in the wide-eyed fledglings and the vampyres who were either armed against him or frozen somewhere between their desire to run from him and their desire to adore him. "Ah, children of Nyx, like me, many of you have stopped listening to your Goddess. When will you learn?"

Then the winged immortal looked to his right. Rephaim was standing there, silently watching his father.

"It is true you have Imprinted with the Red One?"

"Yes, Father. It is."

"And you saved her life? More than once?"

"As she has saved mine in turn, more than once. It was she who truly healed me from the fall. It was she who filled the terrible wound Darkness ripped within me later, after I faced the white bull for her." Rephaim's eyes found Stevie Rae's. "As payment for freeing her from Darkness, she touched me with the power of Light she wields, that of the earth."

"I didn't do that as payment. I did that because I couldn't stand to see you hurtin'," said Stevie Rae.

Slowly, as if it were difficult for him, Kalona lifted his hand and rested it on his son's shoulder. "You know she can never love you as a woman loves a man? You will forever desire something she cannot, will not, give you."

"Father, what she gives me is more than I have ever known before."

Stevie Rae saw pain twist Kalona's face, if only for an instant. "I have given you love as my son, my favorite son," he said so softly she had to strain to hear him.

Rephaim hesitated and when he answered his father, Stevie Rae could hear the raw honesty in his voice, and the heartache the admission cost him. "Perhaps in another world, another life, that might have been true. In this one you gave me power and discipline and anger, but you did not give me love. Never love."

Kalona's eyes flashed, but Stevie Rae thought she saw more pain than anger within their amber depths. "Then in this world, in this life, I shall give you one more thing: choice. Choose, Rephaim. Choose between the father you have served and fol-lowed faithfully for eons and the power that service has afforded you, and the love of this vampyre High Priestess, who will never be completely yours because she will always, always be horrified by the monster within you."

Rephaim's eyes found hers. She saw the question in them and answered it before he could ask it aloud.

"I don't see a monster when I look at you—not outside, not inside. So I'm not horrified by you. I love you, Rephaim."

Rephaim closed his eyes for a moment, and she felt a quiver of unease. He was good—Stevie Rae believed that, but to choose her over his father would change the course of his life forever. He was part immortal, and forever could be a literal thing for him. Maybe he couldn't—maybe he wouldn't—maybe he—

"Father—" Stevie Rae opened her eyes the second she heard Rephaim's voice. He was speaking to Kalona, but he was still looking at her. "I choose Stevie Rae, and the path of the Goddess."

Her gaze darted to Kalona in time to see the grimace of pain pass over his face. "Then so be it. From this day forth you are no longer my son." He paused and Rephaim turned his gaze from her to the winged immortal. "I would offer you Nyx's blessing, but she no longer hears me. So instead I offer you a piece of advice: if you love her with everything within you, when you realize she does not love you in the same way—and she will not, cannot—it will kill everything within you." Kalona unfurled his great wings, lifted both arms, and proclaimed, "Rephaim is free of me! So I have spoken. So let it be!"

Afterward, Stevie Rae would think about that moment and the way the air quivered around Rephaim with his immortal father's release. Then all she could do was to stare wide-eyed at Rephaim as the red tint that had been present in his eyes for as long as she had been looking into them faded, leaving only the wide, dark eyes of a human boy staring at her from the head of an enormous raven.

Wings still extended, body still magnified by power and, Stevie Rae liked to believe, by the grief he had to feel somewhere inside him at the loss of his son, Kalona moved his amber gaze to Neferet. He didn't say one word. He only laughed and then launched himself into the night sky, leaving a trail of mocking laughter behind him and one other thing. From the air a single white feather dropped to the ground at Stevie Rae's feet. It shocked her so much that the barrier she'd erected around Rephaim dissipated, but she was staring at the feather so intently that Stevie Rae didn't even realize her concentration had utterly shattered. She was bending to pick up the feather when Neferet commanded Dragon.

"Now that the immortal has fled, kill his son. I am not fooled by this charade."

Stevie Rae felt the terribly familiar sting of Darkness breaking her connection to the earth, weakening her. She was unable to even cry out as she watched Dragon descend on Rephaim.

CHAPTER TWENTY-THREE

Rephaim

Rephaim hadn't even had time to take in what had happened when Neferet ordered his death. He was watching Stevie Rae in wonder as she stared down at something white in the grass. Then chaos ensued. The green glow that had been surrounding him faded. Stevie Rae turned ghostly pale and swayed dizzily. The Raven Mocker was so focused on Stevie Rae that he didn't even know Dragon was attacking, and then her friend Zoey was suddenly there before him, placing herself between him and the avenging Sons of Erebus.

"No. We don't attack people who choose the path of the Goddess." She spoke in an amplified voice, and the Warriors halted uncertainly in front of her. Rephaim noted that Stark had moved to stand on one side of her, and Darius on the other. Both Warriors had their swords raised, but their expressions spoke volumes; it was obvious neither of them wanted to strike their brothers.

My fault. It is my fault they stand against each other. Rephaim's thoughts were jumbled with self-loathing and uncertainty as he hurried to Stevie Rae.

"Will you have Warrior turn against Warrior?" Neferet asked Zoey incredulously.

"Will you have our Warriors kill someone in the service of their Goddess?" countered Zoey.

"So now you are able to judge what is in another's heart?" Neferet said, sounding smug and wise. "Not even *real* High Priestesses claim such a divine ability."

Rephaim felt the change in the air before she materialized. It was as if a thunderstorm had been contained and its lightning had charged the air around them. In the middle of the surge of power and light and sound, the Great Goddess of Night, Nyx, appeared.

"No, Neferet, Zoey cannot claim such a divine ability, but I can."

Every tentacle of Darkness that had been searching and draining and lurking slithered away at the sound of her divine voice. Beside him, Stevie Rae gasped, like she'd let loose the breath she'd been holding, and dropped to her knees.

From all around him Rephaim heard awestruck whispers of "It's Nyx!" "It's the Goddess!" "Oh, blessed be!"

And then his attention was consumed by Nyx.

She was, indeed, night personified. Her hair was like the full hunters' moon, shining with a silver luminescence. Her eyes were the new moon sky—black and limitless. The rest of her body was almost completely transparent. Rephaim thought he caught a glimpse of dark silk lifting in a breeze of its own, and a woman's curves—and perhaps even a crescent moon tattooed on her smooth forehead, but the more he tried to focus on the Goddess's image, the more transparent and incandescent she became. It was then that he noticed he was the only one still standing. Everyone else had knelt to the Goddess, and he, too, knelt.

He quickly realized that he didn't need to worry about his late response. Nyx's attention was elsewhere. She was floating over to Damien, who, ironically, had no idea she approached because he was kneeling with his head bowed and his eyes closed.

"Damien, my son, look at me."

Damien's head lifted, and his eyes opened wide in surprise. "Oh, Nyx! It's really you! I thought I'd imagined you here."

"Perhaps in a way, you did. I want you to know that your Jack is with me, and he is one of the purest, most joy-filled spirits my realm has ever known."

Tears filled and overflowed Damien's eyes. "Thank you. Thank you for telling me that. It will help me try to get over him."

"My son, there is no need to get over Jack. Remember him, and rejoice in the brief, beautiful love you shared. Choosing to do so does not mean forgetting or getting over, it means healing."

Damien smiled through his tears. "I'll remember. I'll always remember and choose your path, Nyx. I give you my word."

The Goddess's hovering form turned so that her dark gaze took in the rest of them. Rephaim saw Nyx look fondly at Zoey, who grinned.

"Merry meet, my Goddess," Zoey said, shocking Rephaim with the familiar tone of her voice.

Shouldn't she be more respectful—more fearful—when addressing the Goddess?

"Merry meet, Zoey Redbird!" The Goddess returned the fledgling High Priestess's grin, and he thought, for a moment, she looked like an exquisitely lovely little girl—a little girl who was suddenly familiar to him. With a jolt Rephaim recognized her. The ghost! The ghost had been the Goddess!

Then Nyx began speaking, addressing the entire gathering, and her visage shifted to an ethereal being so brilliant and beautiful it was difficult to gaze upon her and impossible to think about anything except the words that she spoke like a symphony over them all. *"Much has happened here this night. Spirit-altering choices were made, which means, for some of you, new life paths have opened. For others, your paths have been sealed, your choices made long ago. And yet others of you are at a life precipice."* The

Goddess's gaze lingered on Neferet, who instantly bowed her head. *"You have changed, daughter. You are not as you once were. Truly, can I still call you daughter?"*

"Nyx! Great Goddess! How could I not be your daughter?"

Neferet did not raise her head as she spoke to the Goddess, and her thick fall of auburn hair completely covered her face, blanketing her expression.

"Tonight you asked for forgiveness. Zoey gave one answer. I shall give you another. Forgiveness is a very special gift, and it must be earned."

"I ask humbly that you share that special gift with me, Nyx," Neferet said, still bowing her head and hiding her face.

"When you earn the gift, you will receive it." Abruptly, the Goddess turned from Neferet, her attention turning to the Sword Master, who closed his fist over his heart respectfully to her. *"Your Anastasia is free of pain and remorse. Will you make Damien's choice, and learn to rejoice in the love you had and move on, or will your choice destroy that which she loved so much about you—your ability to be both strong and merciful?"* Rephaim was watching Dragon, waiting for a response from the Sword Master that did not come, when Nyx spoke his name.

"Rephaim."

He looked Nyx full in the face for only an instant, and then Rephaim remembered what he was and he bowed his head in shame and spoke the first words that flooded his mind. "Please don't look at me!"

He felt Stevie Rae's hand slide into his. "Don't worry. She's not here to punish you."

"And how do you know that, young High Priestess?"

Stevie Rae's grip tightened spasmodically on his hand, but her voice didn't falter. "'Cause you *can* see into his heart, and I know what you'll find there."

"What do you believe is in the Raven Mocker's heart, Stevie Rae?"

"Goodness. And I don't think he's a Raven Mocker anymore. His daddy released him. So now I think he's a-a new kinda, uh, boy-who's-never-been-before." She tripped over the words, but managed to finish.

"I see you are bound to him," was the Goddess's enigmatic response.

"I am," she said firmly.

"Even if your bond means splitting this House of Night, and perhaps, this world, in two?"

"My mama used to prune her roses real fierce, and I thought she was gonna hurt them, maybe kill them. When I asked her about it she told me sometimes you have to cut away the old stuff to make room for the new. Maybe it's time to cut away some old stuff," Stevie Rae said.

Her words surprised him so much that Rephaim turned his eyes from the ground to Stevie Rae. She smiled at him and at that moment, he wished more than anything else, he could smile back at her and take her in his arms like a real boy would be able to do, because what he saw in her eyes was warmth and love and happiness with not even the slightest glimpse of remorse or rejection.

Stevie Rae gave him the strength to look up at the Goddess and meet her infinite gaze.

And what he saw there was familiar because mirrored in Nyx's eyes was the same warmth and love and happiness he'd seen within Stevie Rae's gaze.

Rephaim dropped Stevie Rae's hand so that he could close his fist over his heart, in the ancient, respectful greeting. "Merry meet, Goddess Nyx."

"Merry meet, Rephaim," she said. *"You are the only child of*

Kalona's to turn from the rage and pain of your conception, and the hatred that has filled your long life, and seek Light."

"None of the others had Stevie Rae," he said.

"It is true that she influenced your choice, but you had to be open to her and respond with Light instead of Darkness."

"That hasn't always been my choice. In the past I've done terrible things. These Warriors are right to want me dead," Rephaim said.

"Do you regret your past?"

"I do."

"Do you choose a new future where you pledge yourself to my path?"

"I do."

"Rephaim, son of the fallen immortal Warrior Kalona, I accept you into my service, and I forgive you for the mistakes of your past."

"Thank you, Nyx." Rephaim's voice was rough with emotion as he spoke to the Goddess, *his Goddess.*

"Will you thank me when I tell you that though I forgive you and accept you, there are consequences you must pay for the choices of your past?"

"No matter what comes next, for an eternity I will thank you. This I swear," he said with no hesitation.

"Let us hope that you will have many, many years to live up to your oath. Know then that this is your consequence." Nyx raised her arms as if she could cup the moon in the palms of her hands. It seemed to Rephaim she was gathering light from the stars themselves. *"Because you have awakened the humanity within you, I will, each night from setting sun to rising sun, gift you with this: the true form you deserve."* The Goddess hurled the glowing power that had coalesced between her hands at him. It shuddered through his body, causing a pain so terrible that he

screamed in agony and crumpled to the ground. As he lay there, paralyzed, the Goddess's voice was the only sound that broke through to him. *"To atone for your past, by day you will lose your true form and return to that of the raven, who knows nothing except the base desires of a beast. Consider well how you use your humanity. Learn from the past and balance the beast. So I have spoken—so mote it be!"*

The pain was beginning to recede and Rephaim was able to look up at the Goddess again as she opened her arms to take in everyone and said joyously, *"I leave the rest of you with my love, if you so choose to accept it, and my desire that you will always blessed be."*

Nyx disappeared in what looked like an explosion of the moon. The brightness of it was blinding, which didn't help Rephaim's lingering confusion. His body felt strange, unfamiliar, dizzy . . . Rephaim looked down at himself. His shock was so intense he could not, for a moment, comprehend what he saw. *Why am I inside a boy?* passed through his jumbled mind. It was Stevie Rae's sobs that finally got through to him. He was able to focus on her and when he did, Rephaim realized she was crying and laughing at the same time.

"What has happened?" he asked, still not fully understanding.

Stevie Rae didn't seem to be able to speak because she just kept crying what looked like happy tears.

A hand came into his line of vision and he looked up to see the fledgling High Priestess, Zoey Redbird, smiling wryly at him. Rephaim took her offered hand and stood a little shakily.

"What's happened is our Goddess has zapped you into being a guy," Zoey said.

The truth hit him then and it almost drove him to his knees again. "I'm human. Completely human." Rephaim stared down at the strong, tall body of a young Cherokee warrior.

"Yeah, you are, but only during the nighttime," Zoey was saying. "During the day you're gonna be completely a raven."

Rephaim barely heard her. He was already turning to Stevie Rae.

He must have been knocked away from her when Nyx changed him, because she was no longer by his side. She took one small, hesitant step toward him and then stopped, looking unsure and wiping her face.

"Is it—is it bad? Do I look wrong?" he blurted.

"No," she said, staring into his eyes. "You're perfect. Absolutely perfect. You're the boy we saw in the fountain."

"Will you . . . can I . . ." His voice trailed off. Rephaim was too filled with emotion to find the right words, so he moved instead, closing the space between Stevie Rae and him in two long, strong, *totally human* strides. With no hesitation he took her in his arms, and then he did what he had barely even allowed himself to do in his dreams. Rephaim bent and kissed Stevie Rae's soft lips with his own. He tasted her tears and her laughter, and finally he knew what it was to be truly, completely happy.

So it was reluctantly that he pulled back and told her, "Wait. There's something I have to do."

Dragon Lankford was easy to find. Though everyone was staring at him and Stevie Rae, Rephaim felt the Sword Master's gaze distinctly. He approached Dragon slowly, making no sudden movements. Even so, the Warriors that stood to either side of him shifted, obviously ready to fight by their Sword Master's side once more.

Rephaim stopped in front of Dragon. He met his gaze and saw the pain and anger there. Rephaim nodded in acknowledgment. "I have caused you great loss. I make no excuses for what I was. I can only tell you that I was wrong. I do not ask you to forgive me as the Goddess has." Rephaim paused and sank to one knee. "What I ask is that you allow me to repay the life debt

I owe you by serving you. If you accept me, for as long as I breathe I will, with my actions and my honor, attempt to atone for the loss of your mate."

Dragon said nothing. He only stared at Rephaim as warring emotions passed over his face: hatred, despair, anger, and sadness. Until finally they coalesced into a mask of cold determination.

"Get off your knees, creature." Dragon's voice was emotionless. "I cannot accept your oath. I cannot bear to look at you. I will not allow you to serve me."

"Dragon, think about what you're saying," Zoey Redbird spoke up, walking quickly to Rephaim's side with Stark close by her. "I know it's hard—I know what it's like to lose someone you love, but you have to make a choice about how you go on from there, and it feels like you're choosing Darkness instead of Light."

Dragon's eyes were cruel, his voice cold, as he answered the young High Priestess. "You say you know what it's like to lose a love? How long did you love that human boy? Less than a decade! Anastasia was my mate for more than a *century*."

Rephaim saw Zoey flinch, as if his words had physically hurt her, and Stark moved closer to her side, his gaze narrowed on the Sword Master.

"And that is why a child cannot lead a House of Night. Nor can she be a true High Priestess, no matter how indulgent our Goddess is," Neferet said, moving silkily to Dragon's side and touching his arm deferentially.

"Hang on there a sec, Hateful. I don't remember Nyx actually saying she'd forgiven you. She talked about *ifs* and *gifts,* but correct me if I'm wrong, no *hey there, Neferet, you're forgiven*s," Aphrodite said.

"You do not belong at this school!" Neferet yelled at her. "You are not a fledgling anymore!"

"No, she's a Prophetess, remember?" Zoey said, sounding calm and wise. "Even the High Council has said so."

Instead of answering Zoey, Neferet addressed the crowd of watching fledglings and vampyres. "Do you see how they twist the words of the Goddess, even just moments after she has appeared to us?"

Rephaim knew she was evil—knew she was no longer in the service of Nyx, but even he had to acknowledge how fierce and beautiful she looked. He also had to acknowledge the threads of Darkness that had reappeared and begun to slither to her again, filling her, feeding her need for power.

"No one's twisting anything," Zoey said. "Nyx forgave Rephaim and changed him into a kid. She also reminded Dragon he had a choice to make about his future. And she let you know forgiveness is a gift from her that has to be *earned*. That's all I'm saying. That's all any of us is saying."

"Dragon Lankford, as Sword Master and Leader of this House of Night's Sons of Erebus, do you accept this—" Neferet paused, glancing at Rephaim with loathing. "—this aberration as one of your own?"

"No," Dragon said. "No, I cannot accept him."

"Then I cannot accept him, either. Rephaim, you will not be allowed to remain at this House of Night. Begone, foul creature, and atone for your past elsewhere."

Rephaim didn't move. He waited for Neferet to look at him. And then quietly, distinctly, he said, "I see you for what you are."

"Begone!" she shrieked.

He stood and started to back away from the Sword Master and his group of Warriors, but Stevie Rae took his hand and stopped his retreat.

"Where you go, I go," she said.

He shook his head. "I don't want you to be kicked out of your home because of me."

Looking a little shy, Stevie Rae touched his face. "Don't you know that home is wherever you are?"

He covered her hand with his. Not trusting his voice, he nodded and smiled at her. *Smiling*—it was incredible how good it felt!

Stevie Rae pulled her hand gently from his. "I'm goin' with him," she spoke to the crowd. "I'm gonna start another House of Night in the tunnels under the depot. It's not as nice there as it is here, but it's a whole heck of a lot friendlier."

"You cannot begin a House of Night without approval of the High Council," Neferet snapped.

The watching crowd's whispers of shock reminded Rephaim of summer wind sloughing through the grasses of the ancient prairie—the sound was endless and pointless, unless you were taking wing.

Zoey Redbird's voice broke through the throng. "If you have a vampyre queen, and you agree to stay out of vampyre politics, the High Council will pretty much leave you alone." She smiled at Stevie Rae. "Coincidentally enough, I have just been kinda sorta made a queen. How 'bout I come with you and Rephaim? I'll take friendly over fancy any day."

"I'll come, too," Damien said. He looked one last time on the smoldering pyre. "I choose to make a fresh start."

"We're coming," Shaunee said.

"Ditto, Twin," Erin echoed. "Our room was too small here, anyway."

"But we'll come back for our stuff," Shaunee said.

"Oh, hells yes," Erin agreed.

"Shit," Aphrodite said. "I knew it when this night blew up. I just knew it. It sucks like Tulsa not having a Nordstrom, but I'm damn sure not staying here, either."

While Aphrodite leaned against her Warrior and sighed dramatically, each of the red fledglings stepped forward. Leaving the crowd, they made their way to stand beside Rephaim and Stevie Rae, Zoey and Stark, and the rest of their circle—the rest of their friends.

"Does this mean I can't be Poet Laureate of all the vampyres?" Kramisha asked as she joined them.

"No one but Nyx can take that away from you," Zoey said.

"Good. She was just here and she didn't fire me. So I guess I'm okay," Kramisha said.

"You're nothing if you leave! None of you are!" Neferet cried.

"Well, Neferet, it's like this," Zoey said. "Sometimes nothing and your friends equals a whole lot of something."

"That doesn't even make sense," Neferet said.

"To you it wouldn't," Rephaim said, putting his arm around Stevie Rae's shoulders.

"Let's go home," Stevie Rae said, sliding her arm around Rephaim's totally, completely human waist.

"Sounds good to me," Zoey said, taking Stark's hand.

"Sounds like we got us a bunch of cleaning to do to me," Kramisha muttered as they started to walk away.

"The Vampyre High Council will hear of this," Neferet called after them.

Zoey paused long enough to yell back over her shoulder, "Yeah, well, we won't be hard to reach. We have internet and everything. Plus, a bunch of us will be back because we'll be taking classes. This is still our school, even if it isn't our home."

"Oh, great. It's like we're being bussed in from the fucking projects," Aphrodite said.

"What are the projects?" Rephaim asked Stevie Rae.

She beamed a smile up at him and said, "It means we're comin' from a totally different place that some people don't think is so great."

"I'm hoping for urban renewal," Aphrodite grumbled.

Rephaim knew his expression was a huge question mark when Stevie Rae laughed and hugged him. "Don't worry. We'll have plenty of time for me to explain this modern stuff. For now all you need to know is that we're together and that Aphrodite usually isn't very nice."

Stevie Rae stood on her tiptoes and kissed him, and Rephaim let her taste and touch drown out the voices of his past and the haunting memory of the wind under his wings . . .

CHAPTER TWENTY-FOUR

Neferet

She held herself under the strictest of control and allowed Zoey and her pathetic group of friends to leave the House of Night even though she wanted so very much to loose Darkness on them and crush them into nothingness.

Instead, carefully, secretly, she inhaled, absorbing the threads of Darkness that scuttled about her, slithering deliciously from shadow to shadow. When she felt strong and confident and in control again, she addressed *her* minions, those who remained at *her* House of Night.

"Rejoice, fledglings and vampyres! Nyx's appearance this night was a sign of her favor. The Goddess spoke of choice and gifts and life paths. Sadly, we see that Zoey Redbird and her friends have chosen to take a path that leads away from us and, therefore, away from Nyx. But we will stay through this test and persevere, praying to our merciful Goddess that those misguided fledglings choose to return to us." Neferet could see doubt in some of her listeners' eyes. With a barely discernable motion, she waved just her fingers, pointing the long, red tips of her sharpened nails toward the doubters—the naysayers. Darkness responded, targeting them, clinging to them, causing their minds to be muddled through the confusion of twinges of seemingly sourceless pain and doubt and fear. "Now let each of us retire to our cloistered chambers, each to light a candle the color of the element we feel closest to. I believe that Nyx will hear these elementally channeled prayers, and she will ease us through this time of suffering and strife."

"Neferet, what of the fledgling's body? Should we not continue to hold vigil?" Dragon Lankford asked.

She was careful to keep the disdain from her voice. "You are right to remind me, Sword Master. Those of you who honored Jack with purple spirit candles, throw them on the pyre as you leave. The Sons of Erebus Warriors will hold vigil over the poor fledgling's body for the remainder of the night." *And in that way I will be rid of both the power of the spirit candles as the flames consume them, and the annoying presence of too many Warriors,* Neferet thought.

"As you wish, Priestess," Dragon said, bowing to her.

She barely spared him a glance. "Now I must seclude myself. I believe Nyx's message to me was multilayered. Some of it she whispered to my heart, and she has given me pause. Now I must pray and meditate."

"What Nyx said disturbed you?"

Neferet had already begun to hurry away from the prying eyes of the House of Night when Lenobia's voice stopped her. *I should have known she did not remain because she was snared by my trap,* Neferet acknowledged silently to herself. *She remains to turn the captor into the captive.*

Neferet regarded the Horse Mistress. With one flick of her fingertip, she sent Darkness in her direction, and was then surprised as well as concerned to see Lenobia's gaze darting around her as if she could actually see the seeking threads.

"Yes, what Nyx said did, indeed, disturb me," Neferet spoke abruptly, pulling everyone's attention from the Horse Mistress back to her. "I could tell that the Goddess is deeply worried about our House of Night. You heard her speak of a split in our world—and that has happened. She was warning me. I only wish I could have found the means to keep it from happening."

"But she forgave Rephaim. Could we not have—"

"The Goddess did forgive the creature. But does that mean we must suffer him in our midst?" Gracefully, she swept her arm toward Dragon Lankford, who was standing miserably by the head of the fledgling's pyre. "Our Son of Erebus made the right choice. Sadly, too many young fledglings were led astray by Zoey and Stevie Rae and their tainted words. As Nyx herself said this night, forgiveness is a gift that must be earned. Let us hope for Zoey's sake she continues to have the Goddess's good will, but after her actions here I am afraid for her." While her people were gazing between her and the pitiful, guilty spectacle the Sword Master made, Neferet stroked the air, pulling from the shadows more and more threads of Darkness. Then, with a flicking motion, she threw them out at the crowd, suppressing her smile of satisfaction when the groans and confused, pain-filled gasps reached her ears. "Depart—go to your rooms, pray and rest. This evening has been entirely too taxing for all of us. I leave you now, and as the Goddess said, I wish you to blessed be."

Neferet swept from the center of the courtyard, whispering under her breath to the ancient force around her, "He will be there! He will be awaiting me!" She gathered her power so that she felt swollen, throbbing with the rhythm of Darkness, and then gave herself to it, letting it pick up her newly immortal body and carry her on the colorless wings of death and pain and despair.

But before she could reach the Mayo, and the opulent penthouse where she *knew,* she was *certain* Kalona would be awaiting her, Neferet felt a great shifting in the powers that carried her.

The cold reached her first. Neferet wasn't certain if she commanded the powers to cease and allow her to halt, or whether the coldness froze them; either way, she found herself spewed out onto the middle of the intersection of Peoria and 11th Street. The Tsi Sgili picked herself up and looked around her, trying to get her bearings. The graveyard to her left drew her attention, and not simply because it housed the rotting remains of humans, which amused her. She sensed something approaching from within it. With one movement Neferet snagged a retreating thread of Darkness, hooked into it, and forced it to lift her over the spiked iron fence that surrounded the graveyard.

Whatever it was, she could feel it coming toward her, calling to her, and Neferet ran, darting ghostlike between the aging gravestones and crumbling monuments that humans found so soothing. Until finally she came to the centermost part of it, where four wide, paved pathways converged to form a circle where an American flag hung, the single illumination in the graveyard—except for *him*.

Of course Neferet recognized him. She'd caught glimpses of the white bull before, but he'd never fully materialized and appeared to her.

Neferet was stuck speechless at his perfection. His coat was a luminous white. Like a magnificent pearl it glowed—coaxing, alluring, compelling. She swept off the concealing shirt the pubescent Stark had given her, baring herself to the bull's consuming black gaze. Then Neferet sank gracefully to her knees.

You bared yourself to Nyx. Now you bare yourself to me? Are you that free with yourself, Queen of the Tsi Sgili?

His voice resonated darkly in her mind, sending shivers of anticipation throughout her body.

"I didn't bare myself to her. You, above all else, know that. The

Goddess and I have parted ways. I am no longer mortal, and do not desire to subjugate myself to any other female."

The mammoth white bull strode forward, causing the ground to shake under his great cloven hooves. His nose did not quite touch her delicate skin, but he inhaled her scent and then his cold breath released, surrounding Neferet, caressing her most sensitive places, awakening her most secret desires.

So instead of subjugation to a goddess you choose to chase after a fallen immortal male?

Neferet's gaze met the bull's black, bottomless eyes. "Kalona is nothing to me. I was going to him to exact my revenge for the oath he broke. It is my right to do so."

He broke no oath. It did not bind him. Kalona's soul is no longer fully immortal—he has foolishly given a piece of it away.

"Truly? How very interesting . . ." Neferet's body hummed with excitement at the news.

I see that you are still infatuated with the thought of using him.

Neferet lifted her chin and shook back her long auburn hair. "I am not infatuated with Kalona. I only wish to harness and use his powers."

You are truly a magnificent, heartless creature. The bull's tongue snaked out. He licked Neferet's naked flesh, causing her to gasp in exquisite pain as her body trembled with excitement. *It has been more than a century since I have had such a willing follower. The idea seems suddenly appealing.*

Neferet stayed on her knees before him. Slowly, gently, she reached out and touched him. His coat was frigid as ice, but slick like water.

Neferet felt his body shiver in anticipation. *Ah,* his voice resonated through her mind, and entered her soul, making her head dizzy with the power of it. *I'd forgotten how surprising touch can be when it is not forced. It is not often that I am surprised, and I find myself wanting to show you such a favor in return.*

"I would willingly accept *any* favor Darkness would do for me."

The bull's knowing chuckle rumbled through her mind. *Yes, I do believe I would like to gift you with something.*

"A gift?" she said breathlessly, loving the irony that Darkness Incarnate's words so clearly mirrored those of Nyx. "What is it?"

Would it give you pleasure to know that I could create for you a Vessel, to take Kalona's place? He would be yours to command— yours to use as an absolute weapon.

"Would he be powerful?" Neferet's breathing had increased.

If the sacrifice is deserving, he would be very powerful.

"I would sacrifice anything or anyone to Darkness," Neferet said. "Tell me what you desire for the creation of this creature, and I will give it to you."

To create the Vessel, I must have the lifeblood of a woman who has ancient ties to the earth, passed to her through generation upon generation of matriarchs. The stronger, purer, older the woman, the more perfect the Vessel.

"Human or vampyre?" Neferet asked.

Human—they are more thoroughly tied to the earth, as their bodies return to the earth so much more quickly than do vampyres'.

Neferet smiled. "I know exactly who would be the perfect sacrifice. If you take me to her tonight, I will give her blood to you."

The bull's black eyes glinted with what Neferet thought might be amusement. Then he bent his huge forelegs, making his back accessible to her. *I am intrigued by your offer, my heartless one. Show me the sacrifice.*

"You wish for me to ride you?"

With no hesitation, Neferet rose and walked around to the side of his smooth, slick back. Though he was on his knees, she was still going to have to struggle to mount him. Then she felt the familiar thrill of the power of Darkness. Weightlessly, it lifted her so that she was astride his massive back.

Picture in your mind the place you wish for me to take you— the place where your sacrifice can be found—and I will take you there.

Neferet lay forward, wrapping her arms around his huge neck, and she began picturing lavender fields and a lovely little cottage made of Oklahoma stone with a welcoming wooden porch and large, revealing windows . . .

Linda Heffer

Linda hated to admit it, but all these years her mother had been right. "John Heffer is a *su-li*." She said aloud the Cherokee word for "buzzard," which is what her mother had called John the first night they'd met. "Well, he's also a lying, cheating jerk—but a jerk with zero dollars in his savings and checking account," she said smugly. "Because I drained them today, right after I caught him with the church secretary bent over his office desk!"

Her hands tightened on the steering wheel of their Intrepid and she flicked on her brights as she replayed the terrible scene over in her mind. She'd thought it would be a nice surprise to make him a special lunch and bring it to him at his office. John had been working so many late hours—putting in so much overtime. But even after all those hours at work he still kept up so much volunteer time at church . . . Linda pressed her lips together.

Well, now she knew what he'd *really* been doing! Or rather, *who* he'd really been doing!

She should have known. All the signs were there—he'd stopped paying attention to her, stopped coming home, lost ten pounds, and even bleached his teeth!

He'd try to talk her back. She knew he would. He'd even tried to get her from running out of his office, but it'd been pretty darn hard to chase her with his pants around his ankles.

"The worst part is that he won't want me back because he loves me. He'll want me back so he doesn't look bad." Linda bit her lip and blinked hard, refusing to cry. "No," she admitted aloud to herself. "The worst part is that John never loved me. He just wanted to look like the perfect family man, so he needed me. Our family was never anything close to perfect—anything close to happy." *My mother had been right. Zoey had been right, too.*

Thinking of Zoey was what finally tipped the tears over to spill down her cheeks. Linda missed Zoey. Of her three children, she'd been closest to Zoey. She smiled through her tears, remembering how she and Zoey used to have geekends where they'd curl up on the couch together, eat lots of junk food, and watch either the Lord of the Rings or Harry Potter movies, or even sometimes Star Wars. How long had it been since they'd done that? Years. Would they ever again? Linda hiccupped a little sob. Could they now that Zoey was at the House of Night?

Would Zoey even *want* to see her again?

She'd never forgive herself if she'd let John irreparably mess up her relationship with Zoey.

That was one reason she'd gotten in the car, in the middle of the night, and headed to her mother's house. Linda wanted to talk to her mother about Zoey—about mending her relationship with Zoey.

Linda also wanted to lean on her mother's strength. She wanted help to stand firm and not let John talk her into a reconciliation.

But mostly, Linda just wanted her mother.

It didn't matter that she was a grown woman with children of her own. She still needed her mother's arms to hold her, and her mother's voice to reassure her that everything really would be all right—that she'd made the right decision.

Linda was so deep in thought that she almost missed the turnoff to her mother's house. She braked hard and just made the right turn. Then she slowed the car so that it wouldn't spin out on the dirt road that led between lavender fields to her mother's house. It'd been more than a year since she'd been here, but it hadn't changed—and Linda was thankful for that. It made her feel safe and normal again.

Her mother's porch light was on, and so was one lamp light inside. Linda smiled as she parked and got out of the car. It was probably that 1920s brass mermaid lamp her mother liked to read by late at night—only it wouldn't be late to Sylvia Redbird. Four in the morning would be early for her, and just about getting up time.

Linda was just going to tap on the windowpane of the door before opening it when she saw the note written on lavender-scented paper and taped on the door. Her mother's distinctive handwriting said:

Linda darling, I felt you might be coming, but I couldn't be sure when you would actually arrive, so I went ahead and took some soaps and sachets and things to the powwow in Tahlequah. I'll be back tomorrow. As always, please make yourself at home. I hope you're here when I return. I love you.

Linda sighed. Trying not to feel disappointed and annoyed at her mother, she went inside. "It's really not her fault. She'd be here if I hadn't stopped coming by." She was used to her mother's weird way of knowing whenever she was going to have a visitor. "Looks like her radar still works."

For a moment she stood in the middle of the living room, trying to decide what to do. Maybe she should go back to Broken Arrow. Maybe John would leave her alone for a while—or at least long enough for her to get an attorney and get him served with papers.

But she'd broken her rule about no overnights during the week, and the kids were at friends' houses. She didn't have to go back. Linda sighed again, and this time with her inhaled breath she took in the scents of her mother's home: lavender, vanilla, and sage—real scents from real herbs and hand-poured soy candles, so unlike the PlugIns John insisted she use instead of "those sooty candles and those dirty old plants." And that decided her. Linda marched into her mother's kitchen and went straight to the little, but well stocked wine rack and pulled out a nice red. She was going to drink an entire bottle of wine and read one of her mother's romance novels, and then stagger up to the guest loft, and she was going to enjoy every minute of it. Tomorrow her mother would give her an herbal tea concoction to get rid of her hangover, and she'd also help her figure out how to get her life back on the right track—a track that didn't include John Heffer and did include her Zoey.

"Heffer, what a stupid name," Linda said, pouring herself a glass of wine and taking a long, slow drink. "That name is one of the first things I'm going to get rid of!" She was looking through her mother's bookshelf, trying to decide between reading something sexy by Kresley Cole, Gena Showalter, or Jennifer Crusie's latest, *Maybe This Time*. That was it—the great title decided her because maybe this time she'd do the right thing. Linda was just settling down in her mother's chair when someone knocked on the door three times.

In her opinion, it was entirely too late for visitors, but you never knew what to expect at her mother's house, so Linda went to the door and opened it.

The vampyre who stood there was stunningly beautiful, a little familiar looking, and totally, completely naked.

CHAPTER TWENTY-FIVE

Neferet

"You are not Sylvia Redbird." Neferet looked down her nose disdainfully at the drab woman who had answered the door.

"No, I'm her daughter, Linda. My mother isn't in right now," she said, glancing around nervously.

Neferet knew the moment the human's eyes found the white bull, because they widened in shock and her face drained of all of its sallow color.

"Oh! It's a . . . a . . . b-bull! Is it making the ground burn? Hurry! Hurry! Come inside where it's safe. I'll get you a robe to wear and then call animal control or the police or *someone*."

Neferet smiled and turned her head so that she could gaze at the bull, too. He was standing in the middle of the closest lavender field. If one didn't know better it would, indeed, appear as if he were burning everything around him.

Neferet knew better.

"He isn't burning the field; he's freezing it. The withered plants just look scorched. Actually, they're frozen," Neferet said in the same matter-of-fact tone she often used in her classroom.

"I've— I've never seen a bull do that before."

Neferet lifted one brow at Linda. "Does he truly look like a normal bull to you?"

"No," Linda whispered. Then she cleared her throat and, obviously trying to sound stern, said to Neferet, "I'm sorry. I'm confused about what's going on here. Do I know you? May I help you?"

"There is no need for you to be confused or concerned. I am Neferet, High Priestess of Tulsa's House of Night, and I do most certainly hope you can help me. First, tell me when you expect your mother to return." Neferet kept her voice affable, though her mind was a jumble of emotions: anger, irritation, and a lovely shiver of fear.

"Oh, that's why you look familiar. My daughter Zoey goes to that school."

"Yes, I know Zoey very well." Neferet smiled smoothly. "When did you say your mother would return?"

"Not until tomorrow. Can I give her a message from you? And would you, uh, like a robe or something?"

"No message and no robe." Neferet dropped her mask of affability. She lifted her hand and swept several tendrils of Darkness from the shadows surrounding her, then she flung them at the human woman, commanding, "Bind her and bring her out here." When Neferet felt none of the familiar, painful slice that was the payment for manipulating the lesser threads of Darkness, she smiled at the mammoth bull and dipped her head in acknowledgment of his favor as she approached him.

You shall pay me later, my heartless one, rumbled through her mind. Neferet shivered in anticipation.

Then the human's pathetic screams intruded on her thoughts and she made a motion over her shoulder, snapping the command, "And gag her! I cannot be expected to bear that noise."

Linda's screams stopped as abruptly as they had begun. Neferet stepped into the frozen lavender that encircled the beast, ignoring the cold on her bare feet and against her naked skin as she strode directly up to his great head and stroked one finger down the length of his horn before she dropped to a graceful curtsey before him. When she rose, she smiled into the complete blackness of his eyes and said, "I have your sacrifice."

The bull's gaze flicked over her shoulder.

This is not an old, powerful matriarch. This is a pathetic housewife whose life has been consumed by weakness.

"True, but her mother is a Wise Woman of the Cherokee. Her blood flows in this one's veins."

Diluted.

"Will she serve as the sacrifice or not? Can you use her to make my Vessel?"

I can, but your Vessel will be only as perfect as your sacrifice, and this woman is far from perfect.

"But will you invest him with power that I can command?"

I will.

"Then my wish is that you accept this sacrifice. I will not wait for the mother when I can have the daughter, and the same blood, now."

As you wish, my heartless one. I grow weary of this. Kill her quickly and let us move on to other things.

Neferet didn't speak. She turned and walked over to the human. The woman was pathetic. She wasn't even struggling. All she was doing was sobbing silently as the tendrils of Darkness cut red swaths across her mouth and face, and all around her body where they bound her.

"I need a blade. Now." Neferet held out her hand and instantly pain and cold filled it in the shape of a long, obsidian dagger. With one swift motion, Neferet slit Linda's throat. She watched the woman's eyes widen and then roll to show only their whites as her life's blood drained from her.

Catch all of it. Let none of the blood be wasted.

At the bull's command the tendrils of Darkness writhed all

over Linda, attaching to her throat and to any other part of her body from which blood seeped, and began sucking. Mesmerized, Neferet saw that each pulsing tendril had a thread that returned to the bull, dissolving into his body, feeding him the human's blood.

The bull moaned in pleasure.

When the human was drained to a husk of herself, and the bull was thrumming and swollen with her death, Neferet gave herself to Darkness, utterly and completely.

Heath

"Go long, Neal!" Heath drew back his arm and aimed for the receiver in the Golden Hurricane's jersey with the name SWEE-NEY in bold letters across his back.

Sweeney caught it, and then feinted and dodged around a bunch of guys in crimson and cream OU uniforms to make the touchdown.

"Yeah!" Heath raised his fist, laughing and shouting. "Sweeney could catch a gnat off a fly's back!"

"Are you enjoying yourself, Heath Luck?"

At the sound of the Goddess's voice Heath put away his fist pump and gave Nyx a semi-guilty smile. "Uh, yeah. It's great here. There's always a game I can quarterback—awesome receivers, great fans, and when I get tired of football there's that lake just down the street. It's stocked with bass that would make a pro fisherman cry."

"What about girls? I see no cheerleaders, no fisher*women*."

Heath's smile faltered. "Girls? No. Well. I only have one girl and she's not here. You know that, Nyx."

"I was just checking." Nyx's smile was radiant. "Would you sit and talk with me a moment?"

"Yeah, sure," Heath said.

Nyx waved her hand and the old-school replication of a college football stadium disappeared. Suddenly Heath found himself standing on the precipice of an enormous canyon, so deep that the river that roared through the bottom of it looked like only a thin silver thread. The sun was rising over the opposite bank of the ridge, and the sky was shaded with the violets and pinks and blues of a beautiful new day.

Movement in the air caught Heath's eye, and he noticed hundreds, maybe thousands of sparkling globes that were tumbling down into the gorge. He thought some of them looked like electric pearls, and others like geode balls, and still others were fluorescent colors so bright they almost hurt his eyes.

"Wow! It's awesome up here!" He shaded his eyes with his hand. "What are those thingies?"

"Spirits," Nyx said.

"Really, like ghosts or something?"

"A little. Mostly like you or something," Nyx said with a warm smile.

"Well, that's just weird. I don't look anything like that. I look like me."

"Right now you do," Nyx said.

Heath glanced down at himself, just to be sure he was still, well, *him*. Relieved at what he saw, he looked back at the Goddess. "Should I get ready to change up?"

"That depends entirely upon you," Nyx said. "As you would say in your world: I have a proposition for you."

"Awesome! It's cool to be propositioned by a goddess!" Heath said.

Nxy frowned at him. "Not that kind of proposition, Heath."

"Oh. Uh. Sorry." Heath felt his face getting really warm. Jeeze, he was a retard. "I didn't mean anything disrespectful. I was just kidding . . ." He stuttered to a stop, wiping his face with his hand. When he looked at the goddess again, she was smiling wryly at him. "Okay," he started again, relieved she hadn't blasted him with a thunderbolt or something. "About that proposition?"

"Excellent. It's nice to know I have your full attention. My proposition is this: choice."

Heath blinked. "Choice? Between what?"

"I'm so pleased that you asked," Nyx said with only a little teasing sarcasm in her divine voice. "I'm going to give you a choice between three futures. You may choose one of the three, but know before you hear the choices that once you decide upon a path, the outcome is not set—it is only your decision that is set. What happens thereafter is left up to chance and fate and the resources of your soul."

"Okay, I think I get that. I get to pick something, but once I pick it I'm pretty much on my own?"

"With my blessing," she added.

Heath grinned. "Well, I hope so."

The Goddess didn't return his smile. Instead she met his gaze, and he saw all humor was gone from her expression. "I give you my blessing, but only if you find my path. I cannot bless a future in which you choose Darkness."

"Why would I do that? It doesn't even make sense," Heath said.

"Hear me out, my son, and consider the choices I offer you; you will understand then."

"Okay," he said, but something about the tone of her voice made his gut tighten.

"Choice one is that you stay here in this realm. You will be content, as you have been. You will frolic eternally with my other joy-filled children."

"Content doesn't mean happy," Heath said slowly. "I'm a jock, but that doesn't mean I'm stupid."

"Of course it doesn't," said the Goddess. "Choice two: you fulfill your original intent and are reborn. That may mean you stay here and frolic for a century or more, but you will eventually leap from this precipice and return to the mortal realm to be reborn as a human who will eventually find his soul mate again."

"Zoey!" He spoke the one word that filled his mind, and as he spoke her name Heath wondered why it had taken him so long. What was wrong with him? Why had he forgotten her? Why hadn't he—

Nyx's hand touched his arm gently. "Do not punish yourself. The Otherworld can be intoxicating. You did not truly forget your love—you never could. You simply allowed the child within you to rule for a time. He would, eventually, have given way to the adult, and you would have remembered Zoey and your love for her. Under normal circumstances that is the way of things. But the world today is not normal, nor are our circumstances. So, I'm going to ask the child within you to grow up a little more quickly, if you so choose."

"If it has to do with Zo, then I say yes."

"Then hear me out, Heath Luck. You can find your Zoey again if you choose to be reborn as a human; I give you my promise on that. You and she are destined to be together, whether it is as vampyre and mate, or vampyre and consort. It will happen, and you can choose to make it happen in this lifetime."

"Then I—"

Her upraised hand silenced him. "There is a third option from which you may choose. As I speak to you the mortal world is shifting and turning. The great shadow of Darkness in the form of the white bull has gained an unexpected foothold. Good and evil are no longer balanced because of it."

"Well, can't you just zap something and fix that?"

"I could if I hadn't gifted my children with free will."

"You know, sometimes folks are stupid and they need to be told what to do," Heath said.

Nyx's expression remained serious, but her dark eyes sparkled. "If I begin taking away free will and controlling the decisions of my sons and daughters, when does it end? Will I not simply become puppet master, and my children marionettes?"

Heath sighed. "I guess you're right. I mean, you are a goddess and all, so I'm pretty sure you know what you're talkin' about, but it does sound easier."

"Easier is rarely better," she said.

"Yeah, I know. And that sucks," Heath said. "So what about my third choice? Are you trying to tell me it has something to do with good and evil?"

"I am. Neferet has become an immortal, a creature of Darkness. This night she has allied herself with the purest evil that can manifest in the mortal realm, that of the white bull."

"I know about that. I saw something like that try to get to us when I was first dead."

Nyx nodded. "Yes, the white bull was awakened by the shifts of good and evil in the mortal world. It has been eons since he roamed between realms as he is doing today." Heath was disturbed to see the Goddess shiver.

"What's going on? What's happening down there?"

"Neferet is being gifted with a Vessel, an empty, golem-type creature, created by Darkness through a terrible sacrifice and lust and greed and hatred and pain—that she can control completely. He will be her ultimate weapon, or at least that is what she desires. Had her sacrifice been more perfect, the Vessel would be the perfect weapon of Darkness, but there is a flaw in his creation, and that is where your choice comes in, Heath."

"I don't get it," Heath said.

"The Vessel is meant to be a soulless machine, but because

the sacrifice that fed his creation went awry, I am able to touch him."

"Like he has an Achilles' heel?"

"Yes, a little like that. Should you choose this option I would use the flaw in the creature's creation, and through that weakness I would insert your soul into an otherwise empty Vessel."

Heath blinked, trying to take in the enormity of what the Goddess was saying. "Would I know I'm me?"

"You would only know that which all reborn souls know—the most refined essence of what you are. That never fades, no matter how many lifetimes you circle through." Nyx paused, smiled, and added, "And, of course, should you choose, you will also know love. That, too, never fades. It is only suppressed or missed or set aside to circle back around."

"Wait, hang on. This creature is in Zoey's world? Right now?"

"He is being created this night in Zoey's modern world, yes."

"By Neferet, Zo's enemy?"

"Yes."

"So Neferet is gonna use this guy against my Zo?" Heath felt totally pissed.

"I am quite sure that is her intent," Nyx said.

"Huh," he snorted. "With me inside him, she can try, but she's not gonna get very far."

"Before you make your final choice, you must understand: you will not know yourself. Heath will be gone. Only your essence will remain—not your memories. And you will be dwelling within a being created to destroy that which you love most. You may very well succumb to Darkness."

"Nyx, bottom line: does Zo need me?"

"She does," the Goddess said.

"Then I pick the third choice. I want to be put in the Vessel," Heath said.

Nyx's smile was radiant. "I am proud of you, my son. Know that you return to the modern world with my very special blessing."

From the air above her, the Goddess plucked a single strand of something that Heath thought looked like a shimmering thread of silver so bright and shining and beautiful that it made him gasp. She circled her fingers, so that the strand grew to a quarter-sized orb that glistened and glowed with an ancient, special light like a moonstone illuminated from within.

"That's so totally cool! What is it?"

"Magick of the oldest kind. It is rarely present in the modern world; it does not suffer civilization well. But the white bull's ancient magick created the Vessel, so it is only right that *my* ancient magick be there, too."

As Nyx continued to speak, her voice took on a singsong tone that seemed to mix with and complement the beauty of the orb.

> *A window within the soul to see*
> *Light and Magick I send with thee*
> *Be strong, be brave, make the right choice*
> *Though Darkness shouts with a terrible voice*
> *Know that I am watching from above*
> *And that always, always, the answer is love!*

The Goddess flung the glowing orb at him and it filled Heath's eyes, blinding him with its magick light and causing him to stagger backward so that he felt himself toppling over the edge of the gorge and falling, falling . . .

CHAPTER TWENTY-SIX

Neferet

Her body ached, but Neferet didn't mind. The truth was, she enjoyed the pain. She drew in a deep breath, automatically pulling to her the remnants of the white bull's power that slithered in the shadows forming in the gloaming of predawn. Darkness strengthened her. Neferet ignored the gore that covered her skin. She stood.

The bull had left her on the balcony of her penthouse suite. Kalona was not within. But that mattered little to her. She didn't want him anymore because after tonight she wouldn't need him.

Neferet faced north, the direction allied with the element earth. She raised her arms and began weaving her fingers through the air, combing invisible, powerful, ancient threads of magick and Darkness. Then, in a voice devoid of all emotion, Neferet spoke the incantation as the bull had instructed her.

> *From earth and blood you have been born*
> *A pact with Darkness I have sworn*
> *Filled with power you'll hear only my voice*
> *Your life is mine; you have no choice*
> *Complete the bull's pledge this night*
> *And always, always revel in his terrible Dark light!*

The Tsi Sgili flung the inferno of Darkness that had swarmed to her hands down before her. It hit the stone balcony floor and pillar-like erupted up, swirling, writhing, changing . . .

Neferet watched, mesmerized, as the Vessel took form, its body coalescing from the pillar of brilliance that reminded her so much of the white bull's pearl-colored coat. Finally it stood there—*he* stood before her. Neferet shook her head in wonder.

He was beautiful, an utterly gorgeous young male. Tall, and strong, and perfectly formed. The average person would see no hint of Darkness about him. The skin that covered his mighty muscles was smooth and blemish-free. His hair was long and thick and the blond of summer wheat. His features were perfect—he was flawless in his façade.

"Kneel to me, and I will give you your name."

The Vessel obeyed instantly, dropping to one knee before her.

Neferet smiled and put her blood-spattered hand on the top of his silky blond head. "I shall call you Aurox, after the ancient bulls of old."

"Yes, mistress. I am Aurox," the Vessel said.

Neferet began to laugh and laugh and laugh, not caring that hysteria and madness tinged her voice, not caring that she left Aurox kneeling on the stone rooftop awaiting her next command, and not caring that as she walked away the Vessel watched her with eyes that glistened and glowed with an ancient, special light like moonstones illuminated from within . . .

Zoey

"Yeah, I know Nyx forgave him and turned him into a kid. Kinda, 'cause I don't know about you, but I don't know any other kid who turns into a bird during the day." Stark sounded super tired, but not super tired enough to stop worrying.

"That's his consequence for all the bad stuff he's done," I told Stark, curling up against him and trying to ignore the Jessica Alba poster on the wall. Stark and I had taken over Dallas's room in the tunnels under the depot. I'd done some elemental zapping, and everyone had done a lot of good old-fashioned cleaning. We still had quite a way to go, but at least the place was habitable and a Neferet-Free Zone.

"Right, but it's still weird that up until just a little while ago he was Kalona's favorite son, and a Raven Mocker," Stark continued.

"Hey, I'm not disagreeing with you. It's weird for me, too, but I trust Stevie Rae and she loves him." I squinched up my face, making Stark smile. "Even before he got rid of that beak and those feathers. Jeesh, eew. I gotta get the whole story from her." I paused, thinking. "I wonder what's happening right now between them."

"Not much. The sun just came up. He's a bird. Hey, did Stevie Rae say she was going to put him in a cage, or what?"

I smacked him. "She didn't say anything like that and you know it!"

"Makes sense to me." Stark yawned hugely. "But whatever she does, you'll have to wait till sunset to hear about it."

"Past your bedtime, little boy?" I asked, grinning up at him.

"Little boy? Are you sassing me, girl?"

"Sassing?" I giggled. "Yeah, of course. Heehees!"

"Come here, wumman!"

Stark started to tickle me like crazy and I tried to retaliate by pulling the hairs on his arms. He yelped (like a little girl) and then the whole thing turned into a wrestling match where I, somehow, ended up being pinned.

"Do you give?" Stark asked me. With one hand he had both of my wrists and was holding my arms over my head, tickling my ear with his panting breath.

"No way; you're not the boss of me." I struggled (futilely). Okay, so I admit I didn't struggle very hard. I mean, he was pressed against me and totally not hurting me—like Stark would *ever* hurt me—and he was super hot, and I loved him. "Actually, I'm going easy on you. All I have to do is call my mega cool element powers and your cute butt will be kicked."

"Cute, huh? You think my butt is cute?"

"Maybe," I told him, trying not to smile. "But that doesn't mean I won't call the elements to kick it."

"Well then I better keep your mouth busy so you can't do that," he said.

When he started kissing me I thought about what a strange and wonderful thing it was that something so simple, just a kiss, could make me feel so much. His lips against mine were soft, and an amazing contrast to his hard body. As he kept kissing me I quit thinking about how wonderful it was because he made me stop thinking. All I did was feel: his body, my body, our pleasure.

So I hadn't really been thinking about the fact that he was still holding my arms by my wrists, trapped over my head. I didn't think about it when his free hand slid up the extra-large Superman T-shirt I was using as pj's. I still didn't think about it when his hand moved from under my shirt to the top of my panties. I only started to think about it when his kiss changed. It went from soft and deep to hard. Too hard. It was like he'd suddenly become starving, and I was the meal that ended his famine.

I tried to pull my wrists from his hand, but his grip was solid.

I turned my head and his lips left my mouth to make a hot trail down my neck. I was trying to get my head together— trying to figure out what was bothering me so much—when he bit me. Hard.

The bite wasn't like before, like our first time on Skye. Then it had been something we'd shared. Something we *both* had wanted. This time he was rough and possessive and it was definitely not something we were sharing.

"Ouch!" I jerked my wrists and managed to break one hand free of his hold. With it I shoved at his shoulder. "Stark, that hurt."

He moaned and ground his body against me, like I hadn't spoken or pushed him. I felt his teeth against my skin again and this time I yelled and, with my emotions as well as my body I shoved harder at him—channeling lots of *Seriously! You're hurting me!*

He lifted himself up on his elbows and his gaze met mine. For a flash that lasted less than a second, I saw something within his eyes that made my soul shiver. I flinched back, Stark blinked, and looked at me with a total question mark that turned into shock. Instantly he let go of my wrist.

"Shit! I'm so sorry, Zoey. Jesus, I'm sorry! Are you hurt?"

He was patting my body down a little frantically and I batted away his hands, frowning at him. "What do you mean, am I hurt? What the heck's wrong with you? That was way too rough."

Stark wiped a hand down his face. "I didn't realize—I don't know why—" He broke off, took a deep breath, and started again. "I'm sorry. I didn't know I was hurting you."

"You bit me."

He rubbed his face again. "Yeah, it seemed like a good idea at the time."

"It hurt." I rubbed my neck.

"Let me see."

I moved my hand away and he studied my neck. "It's a little red, that's all." He bent and kissed the sore place uber-gently, and then said, "Hey, I really didn't think I bit you that hard. Seriously, Z."

"Seriously, Stark, you did. And you wouldn't let go of my wrists when I told you to."

Stark blew out a long breath. "Okay, well, I'll be sure that doesn't happen again. It's just that I want you so much, and you turn me on so much—"

He paused and I finished his sentence, "—that you can't control yourself? What the hell?"

"No! No, that's not it. Zoey, you can't think that's it. I'm your Warrior, your Guardian—it's my job to protect you from anyone who might hurt you."

"Does that include yourself?" I asked.

His gaze met mine and held. In his familiar eyes I saw confusion and sadness and love—a lot of love. "That includes myself. Do you really think I'd actually hurt you?"

I sighed. What the hell was I making such a big deal about? So, he'd gotten carried away, grabbed my wrists, bit me, and not jumped the second I told him how high. He was a *guy*. What was that old saying? *If it has tires or testicles, it's gonna give you problems.*

"Zoey, really, I would never let you be hurt. I gave you my oath, plus I love you and—"

"Okay, sssh." I pressed my finger against his lips, shutting him up. "No, I don't think you'd let anything hurt me. You're tired. The sun's up. We've had a crazy day. Let's just sleep and agree to no more biting."

"That sounds good to me." Stark held open his arms. "Would you come here?"

I nodded and spider-monkied him. His touch was normal: strong and secure, but very, very gentle.

"I've been having sleep issues," he said hesitantly, after he kissed the top of my head.

"I know you have—I've been sleeping with you. It's been kinda obvious." I kissed his shoulder.

"Not going to ask me if I want to go into therapy with Dragon Lankford this time?"

"He stayed. He didn't leave the House of Night with us," I said.

"None of the professors did. Lenobia stayed, and you know she's one hundred percent behind us."

"Yeah, but she can't leave those horses, and there's no way we can get them down here," I said. "Anyway, Dragon's different. He feels different to me. He wouldn't forgive Rephaim, even after Nyx basically told him he should."

I could feel Stark nodding. "That was bad. But, ya know, I wouldn't be into forgiving someone who killed you, either."

"It would be like me forgiving Kalona for Heath," I said quietly.

Stark's arms held me closer. "Could you do that?"

"I don't know. I honestly don't know—" I hesitated, my words stumbling.

He nudged me. "Go ahead. You can tell me."

I threaded my fingers through his and said, "In the Otherworld, when you were, uh, *dead*"—I could hardly speak the word and hurried on—"Nyx was there."

"Yeah, you told me that. She made Kalona pay his life debt for killing Heath, and bring me alive."

"Well, what I didn't tell you was that Kalona got super emotional in front of Nyx. He asked her if she would ever forgive him."

"What did the Goddess say?"

"She said to ask again if he was ever worthy of her forgiveness. Actually, Nyx sounded a lot like she did tonight when she was talking to Neferet."

Stark snorted. "Not a good sign for Neferet or Kalona."

"Yeah, no kidding. Anyway, my point is, well, not that I'm pretending to be a goddess or anything like that, but my answer about forgiving Kalona is a lot like Nyx's to him and Neferet. I think real forgiveness is a gift someone has to earn, and I don't even have to worry about Kalona asking for my forgiveness unless he's worthy of even considering it, and I just don't see that happening."

"He set Rephaim free tonight, though." I could hear the conflicting emotions in his voice. I understood them. I had them, too.

"I've been thinking about that, and all I can figure is that somehow setting Rephaim free is going to benefit Kalona," I said.

"Which means we need to keep an eye on Rephaim," Stark said. "You gonna mention that to Stevie Rae?"

"Yeah, but she loves him," I said.

He nodded again. "And when you love someone you don't always see them realistically."

I drew back just far enough to give him The Look. "Are you saying that from experience?"

"No, no, no," he said quickly, giving me his tired, but cocky grin. "Not experience, just observation." Stark pulled gently and I curled against him again. "It's time for sleepin' now. Lay yur head, wumman, and let me get my rest."

"Okay, seriously, you sound creepily like Seoras." I looked up at Stark and shook my head. "If you start growing a white goatee beard thingie like his I'm gonna fire you."

Stark rubbed his chin with one hand like he was considering it. "You can't fire me. I've signed on for life."

"I'll stop kissing you."

"Nae beard for me, lassie." He grinned.

I smiled back at him, thinking how glad I was he'd "signed up for life," and how much I hoped that meant he had his "job" for a very, very long time. "Hey, how about this: you fall asleep first, and I'll stay awake for a while?" I cupped his cheek. "Tonight I'll guard the Guardian."

"Thank you," he said, being way more serious than I expected. "I love you, Zoey Redbird."

"I love you, too, James Stark."

Stark turned his head and kissed the inside of my palm and the intricate tattooing the Goddess had placed there. As he closed his eyes and his body began to relax, I stroked his thick brown hair and wondered briefly if or when Nyx would add to my incredible tattooing. She'd given me Marks, taken them away—or at least my friends said they went away while my soul was in the Otherworld—and then Nyx returned them to me again when I returned to myself. Maybe I was set now—maybe I wouldn't get any more. I was trying to decide whether that was a good or a bad thing when my eyelids got way too heavy to keep open. I thought I'd shut them, just for a little while. Stark was definitely sleeping, so maybe it wouldn't hurt anything . . .

Dreams are so weird. I was having a dream that I was flying like Superman—you know, with my hands out in front of me kinda guiding me, and the theme music for the cool old Superman movies, the ones with the awesome Christopher Reeve, was playing in my head when everything changed.

The theme song was replaced by my mom's voice.

"I'm dead!" she said.

Nyx's voice responded right away, "Yes, Linda, you are."

My stomach clenched. *It's a dream. It's just a really bad dream!*

Look down, my child. It is important that you bear witness. When the Goddess's voice whispered through my mind I knew reality had seeped into the Realm of Dreams.

I didn't want to. I really, really didn't want to, but I looked down.

Below me was what I'd come to think of as the entrance to Nyx's Realm. There was the vast Darkness into which I'd jumped to get my spirit back into my body. Then there was a carved stone archway above hard packed dirt, and on the other side of the arch stretched Nyx's magickal grove, beginning with the ethereal hanging tree that was a magnified version of the one

Stark and I had tied our dreams for each other on during that wonderful day on the Isle of Skye.

And just inside the Otherworld arched entrance stood my mom, facing Nyx.

"Mom!" I called, but neither the Goddess nor my mom reacted to my voice.

Bear witness silently, my child.

So I hovered above them and watched while soundless tears washed down my face.

My mom was staring at the Goddess. Finally, she said in a small, scared voice, "So is God a girl, or did my sins send me to Hell?"

Nyx smiled. "Here we are not worried with past sins. Here, in my Otherworld, we care only about your spirit and what essence it chooses to carry with it: Light or Darkness. It is a simple thing, really."

Mom chewed her lip for a second, and then said, "Which does mine carry, Light or Darkness?"

Nyx's smile didn't waver. "You tell me, Linda. Which have you chosen?"

My heart squeezed as I watched my mom start to cry. "Until recently, I think I've been more on the bad side."

"There is a great deal of difference between being weak and being evil," Nyx said.

Mom nodded. "I was weak. I didn't want to be. It's just that my life was like a snowball rolling down a mountain, and I couldn't find my way out of the avalanche. But I was trying there at the end. That's why I was at Mother's house. I was going to make my life my own again—and get back together with my daughter Zoey. She's—" Mom stopped. Her eyes widened in understanding. "You're Zoey's Goddess, Nyx!"

"I am, indeed."

"Oh! So Zoey will be here someday?"

I wrapped my arms around myself. *She loved me. Mom really loved me.*

"She will, though I hope not for many, many years."

Hesitantly, Mom asked, "May I come in and wait for her?"

"You may." Nyx spread her arms wide and declared, "Welcome to the Otherworld, Linda Redbird. Leave pain and regret and loss behind, and bring with you love. Always love."

And then my mom and Nyx disappeared in a brilliant flash of light. I woke up, lying on the edge of the bed, arms wrapping around myself, crying steadily.

Stark woke instantly. "What it is?" He scooted over to me and pulled me into his arms.

"It's m-my mom. S-she's dead," I sobbed. "S-she really did love me."

"Of course she did, Z, of course she did."

I closed my eyes and let Stark comfort me while I cried out pain and regret and loss, until all I had left was love. Always love.

THE END

The story continues in

Destined